A FOOL OF SORTS

FALL OF THE COWARD, BOOK TWO

TAYLOR O'CONNELL

TAYLOR O'CONNELL BOOKS

Dad and Mom, you are two of the most exemplary individuals I have ever had the privilege of knowing. Thank you for always being there for me. This one is for you guys.

CONTENTS

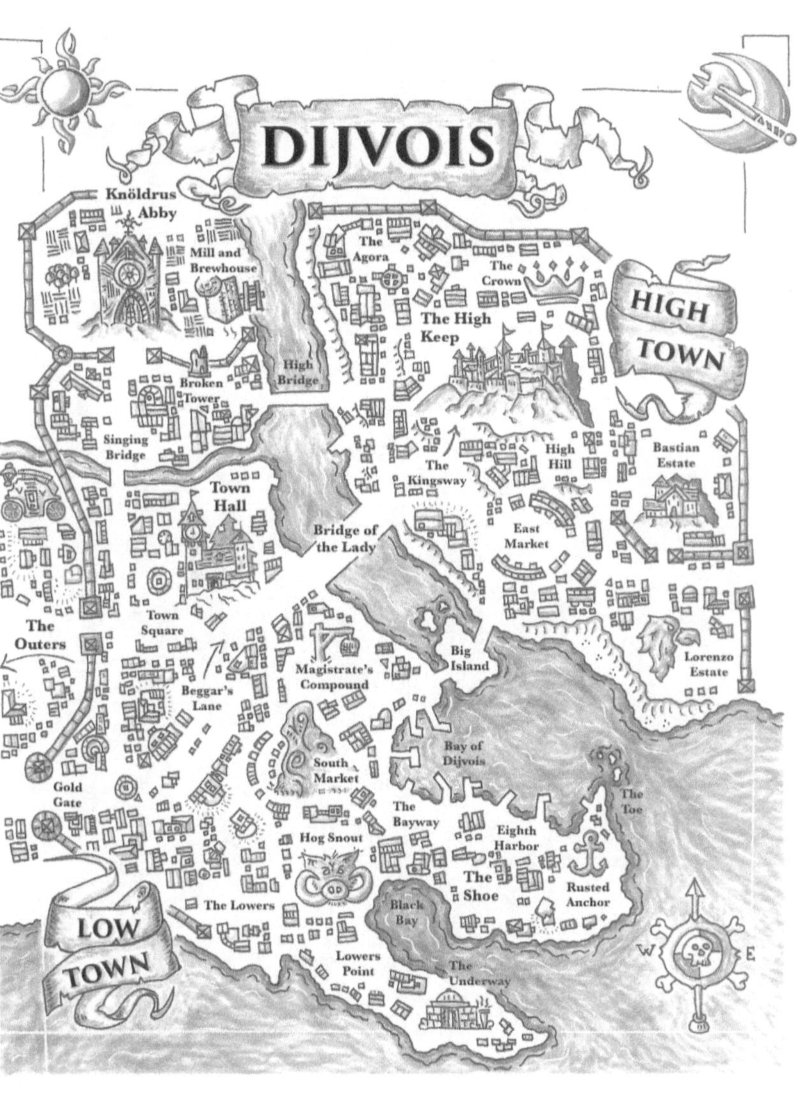

DIJVOIS
HIGH TOWN
LOW TOWN
Knöldrus Abby
Mill and Brewhouse
The Agora
The Crown
The High Keep
Broken Tower
High Bridge
Singing Bridge
Town Hall
High Hill
Bastian Estate
The Kingsway
East Market
Bridge of the Lady
The Outers
Town Square
Big Island
Lorenzo Estate
Magistrate's Compound
Beggar's Lane
Bay of Dijvois
South Market
The Toe
Gold Gate
The Bayway
Eighth Harbor
Hog Snout
The Shoe
Rusted Anchor
The Lowers
Black Bay
Lowers Point
The Underway
W
E

I

THE FOOL

The boy looks out upon the vista of his future, yet it is the fool who takes the first step and journeys unto manhood.
—Emperor Ashwyn, First of his Name

Every fool is a fool of sorts.
—Bartholomew Shoaly

OUT FROM THE SHADOWS

Rainfall pounded the weatherworn limestone of Knöldrus Cathedral. A pair of adjacent towers protruded endlessly heavenward as they pierced the black storm clouds and vanished beyond. Between the towers, a rosary window of brilliant stained-glass, illuminated by flashes of lightning. Gargoyles perched about the façade glared down in judgment, runnels of rainwater pouring through their open maws, splashing upon the cobblestones below.

Hidden beneath the shadows of the cathedral, broken down on all fours, Sal felt the wet stone underhand. Acid burned his throat as he heaved forth another spurt of bile. A shiver coursed through his body, pain so severe it felt as though a hole had torn through his stomach.

Too weak to stand, he crawled, fingertips digging into mud-sheathed cobblestones until the massive doors of the cathedral loomed before him. Sal reached a trembling hand and grasped the oversized bronze knocker, which he used to right himself. A resounding creak echoed through the nave as the heavy door swung open. Candlelight cast flickering shadows to dance across the lime-stone walls. Still shaking, Sal took a cautious step into the cathedral.

His racing heart slowed as a sigh escaped him. He'd made it.

He'd not been caught, not been seen. A miracle, no doubt. He wouldn't have been hard to spot, dropping into the mud and vomiting as he had. Still, it seemed he'd not been pursued.

Sal walked farther into the cathedral but rested at the first pillar, allowing it to support his weight. He looked back over his shoulder. The door had swept shut behind him. No one had pursued, not the man, nor his victim, nor the blood-curdling scream the victim had unleashed. The scream swallowed by the storm and the night. Sal doubted anyone had heard, anyone but himself.

He had to press on, had to find someone to help. His wet boots were slick upon the floor. He reached for the next pillar, staggered, and slipped on the flagstones. Sal put his hands out to catch his fall, but it was too late. His face hit the floor with a wet smack.

"Another skeever?" said a man with a rather shrill voice.

"A lost lamb seeking shelter from the storm," answered a deeper voice.

"You should have thrown him out," said the first man. "See how he sweats, his body craves the substance."

"Is it not our responsibility to care for the sick? Give me your destitute, your—"

"Do not quote scripture to me. I know the book as well as you, Jacques. But these skeevers cannot be trusted. Stealing and lying are but second nature to their kind."

Sal was parched, sick to his stomach, and exhausted. He wanted to be out of the damp sheets, but he dared not move should they notice he'd woken.

"By the Light, the young man has yet to commit any acts of sacrilege," said the man with the deeper voice. "As for the stealing, how can one steal what is gladly given?"

"You make mock, but take note when I tell you no good comes of keeping company with this sort. Where did you find the creature, looting the larder?"

"Far from it. Phillip here found him in the Cathedral, searching for a place to pray."

"I'd name you fool did I not know you for a liar, Jacques. Phillip, you're young, new to the order, you do not yet understand how things work. The election is coming. You would do well to distance yourself from men such as our Master Infirmarer. Wiser, place yourself favorably among men of import, men who may soon occupy positions of influence come the casting of the votes."

"I'll keep it in mind," piped up a young voice. "Though, the election is a fortnight away and nothing is certain as of yet. I am young as you say, but even initiates have heard the stories. When the brothers of Knöldrus Abbey cast the stones, there is no telling where the votes will land."

"You dare threaten me?" said the man with the shrill voice.

"The boy meant nothing by it, Brother Leobald. No one here doubts your political ambition. Though, one might wonder as to your interest in this young man."

"I care not for the skeever nor your bandying of words. If you wish to say something to me, Jacques, say it to me now."

"I would say only this. We are in the infirmary. I am here because I am Master Infirmarer. Phillip is here because he brought in the patient, and the patient is here because he is in need of my arts. Remind me, Brother Leobald, why it is that you are here?"

Sal heard a loud scoff. "When I am abbot, we may find we have a new Master Infirmarer."

"I thank you for the warning, and it shall be duly noted. If a time truly comes when our brothers name you abbot, you may find I will not be difficult to remove. Now, if you don't mind providing me the same courtesy, as I see the patient may not be so asleep as we had assumed."

Sal cursed to himself, wondering what had given him away.

"Remember what I said, Philip," said the man with the shrill voice. "You do yourself no favors backing the wrong man."

"You may leave as well, Philip," said the man with the deeper voice. "Idle hands make waste."

Sal peeked when he heard the door close, but the exposure to light sent his head spinning, and he quickly closed his eyes.

"As I suspected," said the man with the deep voice. "I shall leave you to the dark. The door will be locked from without. Do try to get some sleep. I'll return come dawn's break."

Waking in sheets dampened by sweat, Sal took in his surroundings. The space was spare, adorned with a single stained-glass window and a sconce holding a lone beeswax candle that had melted to little more than a stump. Morning's light shone through the stained-glass, casting resplendent hues of red and yellow upon the adjacent wall. Three other beds, identical to the one he occupied, were crammed within. The clothing he'd worn the night before hung atop a rack near the hearth.

The door crept open, and a man entered. He had a tonsured pate and wore the drab, brown robes of a brother belonging to the Vespian Order. He was tall, thick-chested, and broad of shoulder, built more like a soldier than a man of the cloth. His features were strong, rigid, as though chiseled from the very stone of the cathedral.

"Ah, you're awake. Are you well?" The man's resonant tone rang of familiarity, one of the monks from the night before, the Master Infirmarer.

"Better, though my head feels like it's to burst."

"No surprise," the monk said with a slight chuckle, "you took a nasty spill. I had feared you would be addled. It's good to know you still possess the ability to speak."

Sal felt his brow. A sizable knot had formed above his left eye. A slight tremor coursed through his body. Would that he had a cap of skeev to soothe the throbbing in his skull. "You're a Master of the Vespian Order?"

"I am," replied the monk. "My name is Jacques. I am Master Infirmarer of Knöldrus Abbey. What might your name be, my son?"

My son. The words cut deep. He was no man's son. "My name is Salvatori Lorenzo."

The monk gave him an inquisitive look. "Lorenzo, you say, who might your father be?"

Sal hesitated, then smiled in hopes that the heir of humor would soften the awkwardness of his reply. "Would that I knew myself."

"I see," said Jacques. "I only thought because of your look that you might have been—well, it's of no import. Do you hail from Dijvois?"

"Listen, Jacques, I don't mean to be rude. But my throat is parched, and my lips feel dry enough to crumble. You wouldn't have something on hand that I might drink, would you?"

"I fear I come empty-handed. Though, my brothers have only just finished their morning prayers and gather this very moment to break their fasts. If you would join us, you would be welcome to your fill."

Sal's insides turned over, as if answering the monk's inquiry. "I would greatly appreciate a fine meal."

The monk smiled. Despite the man's hard features, it was a comforting smile that put Sal's frayed nerves at ease. "I dare say, no such thing as a fine meal has been served within the walls of Knöldrus frater since the passing of our dear abbot. That is not to say it is not passing fare. It does serve to fill the belly. Although, the first man to suggest a more palatable menu would have my vote in the upcoming election, that he would."

Sal couldn't help but smile. He liked Jacques. Speaking with the man was rather like sitting by a warm hearth on a rainy day.

"When you've dressed, join me in the hall, and I'll guide you to the frater." After placing Sal's clothing at the foot of the bed, the monk turned and stepped from the room.

As Sal dismounted the bed, he felt unsteady, weak with exhaustion. A meal would serve nicely, but what he truly needed was a cap. He dressed quickly and joined the monk in the hallway.

Motioning for him to follow, Jacques headed for the opposite end of the hall. They crossed a lawn and entered a high-ceilinged building.

"The frater," said Jacques.

The frater was the size of a great hall, more suited to a king than men of the cloth. The ceiling was timber, blackened by years of oven smoke. It was filled with tables and benches that seated row after row of monks.

"Knöldrus is the largest monastery in the kingdom of Nelgand" Jacques said proudly, gesturing to the rows of monks seated at the tables. "There are over four hundred brothers in service of our holy order living within these walls."

"Ahem," coughed a slender monk standing in Sal's immediate path. The man was tall, his close-set eyes and hooked nose resembled a predatory bird. "I see the skeever lives," he said in a shrill voice. "How long must we suffer his presence, Jacques?"

Jacques crossed his thickly muscled arms. "Such coarse terms are beneath a brother of the order, Leobald. Now make way, we are ready to break our fast."

The hawkish monk narrowed his eyes to thin slits. Sneering in disgust, he shouldered past Sal and exited the frater.

"Never you mind Brother Leobald," said Jacques reassuringly. "Amid the politics of the monastery, some of us forget our order exists to serve. Even though Knöldrus Abbey is within the city walls, we tend to remain isolated from the general population, and isolation will brew fear in the bellies of suspicious men."

Sal unclenched his fist, wondering what would have happened if he had punched Leobald in the back of his tonsured head. Instead, Sal gritted his teeth and adjusted his shirt. When something suddenly occurred to him. His hand snapped to his collar. The locket, it was gone. With everything that had happened, he'd not even thought to check for it.

"Jacques," Sal said, doing his best to keep the panic from his voice, "when you took me in, was I wearing a locket?"

"Ah, yes, I'd nearly forgotten. I put the little pendant in a safe place while you slept. When we've finished breaking our fast, we shall return to the infirmary." Jacques led him through the vast hall, nodding to those who greeted him. "Good morrow, my brothers," said Jacques, taking a seat across from a pair of monks. He patted the empty spot next to him on the bench, signaling for Sal to follow suit. "What news from the brewery, Brother Tanao?"

A podgy, red-faced monk looked up from his porridge. He had a nose of burst purple veins and eyelids that drooped, giving him a melancholy look. Wiping his thick, grey mustache with the sleeve of his robe, he said, "A new harvest was brought in just this morning. With this new batch finishing later in the week, I presume the abbey stores will be full come winter."

"Supposing Tanao doesn't drink it all first," said a mousy, buck-toothed monk seated across from Sal.

Tanao scoffed and puffed out his chest as he fixed the mousy monk with a withering look. "I seem to recall I was not the only one in the brewhouse before dawn's break. On more important business, have you heard the morning count?" the podgy monk asked, turning back to Jacques. "They are saying Leobald has acquired ten new votes."

"Another ten votes won't win him the office," said the mousy monk. "The man is still a horse's ass."

"Troubling news, no less," said the red-faced Tanao. "It shows he is gaining support. I need not remind you, if Leobald becomes abbot, it would spell trouble for us all."

A young acolyte arrived at Jacques's signal. On his tray, he carried a stack of wooden bowls and a pot of porridge. Rich, buttery aromas wafted from the steaming pot. Jacques took two bowls and filled them with the cream-colored slop, then handed Sal a bowl and a wooden spoon. Sal was no stranger to breaking his fast with porridge. Still, he'd never much liked the stuff.

"And who is Leobald's opposition?" Sal asked, growing rather interested in the talk of the monastic elections. After all, abbots served for life, it was a rare thing for any citizen of Dijvois to witness more than one election for the abbot of Knöldrus Abbey.

"Brother Martin and Brother Henry," said Jacques.

"Martin is too old," said the mousy monk, "and Henry has the wit of a dung heap. Neither will gain more votes than Leobald. Jacques here is the best fit for the job. Though, he has shrugged off our best efforts at persuasion. I have begun to suspect his mother is a mule. After all, he certainly bears the look, does he not?"

Tanao looked at Sal as though he had only just noticed him. "And who might this young man be?" said the red-faced monk.

"This is Salvatori Lorenzo," said Jacques, "a guest of the infirmary."

"Found him praying on his face in the cathedral, I did," said the young, mousy monk.

"You—I mean, thank you. I owe you a great debt."

"Pay your gratitude to the Lord that is Light. It was *he* that saved your hide, not I."

"Right," said Sal, a touch uncomfortable.

"The names Philip, by the way. Salvatori Lorenzo, did you say?"

Sal nodded. Like Sal himself, Philip looked to be of Pairgu stock. Nineteen, if he was a day. Philip was short and slender, with a pair of bucked-teeth that gave him a somewhat rodent-like appearance.

The pudgy, red-faced monk, Tanao, squinted his droopy eyelids and looked Sal up and down. "Gentle-born, I've no doubt."

Jacques looked at Sal with one eyebrow cocked, as though asking a silent question.

"Not of the Dijvois gentry," said Philip.

"You know every noble in the city, do you?" asked Tanao.

"Aye, well, I'm one of them, aren't I?"

"Not any longer," said Jacques. "You took our vows, and now you bear but one name."

Philip looked abashed, his young face turning nearly as red as that of Brother Tanao. "Noble or initiate, I've sense enough to know Lorenzo is not a name of the Dijvois gentry. They're merchant class."

"Ah, but by his features, I would have thought—but no matter," said Tanao.

Philip snapped a finger. "Lorenzo, Stefano Lorenzo, no?"

"My uncle."

"Ah, but I knew the name was familiar," said Philip.

The mention of his uncle cast a spell of silence over the table, as it always did when the name Stefano Lorenzo was spoken aloud.

"Why is it you're not running for abbot?" Sal asked Jacques in an attempt to break the silence.

"A sorted answer is the best I can give. I've never been much of a man for leading. It's true, I garner the respect of some, and the position of abbot is an honorable post, but many and more know my true passions lie with my work in the infirmary and my work for the Lord that is Light. If I were to be elected, my life would be filled with bureaucracy and beadledom, long days and short nights. When it is all considered, I feel my life is better spent where I am."

"And if you don't enter your name in the running, the lives of the men at this table could very likely be filled with emptying chamber pots," said Philip.

"Surely that couldn't happen," said Sal.

"Ah, but it could," said Philip. "You see, abbot is an elected position. As the highest authority within the abbey, it is only appropriate that my brothers and I have a say as to who will wear the collar of office. Aside from our abbot, the rest of the positions within the Enlightened Council are appointed and revoked by the abbot himself."

"Therein lies the rub," said Tanao. "All the power lies with he who wears the collar of office, and as such, it is imperative that Jacques enters himself in the election."

"What you men seem to forget is that Leobald must first win the election. As you said, young Philip, abbot is an elected position. Leobald seems to think that, as prior, he will simply step into the position of abbot as though it is his rightful inheritance," said Jacques. "I'll admit, there are fools among our order who would vote for such a man, but do you truly believe the fools outnumber those among us with sense?"

"Many men of sound mind have pledged Leobald their votes," said Philip.

"Pledges mean nothing. They are only words," Jacques snapped, the first crack in his limestone demeanor. "Until the stones are cast, nothing is set. Keep in mind, when the last election was held, our brothers did not elect Leobald. They chose abbot Tarquin, who proved to be one of the most amiable men to ever wear the collar."

"Aye, it's true, our brothers ought to elect a man worthy of the position. A man of strong will, good sense, and a humble heart," said Tanao. "Yet, no such man has put forth his name, and when there are no good options, men will reach for the familiar. You know this as well as I, Jacques. As prior, Leobald has naturally been looked to as the transitory abbot and will remain so until the election. If things go smoothly until the time of the election, the brothers may say to themselves that things should stay as they are. They may know in their hearts Leobald is rotten to his black core, but they may forgive this fault if he can give them more of the same."

Jacques sighed and put his face in his hands dramatically. He drew in a breath, sat up tall, and turned to Sal. "Master Salvatori, I must apologize on behalf of my companions. It seems they forget themselves, even in the presence of an honored guest. Let us be done speaking of politics, my brothers."

Sal spooned another mouthful of porridge, his hand shaking involuntarily, his body weak and craving something with a hunger that food could not fill. What he wouldn't do for skeev was anyone's guess. "Forgive my ignorance, but what happened to the last abbot?"

Jacques took on a somber expression, and Tanao busied himself with his food, but Philip scooted to the edge of the bench, elbows on the table as he leaned close to Sal and rubbed his palms together. "Sickness of the belly, consumption, wasn't it, Jacques?"

Jacques looked away, his eyes seeming to have welled up. "It began as a sickness of the belly, but when he developed a persistent cough, I knew what I was dealing with. Though, by then, it seems it was too late. Soon after I relayed my discoveries to the Enlightened Council, the sickness took our abbot swifter than anything I've experienced in my years as Master Infirmarer."

"Well, there've been rumors," said Philip conspiratorially. "In the initiate housing, some of the other boys—"

"Philip!" said Tanao, placing his spoon on the table and fixing the mousy monk with a leer like a mad dog. "You do forget yourself in our company. Put a hand upon that shaved spot atop your empty skull and keep in mind, the Lord that is Light sees all from above. Would you profess your servitude to our Lord with your talents as rumormonger?"

Philip opened his mouth, but whatever he was about to say, they would never know. At that moment, commotion spread through the gathered monks like the rush of a storm over calm water.

When the message reached their table, it was delivered by a little monk with a lazy eye. "Prior Leobald has asked that the masters of the Enlightened Council gather at the orchard."

"A most unusual request," said Jacques, arching an eyebrow.

"Does the prior not know this is the hour at which we break our fast? I will join him when I've had my fill," said Tanao, raising his hand to summon one of the serving boys.

"I'd not keep the prior waiting," said the little monk with the wandering eye. "It seems to be a matter of urgency."

"Very well," said Jacques, standing. "Come, Master Brewer. It seems we are required in the orchard."

Tanao stood, scowling. "Would that I'd broken my fast in the brewhouse, where dodgy eyed imps seldom come with summonses from their master."

"Light's blessing upon you, Brother Tanao," said the little monk with the wandering eye.

As the two monks began to walk away, Sal felt a pang of anxiety. He wasn't going to let Jacques out of his sight until he got his locket back. He stood, and when no one stopped him or said a word in protest, Sal followed the two masters out the frater doors.

Jacques and Tanao joined another cluster of three monks. The group crossed the yard and made for the orchard, where they saw another group of seven monks some ways into the trees. The others were gathered about the massive trunk of a pardimon tree. Soon to be twelve strong, they made up the entirety of the Enlightened Council.

As they neared the massive tree, its gnarled, leafless branches spotted black by carrion birds, a distant scream sounded in Sal's head.

He nearly dropped to his knees. Terror gripped him by the throat with an icy hand. His heart set to racing, his legs weak and shaking. There was something familiar about the pardimon tree, something horribly familiar.

The monks nearest the tree had begun shouting, and it sounded as though a scuffle might break out.

"What is the meaning of this?" said Jacques.

The gathered monks began to part in order to make way for Jacques, who, it seemed, was a rather big deal, even amongst the Enlightened Council.

Sal had never wanted a cap of skeev more than at that very moment. Everything inside him said to run, to be as far from that place as he could get, but he couldn't move. His feet were planted to the spot.

As the monks made way for Jacques and the other newcomers, Sal caught a glimpse of what they'd gathered about. A black heap lying on the ground. No, not black, brown, a man in drab brown robes—a monk.

"Brother Dennis," said Tanao breathlessly.

Jacques knelt to examine the body closely.

Others gasped, one man's breath caught, another began to break down and sob there and then.

Sal felt a tightness in his throat and a hollow pit in his stomach. Something nagged at him, a familiarity he could not pinpoint. A terrible sinking feeling, ominous as black storm clouds on the horizon.

"A demon walks amongst us, brothers," said Leobald in a loud, shrill voice. "I have summoned you here today to witness for yourselves, and so, there can be no denying the truth. Before you is the victim of a violent and senseless act."

"Strangled," said Jacques. "A garrote."

"Brother Dennis," said a tall monk. "One of the initiates reported him missing at the morning prayers."

"This was not brought to my attention," said Leobald.

"I'd not thought it to be of import," said the tall monk defensively.

"It is not uncommon for an initiate to miss the morning prayers," said Tanao. "As they are often undisciplined."

"Your failure to recognize authority is not the issue at hand," said Prior Leobald. "Someone has violated our laws of sanctuary, despoiled holy ground."

"My concern lies, not with the ground, but with the taking of a life," said Jacques. "This boy was our brother, a member of our order. We should not concern ourselves with the theological implications, but those that pertain to corporeal matters. Our concern, my brothers, should be for the safety of the flock."

The collected group began to mutter their ascent.

"The only way to guarantee the safety of the flock," said Leobald bitterly, "is for the shepherds to beat back the wolves. Our path is clear, brothers, it has been illuminated for us by the Lord that is Light. We must hunt for this wolf that has infiltrated our walls. We must kill this wolf and hang his pelt above our gates as a sign to others who would think our sheep ripe for the taking."

"But how can we know?" said one of the monks.

"A servant of Sacrull cannot conceal himself among the righteous for long," said Leobald. "We must be vigilant. We must be aware of all that which may seem queer, if only in the slightest. We must—" Leobald stopped speaking as his scanning gaze fell upon Sal. "What in Light's Name is this creature doing here?"

The others seemed only then to notice Sal.

"Salvatori is my guest," said Jacques. "He has come at my invitation."

"He has come to view his night-work in the light of day!" said Prior Leobald, his eyes burning with something like realization. "I want him seized."

No one moved. The eleven others seemed as shocked as Sal.

Yet, an instant later, two of the monks began to close toward Sal with the clear intent of subduing him.

Before anyone else answered the prior's call, Sal ran for it.

He fled the orchard, crossed the yard, cut through the cloister, and burst through the transept of the cathedral. Taking a sharp turn, he sprinted, disregarding shouts of protest that rang through the nave.

Once he'd pushed past the cathedral's oak doors and out the Abbey Gate, Sal felt the elation of freedom, but he didn't stop. He ran down the cobblestone street, fast as his feet would take him, giving no regard to where he went, so long as it was away from Knöldrus Abbey and the corpse beneath the massive pardimon tree.

2

A HERO'S RETURN

Too tired to run any farther, Sal slowed as he neared the Singing Bridge. His lungs were on fire, his mouth dry as salted meat, stomach twisting and cramping painfully. He put his arms above his head and breathed hard as he walked. Passersby stared, one man leaned toward his companion, pointing at Sal, and both men began to laugh.

The hum of the Singing bridge was soothing, the Oleander's current streaming pleasantly beneath his feet as though in no hurry to meet her mighty sister, the Tamber. He bypassed Town Square, sticking to the less trafficked streets and darker alleys. By the time he reached South Market, the morning's business had slowed to a trickle, the stink of fish was always worst just before the midday heat. The vendors and fish mongers stayed out until the latest possible hour, in hopes of selling the last of the days catch.

The Godstone came into sight, a towering relic of the past. The slate gray pillar stood alone at the center of the market-round. There was sequestered beauty to the secrets held within the ancient ivy-wrapped stone, a boundless unknowing that had intrigued Sal since the first time he'd set foot in South Market as a small boy, gripping tight to his mother's finger, eyes wide with wonder.

A bony hand grabbed Sal by the wrist.

"Fresh redeye, boy! Here, boy, here, fresh, all fresh," said a fish-wife, attempting to drag Sal toward the stinking buckets near her stall. Sal slipped the old woman's grip and pressed on.

He needed only to cross the market-round, a flagstone court-yard, cylindrical in shape and occupied with vendors, carts, and barrels full of anything that could conceivably come from the sea. Although, by this hour, there were more open spaces than vendors and more vendors than market goers, an unfortunate situation for both buyers and sellers.

Sal saw a young nobleman haggling over crabs. He considered a way to brush past the nobleman, but realized, as he planned out the pickpocket, that he likely wouldn't be able to pull it off.

"Oof," Sal blurted, running headlong into a stout, barrel-chested Yahdrish.

The man's fat belly was hard as a rock. He ran his fingers through his curly, black hair and rubbed at his stomach with the other.

"Come, come," said the Yahdrish, wrapping his arm about Sal's shoulders. "The finest creatures to ever swim the great waters. You will see, not even Jasper's lampreys, nor Aliana's cockles, can hold a candle to my stock. Come now, you will see."

Sal tried to slip free, but the man's meaty arm had encircled his shoulders. The stout Yahdrish was strong, but more to the issue, Sal felt weak as a newborn child. He was half dragged to the Yahdrish fishmonger's cart, three barrels, mostly empty aside from the one filled with stinking cloudy-eyed perch, near black with scale rot.

Sal held his breath and looked away from the barrels. He felt the Yahdrish man's grip tighten, the vendor clearly unwilling to pass up the opportunity of a sale. As Sal averted his gaze to anywhere other than the barrels, he saw her.

She walked alone, wearing a simple dress of green wool, a basket in the crook of her arm, likely returning from her morning's venture outside the city walls to forage herbs and wildflowers. Nicola passed right by him, head held forward, eyes set on her destination.

"I'll take a half dozen of the perch," Sal said.

The vendor's grip didn't loosen. When Sal looked the Yahdrish in the eyes, the man hardly seemed to believe what he'd heard.

"A half dozen?"

"Yes," Sal said, putting an edge on the word. "A half dozen, and I'll want something to carry them in, a crate or a bit of netting."

"But of course, right away," said the fishmonger, releasing Sal in order to fill his order.

The moment the Yahdrish released his grip, Sal bolted away. The vendor shouted at Sal's back as he ran, but he didn't stop. By then, Nicola was nearly inside her home, but Sal managed to catch hold of the handle just before Nicola closed the door.

"What in the Light's—Salvatori? What are you—"

"Sister, please."

Nicola let out a sigh. "What do you want?"

Sal put his hands on his knees and tried to catch his breath. "I need help, and I don't know where else to go. I don't have anywhere else."

Nicola's face was deadpan.

"Nicola?" said a man from inside the house. "Who is —Salvatori?"

Sal felt his pulse quicken, the exhaustion of moments before pushed aside by the heat that coursed through his veins. Oliver Flint stood in the doorway behind Nicola, one hand on her hip, the other on her shoulder.

"Your lordship, a touch early for a visit, is it not?" Sal said, giving his sister a look of reproach. "Or might it be that this is late in the visit? In which case—"

"We'll not be doing this, Salvatori," said Nicola. "You've had your chances. I can't do it again, not now."

"Nicola," Sal said, but she turned away and walked inside as tears came to her eyes. "I've kicked the stuff, I'm done," Sal said, but his words fell on deaf ears.

Oliver looked on him with sympathetic eyes. "I'm sorry, mate."

"Right, well, it was nice seeing you, Oliver. But just to be clear, you stick your prick in my sister, I prick my sticker through your eye, yeah?"

Oliver winked, a little smirk playing across his lips as he closed the door.

Sal was crestfallen. He felt alone, but even more, he felt betrayed. He knew this to be a self-serving lie. Deep down, Sal knew he was to blame. It had been *he*, not Nicola, who'd stolen and lied. It had been *he* who'd shattered her trust, *he* who'd betrayed her.

Still, she could have listened. If only she'd heard him out, she would have understood. Should he have told her about the monk, the man who'd been strangled beneath the pardimon tree? Should he have told her men would be looking for him, monks given authority by both church and duke to wield the sword of justice?

In truth, he remembered little and less of the night before. Yet he recalled a scream, the kind of blood-curdling scream that leaves a man so badly shaken, even the memory of the thing makes his blood run cold. Had that dead monk been the one who'd unleashed the scream? Had it been Sal himself? Or had it merely never been, was it something that he'd only imagined, something that had been inside his own mind?

It was impossible to know.

He knew the dead monk had been real. He was an initiate of the Vespian Order, and he had been strangled in the orchard of Knöldrus Abbey. Yet, why the man was strangled, and who had strangled him was unknowable.

Sal had gone to the abbey that night, not to take shelter from the storm, but to rob the place under cover of darkness. He shivered, struck with a bout of shame, before fatigue swept through him. The craving was back, and suddenly, skeev was all that was on his mind. He needed to get a cap, but a cap meant coin, and that was something Sal was desperately short on.

Sal grabbed at his collar as he realized something was missing. The monk, Jacques, Master Infirmarer of Knöldrus Abbey, still had Sal's locket.

He would need time to come up with a plan to retrieve his locket, but for the moment, sick and shaking as he was, Sal needed to do something about his failing body before he could worry over the locket.

Sal let his feet lead him. Conscious of his efforts or not, his feet took him to the one person Sal knew he could find.

The Cauldron was easily one of the least desirable districts in Dijvois, a kind with places like the Narrows and the Lowers. Brown water ran through the main thoroughfares, cobblestones washed over with mud, filth, and night soil. Just outside the reach of the Black Bay tide, the Cauldron was not the sort of place one would expect to find a noblewoman.

Her favorite spot to run her little charities was a cul-de-sac of abandoned buildings on the southern end of the district. The buildings had been abandoned and allowed to sink into disrepair long ago. Yet still they stood, defying their former occupants, along with time itself. Since they'd been abandoned before Sal had even been born, he had little sense of what the buildings might have been used for in the past, but at present, they served as a place to house gangs of ragged street urchins.

As Sal approached the abandoned cul-de-sac, he softened his steps, trying his best not to make any more noise than necessary. He heard her before he saw her. A voice like mulled wine, it warmed him like a hot coal in his chest and swooned his head with drunken pleasantness.

A big man stood at the center of the cul-de-sac, a bastard sword slung across his back. A searching look in his eyes, his mustache quivered when he spotted Sal.

Damor Nev was Lilliana Bastian's personal bodyguard, and while the Bauden man-at-arms wasn't so fond of Sal, they shared a sort of grudging respect due to their mutual interest in Lilliana's wellbeing.

Damor was surrounded by a pack of urchins, a dangerous scenario for the typical citizen of Dijvois, but no pack of urchins, no matter how hungry and numerous, would dare challenge Damor Nev and his bastard sword.

It wasn't until Lilliana stood that Sal saw her. Raven black hair that fell to her shoulders, eyes like depthless pools of lapis lazuli, and lips that tasted like candied ginger. She wore a dress of sapphire blue, a make that could only come from the Far East.

Sal approached slowly, watching Lilliana as she handed out clothing to each and every child in the mob, addressing them one at a time with the patience of a divine being.

"One for my sister too," said a little girl in stained rags, a red rash on one side of her face. "She's not feeling well, she's not, or she'd have come herself. It's the wet cough, hasn't been out of bed in two days."

Lilliana handed the girl another bundle.

"Which building is she in?"

The little girl scuffed a shoe on the cobblestones, biting her lip.

"I want to send a mender by to make certain she will be alright," said Lilliana reassuringly.

"That one there," said the little girl.

Lilliana nodded, and the little girl moved off as another urchin stepped up to receive his bundle.

Sal watched her speak with another five, handing them bundles of winter clothing and words of reassurance. He approached tentatively, not wanting to startle any of the urchins and insight panic.

Lilliana turned slowly, as though sensing his presence before seeing him.

"Salvatori," she said in surprise, "what are you doing here?"

"I—can we talk?"

Lilliana arched an eyebrow.

A little boy with soot-blackened hands tugged at the hem of Lilliana's dress.

"Oh," she said, handing the boy the bundle in her arms. "Look now isn't—"

"Please, Lilliana, hear me out."

Lilliana picked up another bundle and handed it to a skinny girl. "Damor, take over for me. I'll only be a moment."

"My Lady," said the bodyguard, lowering his head deferentially.

Lilliana followed Sal out from the cul-de-sac and into an alley that was quickly deserted by a pair of urchins.

"What is it, Salvatori, what do you need?"

Sal wasn't certain how to answer the question, as he didn't know what he needed. Help, that was clear, but what sort of help?

What kind of help could Lilliana offer? Even her father wouldn't have the political sway necessary to assuage the monks of Knöldrus Abbey. Not even the duke could go against them, lest he dared the wrath of the entire Holy Vesipian Order and the might of Aduah.

"I need you, Lilliana."

She scoffed. "Yes, well, be a gentleman and speak to my father about my price like the rest of them."

"I don't want to buy you."

"No, you only want to try me out when it suits you?"

"That's not the way of it."

"Isn't it? Tell me then, where have you been? I've not seen you for months, and now you turn up wanting—well, just what is it you what?"

"You, Lilliana, I want only you."

"Only me? That's not possible. You cannot have only me, because that is not all that I am. Much comes with my name and my blood, and with that, a certain responsibility."

"We could be, you and I, we could be together."

"How?" she said flatly, disbelieving.

"We could leave," Sal said, giving serious consideration to leaving the city at that moment. "There are other places in Nelgand where we could be happy. Better, cleaner places, where a man eats what he earns and isn't cheated out of house and home by the duke's taxes."

Lilliana fixed him with narrowed eyes. "You'd have me run away with you?"

"I would."

"And why should I run? For that matter, why should you run? What are you running from, Salvatori?"

If he told her, would she agree to go? It was unlikely but not entirely out of the question. She'd given him chances before, hadn't she? That is, until the day he'd given up. But that had changed, he had changed. Or so he hoped.

"We'd not be running away but running toward something better."

"The nuance doesn't matter. Run toward or away, but I'll not run with you. It's not in my nature."

The words hit him like the blow of an axe, definite and fatal. The finality of them cleaved through his argument and struck him directly between the eyes. At that moment, Sal wanted nothing more than a cap.

He went quiet, and though he knew she expected him to speak, nothing came to mind. After all, what else could he say that he'd not already said a hundred times before? Then, it came to mind, the one thing he could say to salvage the situation.

"I love you, Lilliana." Even as the words left his mouth, he regretted what he'd done. Like throwing a stone into the bay and expecting it to cause a wave that might wash away the shore. The words were but another drop in a sea of broken promises.

She didn't scoff, nor did she grow upset. Instead, she seemed to frost over, to go cold inside, so much that Sal imagined her eyes had changed from the warm lapis to a pale ice blue.

"How can you say that?" Lilliana asked, "After what you did. You made your choice." At that, Lilliana stepped past him and out of the alley. Sal watched in a sort of stunned silence as she went back to the cul-de-sac and resumed her work.

Sal turned and slowly walked away, resigned that there was a very good chance he'd lost Lilliana for good and all, and despite all of the foolish things he'd done in his life, losing Lilliana may have been his crown achievement.

Still, he didn't know how much longer he could go without a cap. He'd kicked the stuff, gone a full two days without it. Yet, the climb out from the pit meant less and little if Lilliana would not wait for him atop the precipice. The thought of never being with her made Sal want to let go and sink back into the bottom as far as he could, down to a place where there was no longer thought or feeling. He wanted to melt away, wanted to burn all that came before, until his future was not but black and ash.

And yet, somehow, he knew he wouldn't allow it. He had come too far to turn back. He would fight. He would fight for Lilliana and his right to her favor. Only, he would wait until after he'd had a cap.

Sal started as a hand clapped him on the shoulder. A large hand with a strong, firm grip.

"You'd do best to stay clear of her," said Damor Nev. "A woman like that is not meant for the likes of you."

Sal turned. "You've left her alone with that horde?"

"Lilliana's a tough one. She could hold her own against a few urchins until I get there and start cleaving the little buggers in two."

Sal couldn't help but shift his gaze to the bastard sword slung on the big Bauden's back.

"Fond of slaying children, are you, Nev?"

"Fond?" said the bodyguard, quivering his mustache. "Not in the least. Yet, if the dog bites the hand that feeds it, I must be the boot that kicks the dog."

"These are children, not dogs."

Damor shrugged. "And you are a man. An undersized runt of a man, but a man no less, and still, I would not hesitate to take your life should it prove necessary."

"Are you anticipating such an event in the near future?"

"Only the gods know what will come to pass, but so far as I can predict, you would do best to keep clear of Lilliana Bastian. Ignore my advice, and wait for her father to learn of you, what you are, and your relations with his daughter—I'd suspect you had a short time to live."

Sal feigned a smile, winked, and left Damor Nev in his slow wake.

As much as he didn't want to admit it, Damor Nev was right. Sal had no business with a woman like Lilliana Bastian. Even if he was not the lying, thieving skeever that he was, his illegitimate birth alone disqualified Sal from the running for Lilliana's hand. He was a nobody from nowhere, and he'd better get that through his thick bastard skull before thinking with his manhood got him killed.

Besides, there were other things to worry about, his locket the most prevalent. As he'd left it behind at Knöldrus Abbey, it was going to be difficult to get it back. Supposing Jacques had not told anyone of the locket, there was a chance it remained in the infirmary. Sal could simply climb the abbey walls and break into the infirmary, but then what? Would he search every corner of the building, rifle through every drawer, nook, and cranny with no inclination as to where it might be or might have moved? Would they not expect him to return for the locket? Even if they had thought him as good as gone, would he be mad enough to return?

It was a fool's errand, and Sal knew it. And yet, he knew deep down, he would have to go back for the thing, somehow.

It didn't take him long to find his way to his destination at the north end of the Shoe, a single-story hovel built of old stone, crumbling mortar, and loosely laid thatch. Sal knocked on the door with all the confidence and energy he could muster, hoping beyond hope he would get an answer in return. By the Lady's fortune, Sal heard shuffling and the lifting of a beam. The poorly fitting door grated on its hinges.

Vinny's frame filled the doorway, blocking Sal bodily from the threshold.

"Salvatori?" Vinny said with the hint of a smile, "Can it be?"

"Who else?" Sal asked, unable to look Vinny in the eyes.

"I thought you might never come around again. Not after what you did."

"Right, well, I am sorry for that. I feel awful about it, and I swear I mean to get you every krom—"

Vinny held up a hand for silence, then clapped Sal friendlily on the shoulder. "You've nothing to be sorry for, mate. Come in." The one-room hovel smelled of stale rushes and wood smoke from the hearth. "Have you eaten?"

Sal nodded, yet midday was nearly upon them. "Might be I could do with a bit more fodder. What did you have in mind?"

"The Hog Snout sounds fine right about now. I'm in need of an ale."

Sal's face must have given away what he was feeling at the sound of the Hog Snout. It was a fine enough place. Yet, there were memories Sal had of the Hog Snout that he never cared to think about.

"It's been half a year," Vinny said. "One of these days you'll have to accept that he's gone."

"I've accepted it, but I won't go back to the Hog, not yet."

"The Anchor it is," Vinny said, dropping the argument.

Sal shrugged. He supposed the Rusted Anchor was as good a place as any to spend an evening. If he wasn't going to get skeev, ale might have to do.

Without even the chance to sit, Sal found himself back on the cobblestone streets of Dijvois once more, but for the first time in a while, he found himself walking in the company of a true friend.

"You've been getting work?" Vinny asked.

"Little enough," Sal said, unwilling to tell the whole of the truth. "Yourself?"

"Valla has kept my pockets lined. The woman seems to set up a big job every month or so."

"That kind of work is going to attract the wrong kind of attention from the Commission. How's she avoiding the leg-breakers?"

"She's not, of course," Vinny said, smiling uncertainly.

"What do you mean?"

"You really don't know?"

Sal shook his head.

"Gods, you have been away from things. Valla got herself made."

"Truly?" Sal asked. "You're not japing? Valla is a made man?"

"Why should I jape? She's running with the Moretti family. A regular old earner she is."

"And you," Sal said, searching Vinny for any new tattoos, "have you gone and gotten yourself made while I was gone?"

Vinny chuckled. "No need. With Valla giving me steady work, I can hire out without paying Commission dues of my own. They cut Valla seven of ten after every job. It's not right, but who's going to speak up? Good as Sacrull's kiss, that would be."

"Best to keep silent, unless you want a red smile," Sal agreed.

"Best to avoid it altogether if you can, but listen, if you need work, I'm certain Valla would be willing to cut you in. She's already made the offer once, and we've been in need of a good second-story man. This new snatcher Odie brought in has a light touch like a troll, last week, she nearly set the whole City Watch on us."

Sal laughed. It felt good to laugh. "Sounds like you've a crush," he mocked.

Vinny scowled. "You want the work, you'd best knock that right off."

"Well, it might be I could use some work. So long as this snatcher of yours doesn't get us all thrown in crow-cages."

Vinny shook his head, smiling. "If she does, I swear I'll hunt that girl to the bottom of Sacrull's hell."

3

BARTHOLOMEW

INTERLUDE, SEVEN YEARS EARLIER

Sal never much liked the Lowers. The place terrified him, Lowers Point most of all. The cobbles were slick with mud. The streets were narrow and winding, cast into shadow by the towering stack-houses. Wind continually blew through Lowers Point with the sound of a howling madman that sent a chill through the soul as much as the flesh.

Sal took cover behind a rubbish pile. One was never far from a rubbish pile in the Lowers, especially this close to Lowers Point. However, the particular pile Sal had chosen smelled of rotten fish, enough that he gagged.

Sal stood halfway up, intent on moving, when he spotted something in his periphery. He dropped back down as a pair of thugs walked past his hiding place and entered the White Eyes den across the street.

The White Eyes were one of the many factions of the Dijvois criminal element. They weren't a Commission sanctioned family, but they were among the larger of the street gangs.

Sal held his position behind the rubbish pile, the stench of rotten fish strong enough to linger on his tongue. He watched the door of the White Eyes den with the patience of a hunter. Watching was a skill he had worked on as of late. He'd heard the big jobs paid well for good scouting, and Sal was confident he could master the skill with time. It would be a good way to get off the street level work. A good way to move from picking pockets to scouting for a real crew, supposing Anton didn't kill him first.

When the door to the White Eyes den next opened, Anton stepped out into the street. The tall, slender Pairgu pulled up the hood of his cloak to fend off the chill of the sea air.

Anton passed by Sal's hiding place, no more aware of him than the previous pair of thugs. Slowly, Sal crept from behind the rubbish pile, his feet fleetingly silent as he closed in on his victim.

"You've really got to learn to move quieter," said Anton as he continued on down the street.

"Damnit," Sal cursed. "When did you make me?"

"When I stepped outside and saw your head duck behind that shit pile," Anton said, turning on Sal without his usual smile. "You bring my money?"

"I've been meaning to talk with you about that."

"What's to talk about?"

Sal looked to the cobbles. "I would appeal to your better nature."

Anton's eyes narrowed, but a sound at the door of the White Eyes den stole his attention as his head snapped in the direction of the noise. Anton nodded for the nearest alley. "Let's discuss this as we walk."

Sal didn't have to be told twice. He moved up beside Anton, and they headed north, out of the Lowers and away from Lowers Point.

"Alright kid, which thumb am I going to take?"

Sal sighed. "I suppose I'd have to say the left one, as I need the right for wiping my ass. Ever tried wiping without thumbs? Wicked difficult I tell you."

"Everything is a jape with you."

"Life is a jape, mate," Sal said. "I mean, what's the point of it all, truly?"

"There are no japes where my coin is concerned," Anton said, his sharp, angular features deadly serious.

"Oh, but is not coin the biggest jape of all? Think about it. We spend our lives scrimping for krom to buy our next scrap, all just so we can keep on living to scrimp for the next scrap. Tell me, is that not a joke?"

"I fail to see the humor," said Anton. "You owe me nine krom, kid. If you don't have it now, you're going to rack another two krom a day until I have the principal in full."

"Two a day," Sal said. "Come now, you know I haven't got it now, but I'll have the nine before the end of the week. I have a plan."

"Left, you said, wasn't it?" Anton grabbed Sal's wrist and pulled him close.

Sal was powerless to fight him off as Anton jerked out a hooked knife and placed the sharp edge against Sal's left thumb.

"Gah, please, Anton—"

"What, no japes?"

Sal struggled but couldn't pull free. Anton was too strong.

"Please, Anton—"

"Oh, but this isn't your wiping thumb," Anton said, applying pressure until a bead of blood dripped down the blade.

"Anton, I—"

The bigger man let go and shoved Sal away.

"Whoreson!" Sal cursed and clutched his thumb. The cut was shallow, but it stung like hell.

"The next time, I take the bloody thing," Anton said. "And that is no jape, kid."

"You'll get your due tomorrow, by evenfall," Sal said.

"Oh, and how is that?"

"I have a plan," Sal said, nursing his thumb.

"Have a plan, do you?"

"Was going to tell you before you started hacking limbs, but it seems I was a tick slow on the draw."

"Well, what's the plan? And don't you lie to me, not again."

"Not again? Anton, when have I ever lied to you?"

"Playing the fool? Or are you truly as stupid as that?"

Sal swallowed, jogging his memory for anything he might have lied about recently, but there was only one lie that came to mind. One lie he'd told Anton, just after they'd met. "I don't think of myself as a fool, though I'd wager the witless ones never do."

"It's only the truly stupid that think themselves smarter than everyone else. When one is too short-sighted to see further than the tip of his own nose, the world looks small and quite easily manipulated."

Sal shifted his weight uncomfortably as he waited for the other boot to drop.

"If you don't think yourself a fool, Salvatori, then you must think me one."

Sal smiled uncomfortably, trying to look as though he were not terrified.

Anton still held the hooked knife. He cleared his throat and arched an eyebrow. "Well?"

Sal shrugged.

"Not willing to come clean?"

"I'm not certain I know just what it is you want me to say?"

"How about you say something like, Antonio Russo—dear, sweet, indelibly handsome Antonio—by all the Gods on high, forgive me, for I have lied. I am a little shit-heel twerp and do not know when to start telling the truth."

Sal sighed. "How did you find out?"

"I'm connected, how would I not find out?"

"Didn't expect you'd ask around, I suppose."

"Right, well, I don't take on urchins until I've made certain they've not worked anyone over before. Why lie to me?"

Sal shrugged. "I thought that if I told you he was my uncle, you might not give me the work."

"And you're bloody right about that. Light's name, do you have any idea what a man like Stefano Lorenzo would do to me if anything happened to you?"

"He wouldn't care," Sal said. "If anything happened to me, that is."

Anton spat, "That's not a wager I'd care to take."

"I take it my thumbs are safe, then?" Sal asked with a smirk.

Anton smiled back. "Not if I don't get my krom, kid, and I mean that. I may not take your thumbs, but if I go to your uncle to collect your dues, I suspect he may."

The threat sunk deep. Sal may be safe from harm by Anton's hand, on account of his uncle, but there was no one to stay his uncle's hand.

"Like I told you," Sal said, "I've got a plan."

"Sure, and you had better hope it works out just right," Anton said. "You'll find me at the Rusted Anchor when you have my coin."

"Hold on, yeah? You don't want to hear the plan?"

Anton shook his head. "Evenfall, and not a turn after."

Sal nodded. "I'll be there."

Sal crossed Town Road, narrowly avoiding an oxcart that trundled past. He ignored the shouts from the driver and slipped into Town Square as he kept sight of his mark.

The plan was simple, snatch and run. It was dangerous, but Sal was confident he could get in and out without anyone even noticing, so long as he was quick enough.

The mark was a bagman. Not just any bagman, but a Svoboda lackey by the name of Oldrez Venturi, one of Don Svoboda's personal collection mules. Sal had followed the man for neigh on a week. Noting every habit, tick, and fancy the bagman had. Most importantly, he took note of the stops which Oldrez made.

Each day began the same, a stop to the chamber pot and a mug of ale to break his fast. The bagman would make his routes, collecting from the various shopkeepers and business owners that paid tribute to Don Svoboda. The course varied each day of the week. The bagman wended his way through Svoboda controlled districts, street by street, his coin purse growing heavier with each stop. However, there was one stop that held consistent each day. The bagman would finish his routes in a little Dahuaneze teashop on the north end of Town Square.

Sal suspected Oldrez favored the teashop, not for the tea, but for the young Dahuaneze serving girl—with whom, he would spend the majority of his time in the little shop making conversation. All the while, the coin purse sitting on the table, just waiting to be snatched.

Sal looked out on Town Square as he leaned up against a trinket seller's wheeled cart. The vendor was Vordin, or maybe Norsic. Sal always had trouble telling the difference between the two. Not only did they look quite similar—tall and broad-shouldered, blonde-haired and fair-skinned—but all Skjorund accents sounded the same to Sal's ear. Though, judging by the way the vendor pointedly ignored Sal, he took the man for a Vordin.

The great fountain at the center of Town Square was vast enough to swim in. Something which orphans often did, until chased off by patrolling steel caps. In the middle of the fountain, the bronze statue of the ancient hero monk, Uthrid Stormbreaker. A former abbot of Knöldrus Abbey, the Vespian Order claimed the old monk once slew a demon or some such nonsense. Whatever the man really did, his statue stood taller than any other in the city, second only to the statue of Bethelwold the Great.

Sal's attention was grabbed by a beautiful woman perusing perfumes, when he noticed he was not the only one eyeing the woman. A pair of steel caps elbowed one another as they chatted in low tones and laughed, their eyes like hungry predators. Sal didn't like seeing the City Watch, but so long as the steel caps' attention remained on the woman and not on Sal, he didn't much mind. Still, their presence would make his plans all the more difficult.

Oldrez had short legs and a fat round belly. Sal didn't think he'd have any trouble outrunning the man once he had the coin purse. The City Watch was another matter. One often found himself outrunning one pair of steel caps, only to run right into rein-forcements.

The bagman passed the fountain, his coin purse tucked under his arm, his trajectory aimed directly for the little Dahuaneze teashop. Sal took a moment to steel his nerves before he moved closer. The pieces were falling into place, everything was going to plan.

Oldrez put his hand on the door of the teashop and pushed, when someone darted in and snatched the coin purse right out of the bagman's thick fingers.

Sal cursed, hardly able to believe what had just happened. The thief was a Yahdrish by the look of him, short but quick, as he easily outpaced Oldrez, who had shouted and stumbled over in his attempt to make chase.

The Yahdrish kid seemed to be making for the south entrance, directly between Sal and the pair of steel caps that had been gawking at the woman. The steel caps noticed the commotion and moved for the Yahdrish.

Without thought to what he was doing, nor to why he was doing it, Sal shoved the trinket vendor's cart. The Vordin vendor let out a cry of dismay, but Sal ignored the man, putting all his weight into the thrust.

The cart rolled, picking up speed as it slammed directly into the pair of steel caps.

The trinket vendor made a swipe at Sal, but he dodged the hand and sprinted to catch up with the Yahdrish boy. That bastard had his coin purse, and Sal meant to take it.

"Sacrull's balls, but you really got them, didn't you?" asked the Yahdrish as Sal moved up alongside him. "Come on, I know of a good place to hide."

Caught off guard by the invitation, Sal hesitated before he reached out to take the purse.

"Fuck!" shouted the Yahdrish as three steel caps surged through the south entrance.

Sal grabbed him by the arm and steered him west. "This way."

Oldrez, it seemed, had resumed the chase, coming down on them from the north. The two previous steel caps had recovered from their bout with the trinket cart, and they closed in from the east. From the south, the three new steel caps joined in.

Sal and the Yahdrish boy ran as fast as their feet would take them, out the west entrance of Town Square and up the Singing

Bridge. Once they'd hit the Cathedral District, Oldrez and the armored steel caps were nowhere in sight, but neither Sal nor the Yahdrish kid slowed their pace. They took the Street of Steel up to Knöldrus Road and cut dead east.

Suddenly, the Yahdrish grabbed him by the arm and tugged. "In here."

Sal was nearly pulled off his feet but managed to keep from falling over as he stumbled around the rubble and wreckage about the tower and ducked through the door. The Yahdrish slammed the door shut and plopped down on one of the stone steps, the coin purse still clutched tight under his arm. They were within what had once been a watchtower but was now a decrepit ruin connected to the perimeter wall of Knöldrus Abbey.

"I didn't realize anyone could get in here anymore," Sal said.

"You couldn't," the Yahdrish replied. "Took me a week to get in. I had to dig out that door there before I could do anything. And the Sacrull damned nails those monks used—anyway, thanks for saving my skin back there. You were brilliant, the way you pushed that cart right into those bloody steel caps."

"Don't mention it," Sal said, his gaze shifting to the coin purse. "Those steel caps would have beaten you bloody if they'd caught you, then I'd have probably seen you winched up in a crow-cage by morning. Which is a whole lot better than what would have happened if Don Svoboda's bagman had caught up with you."

"That fat Pairgu?" the Yahdrish asked. "That stuffed sausage didn't stand a chance of catching me. More than likely, he keeled over just before the Singing Bridge."

"What were you thinking, anyhow?" Sal asked.

The curly haired Yahdrish shrugged. "Saw the fat man with the purse and I figured I could make a clean getaway."

Sal shook his head. The Yahdrish was a damned fool, but Sal couldn't help from liking the kid. He was short and somewhat squirrely, had black curly hair and a hooked nose, green eyes, and olive skin.

"I'm Salvatori," Sal said, reaching out a hand.

"Bartholomew Shoaly," said the Yahdrish boy.

4

WHEN HOUNDS BAY

"But it would rain this night of all nights," said Vinny, brushing long, wet hair from his eyes. "This should clear soon enough. Though, if it doesn't, we'll find ourselves out a fortnight's planning."

Sal was rusted as old chainmail so far as second-story work was concerned, and the wet wasn't going to help. He'd wanted the details planned out as meticulously as possible, which had taken a significant amount of time, much more than the average job. A full fortnight in which Sal had forsworn the use of skeev. Eight days of headaches and sporadic moments of sweating, followed by chills that ran to his very core. The one consolation of the past fortnight had been when Lilliana finally agreed to meet with him once more.

"East Market," Lilliana had told him. *"Two hours before midday, and don't be late."*

He had no intention of being late for their meeting. He had waited too long, come too far back from his mistake, to mess things up again.

"The rain will certainly make the climb more difficult," Sal admitted, "but I'm willing to roll the bones if you are."

Vinny scratched the bit of blonde stubble poking from his chin. He cupped his other hand and collected droplets of rain. The rainfall had increased, hampering the line of sight afforded by their shuttered lanterns to less than an arm's reach. "No one will be looking for second-story work tonight, not in this weather. Might be this rain is in our favor if we play things right and avoid the rooftops until we need."

Sal nodded. If it was difficult for them to see, it would be equally difficult for the steel caps.

They crossed the Tamber by way of High Bridge, often under-manned by the City Watch, as most of High Bridge's traffic came from the monks of Knöldrus Abbey or the craftsmen from the Street of Steel. Though in this weather, the bridge was entirely deserted of foot traffic. When they reached the east bank, the steel caps remained inside the warm, dry bridge tower, not bothering to pose a question to either thief.

Sal and Vinny made their way along the curve of the Kingsway until they reached High Gate. Conveniently, the home they planned to enter was built with the intent of taking advantage of the struc-tural integrity of the city wall. Meaning, the home was built to butt up flush against the wall. The disadvantage of this, so far as the owner was concerned, was that it made the roof of the home quite easily accessible.

The crumbling mortar of the stone wall provided plenty of handholds, allowing the pair to scale it with ease. A quick step up to the roof and Vinny was working at the locked window with a pry and tapper. The method was rudimentary, and though loud, it was reliable.

Within the span of ten heartbeats, Vinny pried open the window. A loud bang sounded, accompanied by a flash of light.

"Gah!" Vinny cried out and stumbled back a step, shielding his eyes with a raised arm. "Bloody ward."

"You oaf," Sal chuckled and examined Vinny for any burns, but it seemed the half-Norsic had only been startled by the small explosion.

After checking the window sill for any untriggered wards, the pair climbed inside. They entered into the solar of Lord Marcus Horvat, Seventh Seat of the High Council and a man of great wealth in his own right. Lord Marcus' home seemed no more special than the next when looked upon from without, but from within, it was clear at a glance that Marcus Horvat was a man of expensive tastes.

Though they'd not seen the inside until that moment, the fortnight spent in preparation revealed many insights about his lordship. He was frugal but not unwilling to pay good coin for quality. Unlike much of Dijvous nobility, Lord Marcus preferred function to opulence, his clothing well cut and finely made, yet not ostentatious —his home much in the same. Still, it might have been worth the extra krom to invest in better security. One never knew when someone might slip through a window.

Vinny tilted his head toward the door.

Sal nodded and began to rifle through the solar as Vinny went for the bedrooms.

The rain stopped suddenly, and Sal smiled to himself as he dripped water on the floorboards.

The solar was organized, everything in its respective place within the drawers of the ebony wood writing desk. A golden letter knife with a pearl handle caught his eye, and he pocketed it, when the parchment beneath the letter knife became apparent to him.

Sal had learned to read as a young child; his uncle had insisted upon it. He'd claimed no man would ever rise high in the world without his letters. Sal picked up the piece of parchment and began to read. It was a shipping manifest, but the bit that interested Sal was that the consignor of the document was scratched out as the Holy Vespian Order of Knöldrus Abbey.

Just then, Sal heard a woman's scream.

He dropped the manifest and ran to the door, poking his head out to see what had caused the commotion.

Vinny bolted up the stairs, headed directly for Sal.

"Run!" Vinny yelled at him.

Sal turned and made for the window. He heard another scream.

"Help, help, I'm being robbed!"

Sal nearly leaped headlong through the open window. Vinny

followed swiftly behind, and they began to move as quickly as they could across rain-slick shingles.

He saw lanterns lighting as they ran along the top of the wall, then onto a roof. Sal leaped and landed on the next rooftop, when he began to hear the baying and barking of dogs amid the shouts and general commotion of the High Town residents.

"Thief!" someone shouted. "Thief on the rooftops!"

His chest began to burn, and his breath quickened. He did his best not to slip as he ran, but he wanted to distance himself from the Horvat residence as quickly as possible. The baying of the hounds drew ever closer. Dogs were the last thing Sal wanted to deal with.

He leaped and landed on the roof of the next home. Only, he didn't land. Instead, he went directly through the thatching.

Sal landed upon a table, which drove the air from his lungs and sent stars popping behind his eyes. He quickly came to as one of the table legs gave way, dumping him unceremoniously upon the dirt floor. The ringing in his ears slowly dissipated, and suddenly, he realized a woman was screaming. He turned to see the woman crouched on a straw mattress, clutching a blanket to her bare chest. There was a man, naked as his name day, moving to position himself between Sal and the woman, as if to protect her.

The door burst open. Hounds barked, and the woman continued to scream as two snarling mastiffs burst through the open doorway.

Sal ducked behind the broken table, and the beasts continued past him, leaping at the naked man.

By that point, the naked man had managed to retrieve a short sword. As the hounds leaped, the man took a wild swing.

One of the hounds snapped its powerful jaws around the man's sword-arm. The other clasped him about the upper thigh.

The woman screamed even louder.

The man cried out in pain.

A whistle drowned them both out, and the dogs disengaged without hesitation.

Four steel caps surged into the home, poleaxes lowered, looks of pure malice upon their faces.

Sal ducked back behind the table, hoping by the Lady's luck he'd not been seen.

The naked man slumped to the floor. The puncture wounds in his arm and thigh pouring rivers of blood.

Sal felt an ironclad hand grip him by the wrist and wrench it behind his back as he was pinned to the floor.

"Bind that man's wounds," said one of the steel caps. "Get him to the mender, quickly now!" The steel cap turned to look at Sal. He wore the midnight blue tabard of the City Watch, the axe and moon sigil of the magistrate sewn proudly upon his chest, the gold armband about his bicep signifying his rank as a Watch lieutenant. He had a thin mustache that perfectly outlined his leering smile.

The woman continued to scream, and the lieutenant's attention was momentarily occupied.

"Madam, I dare say we apologize for any inconvenience we have caused. Compensation will be offered at the Magistrate's Compound should you choose to seek it," said the lieutenant, turning back to Sal. "As for you. I think the under-cells will serve quite nicely."

5

FIRE-WINE

INTERLUDE, SEVEN YEARS EARLIER

The sun rose with alacrity, cresting the horizon while Sal and Bartholomew seated themselves upon a pair of stools. Red light reflected off the crystalline waters of the bay as a layer of fog peeled away from the water's surface. The sea air tasted clean and salty and still held the chill of early morning.

"Rumor has it you've got the best cockles in South Market," said Bartholomew.

A Kirkundan on the stool beside the Yahdrish turned. "Aliana's got the best cockles in all of Dijvois, boy."

"Dijvois?" The little, old cockle vendor nearly spat the word. "Aliana has the best cockles in the known world, and don't you doubt this, child."

Bartholomew blushed red as the sunrise.

Sal smirked.

"If you be wanting any cockles, you wipe that smarmy little smear right of your kisser, or you won't be getting a lick."

Sal stopped smiling and sat up straight.

The little cockle vendor turned on the fat Kirkundan. "And

Finlay, you'll shut your lard trap and sit quiet until I've done cooking, else you won't be getting none neither."

Sal looked out on the market-round. He rather liked South Market. It was a vibrant place, filled with all sorts of different people, funny sounding languages, and strange foreign clothes. The market was right off the harbor and in the early morning, was full of fresh fish, exotic fruits, and curious spices.

Aliana strained the cockles from the pot of boiling water and distributed the steaming shells between three baskets. She plopped a dish of vinegar and another of finely ground black peppercorns upon the bar and served out the baskets.

Just the smell put Sal's mouth to watering. He passed on the vinegar but sprinkled his first morsel with a pinch of pepper. The food was well worth the wait. Sal had never been out of Dijvois, but he didn't doubt Aliana's claim to have the best cockles in the known world.

"How did your meeting with that loan shark go?" Bartholomew asked.

"Anton? He's not a loan shark, more an employer that threw me a few krom in a pinch."

"He's with one of the street gangs, isn't he?"

"The White Eyes, but of late, he can't stop talking about being made with the Moretti Family."

"Moretti? They're a Commission family."

Sal nodded. "Anton's a good earner, pays up the ladder and everything."

"How'd you wind up with someone like that?" the Yahdrish asked, seeming impressed that Sal was associated with someone connected.

"He caught me picking on one of his streets down in the Narrows. Told me I could pay him back for the trespass with my thumbs, or I could cut him a percentage of my work."

"I see you've still got both your thumbs," said Bartholomew with a smile. "You must be quite the snatcher if you're picking for a connected crew."

Sal shrugged but couldn't help a grin from spreading. "I'm not with his crew. I only do side jobs for Anton."

"I'm not a half bad snatcher myself," said the Yahdrish confidently.

Sal scoffed. "I saw that the other day in Town Square."

"Got out of there with the coin, didn't I?"

"I suppose you did, but you know, we should think about laying low for a time," Sal suggested. "Don Svoboda will have his feelers out. He won't appreciate being robbed. Especially not by a couple of urchins like us."

"Wasn't my first Commission bagman," said the Yahdrish proudly.

"Really? And just how many bagmen have you knocked off?"

Bartholomew turned to the little, old cockle vendor. "Oy, you haven't got fire-wine, have you?"

Aliana frowned suspiciously. "I keep some on hand for the Skjörds. You're certain you want it?"

"Aye, my lady, with all my heart. Ever had fire-wine?" the Yahdrish asked, turning to Sal.

Sal shook his head.

The little, old cockle vendor wrinkled her nose and thudded a bottle on the bar. "Charge by the cup. Two copper each. An iron for the opening fee, seeing as this is a fresh bottle."

Bartholomew nodded.

"And I'll not have you getting deep in your cups here. You get clumsy, and I cut you off."

The Yahdrish nodded again. "I'll take a cup, one for my friend here as well."

When she'd poured them each a cup of the fire-wine, Aliana went back to preparing her next batch of cockles. Bartholomew lifted his cup, and Sal followed suit.

"You're going to like this," said the Yahdrish boy.

Sal took a drink and realized almost immediately that he had made a tragic error. The alcohol burned like fire. He panicked and burst into a fit of coughing.

Bartholomew only laughed.

"You actually drink that swill?" Sal asked.

The Yahdrish shrugged and finished off his cup with a long swig. Then he nodded to Sal's cup. Sal nudged the cup over to Bartholomew, who smiled and drank what was left of Sal's fire-wine.

"Whew," Bartholomew said and wiped his mouth with his sleeve. "Got to love that burn."

Sal shook his head. He didn't understand how the Yahdrish could drink that piss-water. He just assumed it had something to do with conditioning.

"So, if Oldrez wasn't your first, just how many Commission bagmen have you robbed?"

Bartholomew smirked. "Leg-breakers are never all that fast, and most of them are so arrogant, it bleeds out their ears."

"Well, how many?" Sal asked again.

"I suppose this was my third."

"Third! Light's blessing, three? Are you bloody mad?"

The Yahdrish boy laughed. "You would think they might be a bit more prepared, but these Commission types are some of the sloppiest fools out there."

"Sloppy?" Sal said, shaking his head. "That's because they know no one is stupid enough to try and rob a Commission bagman. I can't imagine that will be the case much longer."

"Now, hold on just a tick. Didn't you tell me you were going to rob him yourself? I just happened to get there first."

"Right, well, I was desperate. Besides, I have to think my plan, being a bit more sophisticated than a grab and run, might have gone over a touch smoother."

"Had a better plan, did you?" Bartholomew asked, his look skeptical.

"Well, in any case, I was desperate," Sal said.

"We're all desperate on the street."

Sal felt a tinge of guilt. "How long have you been doing this?"

Bartholomew shrugged. "Long as I can remember. Ma' taught me what she knew. You know, a bit of this and that, teasing and picking, before she—you know. Just been me on my own the last four years."

"My mother passed as well," Sal said.

Silence hung between them for a moment, and Sal took a look at the Godstone. The massive gray slab of stone, wrapped in green ivy and carved with runes, brought a sense of wildness to the market place—a memory of the past.

"Ever considered paying up the ladder?" Bartholomew asked. "You know, trying to get yourself made with one of the Commission families?"

"Why would I want to do that?"

"Why not?" Bartholomew asked, seemingly baffled by the question. "Isn't that why you're running with a connected guy? I mean, who wouldn't want to get made?"

Sal shrugged. "I guess I've seen enough to know it's not worth it."

"Not worth it? How could you say that?"

Sal shrugged again and skewered a cockle on his fork.

"I'll be a made man before long," said Bartholomew.

"Will you now?"

The Yahdrish nodded. "Going to be running the Commission one day."

"Running the Commission? You want to be a don?"

"Not just a don. I'll be *the* don, boss of the Five Families."

Sal smiled. "Sure, sure. I suppose if you want it bad enough, why not?"

"You could come along with me," the Yahdrish boy said. "I'll need a loyal underboss. I figure you would fill the position as good as any."

Sal laughed and skewered an especially meaty cockle from its shell.

"Something funny?"

"You are, mate. I told you. I don't have any interest in being made, and I have even less interest in climbing the ladder."

"I mean it. I mean to climb the ladder all the way to the top rung. Come along with me."

Sal shook his head. "No, I think I'm happy right where I am. No need to stick my neck out any farther."

The Yahdrish shrugged. "It's an open offer if you change your mind."

Sal nodded and skewered another cockle.

"So, you said your ma' passed, but what of your da'?" asked Bartholomew.

"Never knew him," Sal said.

"You neither, eh? Guess the world needs bastards like us as much as anyone else."

"I guess you're right," Sal said, looking back out on the bay. "Listen, that name of yours is a real mouthful. You ever go by anything shorter?"

"Ma' used to call me Bartley."

"Bartley, huh?" Sal nodded. "I suppose Bartley will do."

6

A FITTING PUNISHMENT

Footsteps echoed through the stone hallway, stirring Sal from his stupor. *Thump-thud, thump-thud, thump-thud.* A single slender window, barred by iron, was cut high in the stonewall. The only source of light in the dark, dank cell. A full night and half-a-day he'd spent in the cell, and he'd conceived of only one plan. He would needs bull-rush the guards the moment his cell door came open. Mayhap, he could then escape the dungeon and flee.

Should his plan fail, however, they would stuff him in a crow-cage on the Street of Rags, to starve and blister in the sun, until carrion came to pick off his flesh. If only he'd had the locket. The steel caps never would have caught him had he been able to ride away on the lighting.

Thump-thud, thump-thud. The sound of footfalls on flagstones drew closer until they halted before the cell. A faint, flickering glow penetrated the gap beneath the heavy oaken door.

"On your feet," the guard said from without.

The hinges squealed in protest as the door was opened.

There were two jailors. Upon sight of the men, Sal abandoned his plan to charge. One carried a torch and a loop of iron keys, the other a wicked looking cudgel. Neither man wore the livery of the

Magistrate. They were no City Watchmen, merely goalers. The jailor with the cudgel leaned his weapon against the wall and grabbed Sal roughly by the arm, placing manacles about Sal's wrists.

Torch in hand, the turnkey led the way, escorting Sal through a series of locked doors and stone passageways. At the arrival of each door, there followed a pause as the jailor fumbled for the proper key to fit the lock. They climbed a spiral stairwell that seemed to wind on and up endlessly. Sal felt a sinking sensation in his gut. They were in the tower of the magistrate.

Eventually, they arrived before a door for which the jailors had no key. A thick oaken door, studded with iron. Placing the torch in an empty sconce and belting his keyring, the jailor knocked.

A voice called out, telling them to enter.

The room was dimly lit by flickering torchlight. The air smelled of flowery oils. Upon one wall, a patchwork of chains hung loosely, threaded between four metal rings. Directly before Sal was an ornately carved writing desk, upon it, a clay pitcher beaded with condensation so that it shined in the torchlight like a glass chandelier. Sal licked his dry lips, only then realizing how thirsty he was.

Behind the ornately carved writing desk, a little man scribbled something on a sheet of parchment. He wore a gold livery collar that displayed the axe and crescent moon of the Magistrate. As Sal's manacles were removed, he admired the small man's cufflinks for their flawless craftsmanship, polished silver, one a battle axe, the other a crescent moon.

Standing beside the seated man was a stout monk with cheeks like two ripe tomatoes, a bulbous vein splotched nose, and a grey mustache. Brother Tanao.

At the sight of the monk, Sal's heart sunk into his bowels.

Once Sal was seated, the man opposite gingerly laid down his quill, folded his hands on the desktop, and fixed Sal with a smile that showed entirely too many teeth.

"You may leave us," the little man said, with a contemptuous flick of his hand.

The jailors hesitated, but as the little man's smile disappeared the jailors seemed to take their cue, and they turned to leave, closing the door from without.

Brother Tanao snorted, long and loud, wiping at his nose with the sleeve of his drab brown robe.

The little man behind the desk cleared his throat. "My name is Simon Fuller, clerk to his Lordship, Carrow Beveren, magistrate of Dijvois. And this is Brother Tanao, master brewer to the Holy Vespian Order of Knöldrus Abbey. Now, then, you stand accused of the crime of thievery, and for this, you have been detained, subject to judgment upon further notice."

Sal opened his mouth to speak, but it seemed the little man was not finished.

"As of this hour, Brother Tanao has informed me that you are wanted for another crime. He has also brought with him a written request for a transfer of prisoner. Written by the abbot of Knöldrus Abbey and signed by both the abbot and the duke." Simon Fuller fixed Sal with an inquisitive look. "You are hereby transferred to the custody of the brothers of Knöldrus Abbey, to be sentenced by a court of the Vespian Order for the crime of murder."

The news had not hit him so hard as he would have assumed. What else could the presence of the monk have meant?

"Right then, what's to be done with me?" Sal asked.

"You'll come with me," said Tanao. "We will make for the abbey, soon as those irons are removed, and my charge has had a cup of that water."

"Brother Tanao, I would suggest leaving the manacles in place until you have reached your destination. The prisoner could pose a threat to your life."

"Boy, what man of God should fear death? Now, I'll have those irons stripped, or you'll see the true wrath of a servant of the Light."

Simon Fuller leaped to obey, shuffling through his keyring to find the right fit for Sal's irons. The lock clicked sounding the latch's release, and the clerk removed the shackles. Then he grabbed hold of the clay pitcher and poured a cup of water.

Sal opened and closed his hands as feeling painfully rushed into them. He found it difficult to grip the wooden cup when it was handed to him. As he pressed the cup to his lips, the cold water running over his tongue and down his parched throat was the best thing that had ever happened to him. At that moment, any worry he held for the future flitted away. All that mattered was the water and the relief it provided. He felt rejuvenated, the throbbing in his head receded, and the soreness of his throat quelled. He'd not had a thing to eat or drink since he was put in the under-cells, and he shuddered to think how long he'd have been deprived basic necessities had the monk not demanded he get a drink.

"The jailors will escort you from the tower. Good day, Brother Tanao. I will pray for your safe travels. Do be wary of this prisoner, it may be that he is more dangerous than he appears."

"See that you pray for men who need such feeble blatherings, I am a man of God. To what end should I fear union with the Light? Let this man attempt to take the life from me, and you shall see what little need I have for your words, scribe. I require no guide, for the Lord that is Light will guide my way."

Simon Fuller seemed to not know just how to respond, and so he nodded, stood from the magistrate's plush chair of office, and crossed the solar to open the door for Sal and the monk.

The pair of jailors waited just outside the door.

"They'll not need your assistance," the clerk said, unable to hide the contempt in his voice. "Brother Tanao knows the way."

"I make no such claims," said Tanao. "For the glory, be unto the Lord that is Light."

As they headed down the tower stair and through the halls of the Magistrate's Compound, it seemed Tanao did know the way.

"How exactly does your God guide you?" Sal asked

"Through experience," Tanao said, winking. "I served twenty years as an under-jailor. When the former magistrate passed and a new constable was brought on, I decided it was a good time for a career change, and I joined the Vespian Order."

Sal smiled. Had Tanao not joined the monkhood, he might have well made a fine living as a mummer on the stage.

Outside the compound, the usual dreary gray storm clouds

covered the sky above Dijvois. The black basalt stone of the Magistrate's Compound loomed behind them like some predatory monster. Sal was glad to be free of the compound. Still, he couldn't help but wonder if he were any better off at the mercy of the monks than he was in the hands of the Ducal Court. The Vespian Order had a long history of harsh judgment and cruel treatment toward prisoners. After all, the birth of the First Inquisition took place from within their order.

"A blessed day be upon the both of you," Tanao said to the pair of steel caps standing guard at the compound entrance. "Salvatori, in the wagon, if you would."

Tanao untied the reigns of his mules from the hitching post. The beasts were fat and well groomed, but the wagon must have been half a century old. Sal would have needed search long and hard to find its like still in use. The wagon's seat was a flat wooden plank. Sal expected it was bound to grow quite uncomfortable as they bounced along on the cobblestone streets.

Tanao flicked the reigns, which put the mules into motion. Despite everything that was yet to come, Sal felt a smile creeping up the corners of his mouth at the thought of leaving the Magistrate's Compound alive.

The crow-cages were six-foot iron cages that hung from gibbeting along the Street of Rags. Six in all, but only two occupied criminals.

One of Sal's worst fears was to be stuck in a crow-cage, a fate he had narrowly avoided, only to wind up rolling the bones once more.

As they passed the cages, Tanao shook his head. "A truly barbaric practice," the monk said mournfully.

Sal couldn't help but agree. He looked at the cages, forcing himself to see the men behind the bars as they begged, fingers poking through the iron grates. Sal realized he knew one of the men. Not well, but he'd seen the man in his uncle's company a time or two. He was a made man, one of Don Svoboda's enforcers. The made man's eyes met Sal's, and Sal looked away, unable to match the Svoboda man's stare.

A pregnant silence fell over them after they'd passed the crow-cages. The wagon bounced as it trundled along the cobblestones, jostling Sal in a most uncomfortable fashion. It wasn't until they had crossed Beggar's Lane that Tanao spoke.

"The pompous prat. I cared not for the cut of his cloth."

"Pardon?" Sal asked, bemused by the outburst.

"The simpering clerk of the magistrate. I'd have liked to wring my hands about his scrawny neck. Though, I had needs content myself with curt words and obnoxious piety," the monk said with a vulpine smile that seemed queer on his innocent, round face.

"Simon Fuller, was he really so detestable?"

"A simpering jackanape, one could see it in the way the magistrate's men looked upon him. Light's name, I'll eat my robes if a single word I spoke pushed through the wax of his ears and took seed within that shriveled raisin he calls a brain."

Sal laughed, more out of propriety than joviality. As the mules clopped on at a steady pace, he looked around, watching people go about their business of the day. Urchins weaved through the crowds as they worked in pairs, teasing and picking any targets they could mark. When the wagon neared Town Square, Sal could hear vendors pushing their wares.

He began to wonder why he'd ridden so far along with the monk. This was his chance to run. All he needed to do was jump from the plodding wagon and escape into the crowd. He wasn't shackled, nothing was keeping him on the wagon but his own hesitation.

"Wondering why you haven't run?" Tanao asked.

The question startled Sal from his thoughts.

"A good question," Tanao said, as though answering his own inquiry. "I surmise you are not a pious man, neither bound by morals nor God. Fear, perhaps? But no, you did not seem frightened when you were told you'd be coming with me. If I am not mistaken, your look was one of relief. Are you relieved to be going back with me, Salvatori Lorenzo?"

Sal shrugged. "I'm not certain."

"So, you are a man of chance? You would gamble on your luck

with a court of the Vespian Order rather than the servants of the Ducal Court, is this the way of it?"

Sal shrugged again, frowning. "Didn't think I had a choice in the matter. Besides, could be I'm only biding my time. Maybe I'd rather escape at a more convenient location."

Tanao's round visage took on a cherubic expression. "I'm thinking that if you'd meant to escape you'd have done it long before now. My guess is, you've decided riding with me to Knöldrus Abbey would be preferred to wasting away in one of those crow-cages on the Street of Justice. Would that be somewhere near the mark?"

"And what if I murdered that monk?" Sal asked. "What if I was the one who'd done murder. Would you truly not fear for your life?"

"Why should a servant of the Light fear for his mortal flesh? I have faith, in my God and my fellow man. Even his lost sheep will return to the flock once they've done their time in wandering." Tanao ruffled Sal's hair. "You are no murderer, Salvatori Lorenzo," The monk said confidently.

Sal wondered if Tanao made a distinction between killing and murder.

Tanao looked to his left, then his right, and to his left again. Sal realized the monk had a hand inside his robes. Apparently satisfied with what he saw, Brother Tanao withdrew his hand to reveal a clear stoppered bottle filled with an amber liquid. "Can't be too careful," Tanao said, pulling the stopper. He took a healthy swig, shivering slightly as he swallowed. Then hastily hid the open bottle behind the billowy sleeve of his robe as a pair of hooded acolytes, belonging to the Keepers of the Flame, walked past the wagon.

"Like a drink, my friend?" Tanao asked once the acolytes were out of earshot.

Sal shrugged and accepted the bottle. He leaned back and took a pull, no easy task in a moving, bouncing wagon. A warm, burning sensation surged down his throat. He shivered and heaved a sputtering cough. Tanao laughed and hastily snatched the bottle that Sal nearly dropped as he coughed.

"A fine batch this one. Apple brandy, all the way from Kirkundy, given to me by a brother from Athulmere Priory. We only brew ale at Knöldrus Abbey, you see, and a man of the times has a thirst for something stronger." Tanao took another swig of the bottle.

They continued to talk and drink, the wagon plodding along for a time, until something came to mind that had been troubling Sal. "Brother Tanao, how is it you knew I was in that cell?"

"Ah, well, the abbot sent me."

"The abbot? How did he—hold on, the abbot's dead, isn't he?"

"Yes, that's true, Abbot Tarquin did pass from this world, but I was sent by the new abbot."

"The new abbot? But how could he have known I was in the Magistrate's Compound? Lady's sake, I was only in there for a night and half a day."

It was Tanao's turn to shrug. "You'd do as well to ask me how the grass grows, or the tide ebbs and flows. I do not pretend to understand how the workings of this world, only that if I see something, I know it is truth."

Something else occurred to Sal, perhaps the most puzzling quandary of all. "Tanao, who *is* the new abbot of Knöldrus Abbey?"

"Why, I am proud to say, Brother Jacques holds that honor," Tanao said, hardly able to contain his excitement at the announcement. "When Brother Henry and Brother Martin both dropped from the race, Jacques was hard-pressed to put forth his name. Naturally, Leobald was furious about the results. He swore up and down about how he deserved a recount of the stones."

Sal smiled at the thought of Leobald throwing a fit when Jacques had assumed the position of abbot. As they neared Town Square, the noise of the market place grew steadily louder, until it was nearly impossible to hear his own thoughts. They rolled past the great bronze statue of Uthrid Stormbreaker, a hero monk of old, whose statue stood in the heart of the center fountain. When Tanao caught sight of the great bronze statue, he began chanting a hymn that drew stares as they clattered along.

"Shatter the storm with earth and Light!

Shatter the storm with Solus' might!
Arise his men, arise.
Here we stand, and here we fight.
Arise his men, arise.
The storm has come, turn to the Light."

Sal stopped listening to the words as he grew unsettled by the attention Tanao was attracting. When a pair of steel caps looked at their wagon, Sal did his best to hide his face behind his hands without being too obvious before he realized, for once, he had no reason to hide.

"Only blood may pay for blood,
and death may pay for life,
but to rid us of the darkness,
there is only sa-cri-fiiiiice!"

Tanao brought his hymn to a close as they clattered across the Singing Bridge and entered the Cathedral District.

They passed through the abbey gates without halting to provide an explanation, but as they drove along, the tonsured heads of the monk's turned and stared at Sal as he passed. The expressions on their faces ranging from surprise to anger. When they reached the stables, Tanao handed the reigns to a young acolyte.

"An extra bit of oats for Lefty tonight, I think," Tanao said to the taller of the two boys, and the acolytes began to unhitch the mules from the wagon.

"Come along. The abbot will be wanting a word as soon as he returns. Though, it could be some time before then. So, for now, you'll come with me. There is always work to be done about the mill and brewhouse."

Sal moved to obey when a voice sounded behind him. "There was a rumor the skeever had returned to us," said a man with a shrill voice. Sal turned to see Leobald crossing the yard, headed in his direction. "I see the rumors prove true. Come to confess to your crime, have you, murderer?"

"Be off, Brother Leobald, you've no business with my guest," said Tanao, hustling to position himself between Sal and Leobald.

"I dare say I do have business. I am prior of Knöldrus Abbey, or have you forgotten, Master Brewer?"

"I have not," said Tanao, arms crossed. "Nor have I forgotten, Brother Jacques is abbot, not you, Master Prior."

"No matter, I'll soon see you flayed, boy," Leobald said. "When your pelt has been cut from your flesh, we will hang it above the gates as a warning to those who would think my brothers easy victims. And once your skin has been shorn from your flesh, I'll let you free to flop about in the mud, a bloody pink fish."

"Come, Salvatori, we've no use for such sickly-sweet words. They sustain neither the mind nor the belly, rather they stick to teeth to rot and fester," said Tanao.

They crossed the yard, in the direction of the mill. As they neared their destination, the brewhouse came into sight. The rushing current of the Tamber worked the great water wheel that turned the mill. Not only did the Tamber serve as the power source, but the monks used the river's water to brew their ale. The brewhouse was little more than a timber shack, packed floor to ceiling with oak barrels, and smelled of a strong odor that Sal could not put his finger on.

Though, he must have wrinkled his nose, because Tanao began to explain. "Fermentation," the monk said with a chuckle. "I tell you, some of the smells that come out of this brewhouse—though, I come to love each and every one in its own right. Good ale requires special attention, and I give attention to each batch as though they were mine own children."

A laugh burst from above. Seated upon a stack of barrels, guzzling from a tankard, was a buck-toothed, rather mousy monk. Philip, Sal thought his name was.

"Your Grace!" Philip shouted, holding the tankard in mock salute before downing the rest of its contents. "Tell me, Tanao, what sort of father makes children and consumes them in the night?"

"I must apologize for the tactless behavior of my drinking

companion," said Tanao, frowning. "Salvatori, might you care for a horn. This is an ale of mine own make."

"Children, he calls them, and yet, now he offers his child like a common whore," said Philip, sliding down from the barrels. "Still, does he not offer a bite of the cheese? We have a wheel of white from our brothers at North Hernshire. Just arrived this morning."

"You truly never tasted a finer cheese," said Tanao. "A soft white, marbled by veins of blackberry wine."

After a few horns of ale and three helpings of what truly was one of the finest cheeses he had ever eaten, Sal actually began to appreciate the odor of the fermenting ale. He noticed underlying scents, notes of piney hops and whiffs of earthy barley.

"And do you work in the brewhouse as well, Brother Phillip?"

"Bah." Tanao scoffed. "Philip hasn't the patience for brewing ale. Though, when it comes to drinking it, he is prodigious in his consumption and thankful before the Lord that is Light for his generosity."

"Alas, I am a scribe and a mere apprentice at that. I illuminate the works of scripture in the library."

"Illumination?" Sal asked, thinking of the vellum pages he used to look at in his uncle's solar. His uncle had a handful of illuminated works within his collection. Sal wondered just how many books there were in the monastic library, hundreds, maybe even tens of hundreds. "Your work must be challenging. Do you enjoy it?"

"I find that I much prefer the perks of the brewhouse to those of the library. Unfortunately, we don't choose where we serve. It is for the Lord that is Light to show us the Way and for the brothers of my order to walk upon it."

Tanao held his mug aloft. "For the Lord that is Light shall guide us. We will lead the charge for men. We shall be the hardened tip of the first spear's thrust into the heart of darkness."

Sal drank along with the monks as they downed their horns following Tanao's pronouncement. He felt dizzy. Mayhap, he'd had too much drink and too little food. The cheese had been the only thing he'd had to eat in nearly two days. He stood unsteadily and leaned against a cask to regain his balance. As his head spun with drunken bliss, he considered that a mere hour before, he had been in shackles—fit to rot in the under-cells, starved and neglected until he was finally judged guilty of theft and stuffed inside a crow-cage to be slowly consumed by carrion.

"Tell me, Salvatori, what think you of my brew?" Tanao asked.

"I've never drunk its equal," Sal said, holding up his horn. "An ale beyond compare."

Tanao smiled, his cherubic face a shade of red so deep, it was nearly purple. "Ah, but it would seem we have made another brother today."

Sal gave him a quizzical look, his vision blurring double.

"Not a brother of the cloth, but a brother of the cup. Salvatori Lorenzo, I name you friend!" Tanao boomed jovially as he refilled the horns.

Sal couldn't help but smile. Things were not going quite the way he had expected. The rumors of the Vespian Order's cruelty toward criminals was beginning to sound more fiction than fact.

"To Salvatori Lorenzo," said Philip, raising his horn. "Friend of the Vespian Order and a better man than I."

Sal drank with the other two. He could only guess what he had done to earn such praise. It had been a long time since he had felt worthy of anything less than a kick in the teeth. Yet, that was a funny thing about alcohol. It had the power to turn otherwise harmless men into monsters and complete strangers into the best of friends, all in the span of a night.

His insides felt warm and fuzzy, his head light, and for the first time in a while, he felt—happy. He must have been more drunk than he'd realized.

"You're simply too humble," Sal said honestly. "I could not have asked for a greater blessing. This day has turned full upon its face, and it is only thanks to you and Abbot Jacques. Still, I don't understand how it is that the abbot could have known I had been arrested."

"Abbot Jacques is a well-liked man in Dijvois, a man with friends. It would seem to me one of his many friends put a word in his ear about a certain man that had been arrested, a man who very much resembled another man that the Vespian Order had been asking about. When news reached the abbot, he summoned me and sent me to the duke with his letter and his seal of office." Tanao held up his left hand proudly to show a silver ring encrusted with rubies, the golden sun of the Vespian Order at the ring's center, emblazoned with an orange garnet.

"And the abbot, where from is he returning?" Sal asked.

"The abbot had business abroad," said Tanao. "The Lord that is Light will guide his Holiness where he is needed. It is not for lesser men such as we to worry over the workings of God but to act when called upon in a manner which is pleasing to the Lord."

"You don't know, do you?" Philip scoffed.

"And you do?" Tanao said defensively.

"I most certainly do not," Philip said. "but whenever you hide behind your piety, it is due to your ignorance, not your devotion, and don't you deny it."

Tanao huffed. "If it pleases you, I do not know where the Abbot has gone and whence he shall return. Though by his order, we await his pleasure. When he returns, we shall be among the first to know."

Sal was not certain he liked the sound of that. Thus far, things had been more than agreeable, but there was no telling what turn his fate could take at the abbot's return. Though Jacques had been kind to him before, his duties as abbot could require he act in a very different manner than he had when he was the Master Infirmarer.

Sal's heartrate quickened. He considered running, but what would be the point? Unless he was willing to leave the city, it would only be a matter of time before he was spotted and would find himself in a worse situation. Still, where would he go? Where could he go? He'd never left Dijvois. It was the only home he knew, the only place in the world Sal knew how to survive. Even were he to leave the city, there was no guarantee of his safety. Deep in his cups as he was, how far would he even get before sober men restrained him and returned him to the abbey?

His best option was to stay where he was and wait for the bones to roll. Should they roll in his favor, all the better. Still, the words that Leobald had spoken to him earlier. His talk of flaying Sal and hanging his pelt above the gate, was it all bluster? The man was, after all, the prior of Knöldrus Abbey, second only to the abbot. There was no telling what sway Leobald's influence held.

"That prior, Leobald, why is it Jacques has allowed the man to keep his post? I mean, the abbot could just give the position to someone else, couldn't he?"

"A preservation of stability in a time of transition," Tanao said. "You must understand, while Jacques won the election, it was still a close thing. Many of my brothers still support Leobald, and should the man be relieved of his position at such a time, there is no telling the possible repercussions that could arise from such an act."

"In other words," said Philip. "Jacques is under the belief that by keeping his enemies closer than his friends, he can keep even the more restless of his critics silent and the likelihood of mutiny to a minimum."

"Mutiny," Sal said, chuckling slightly until he saw the looks on the monk's faces. "Is that a possibility?"

"It has happened before," said Tanao. "During the reign of King Sardej the Third, a brother named Bethelmure was elected abbot. Much like the election of our dear Jacques, the election took place in a time of division between the Vespian Order. Then, as now, it all began as a divergence of belief, which in time festered into a schism between our brothers, a small intellectual nit that in time opened into a sore—creating a seemingly unbridgeable divide between the Vespian Order. Then, as now, the death of a long-seated abbot created a destabilization that threatened to crumble the very foundation stones of our order. Then, as now, a man stood in opposition to the newly elected abbot, spreading unrest through divisiveness and marshaling support through his lies."

"Hannivour," said Philip.

"Hanni-what?" asked Sal.

"Hannivour," said Tanao. "An ancient tradition of our order. It denotes a state of crisis. Hannivour is the measure taken to protect our order at such a time."

"Didn't much work for Abbot Bethelmure though, did it?" said Philip with a wicked grin.

"The difference at present is that unlike Abbot Bethelmure, Abbot Jacques has neither attempted to denounce nor banish his opponent. The abbot has done nothing to lend credence to the legitimacy of his opposition's grievances. He has taken the apathetic approach and simply ignored Leobald rather than placing the abbey in a state of Hannivour."

"Has it worked?"

Tanao held out his hands, palms up. "Only time will tell, but thus far, no coups have been incited."

"Yet, summer fast approaches," said Philip. "Wars are not fought in the snow but beneath the summer heat of the Lord that is Light."

"And should it come to war, which side shall you fight upon?" Tanao asked.

"The side of the Light," said Philip defiantly.

"Hannivour," said Tanao as he fixed the young apprentice with a withering look but was interrupted by the opening of the brew-house door.

"Master Brewer," said a boy of no older than ten and three. He wore drab, brown robes and had the tonsured pate of the Vespian Order.

"Well, boy, spit it out."

"It's the abbot, sir. He asked that I inform you of his return."

"Very well," said Tanao, "you may tell the abbot I harken his call."

The boy stood in the doorway, clearly uncertain of something, as he shifted his weight from foot to foot and bit his lower lip.

"Out with it, boy."

"The Abbot asked I bring you, sir."

"And you shall, though you shall do it from a distance. Hurry back now, and tell the Abbot that we follow at your very heels, go now, Light's blessing upon you."

The boy obeyed, leaving the door ajar as he ran to inform the Abbot of his news.

"So be it," said Tanao, grabbing for the ale horns, "a last cup to warm our bellies and ensure our health."

O utside the brewhouse, the city seemed to be glowing. Sal felt happy and light on his feet. It was difficult to keep his balance as he followed Tanao across the yard. Only, when they passed the orchard, Sal felt sick to his stomach. He could see the gnarled, naked branches of the massive pardimon tree in the distance, a terrible reminder of the fate that awaited him. Drunk as he was, he nearly asked Tanao when the last criminal was flayed by the Vespian Order but decided he didn't really want to know.

The abbot's home was on the far end of the abbey. A small stone structure, sturdy and well maintained, but nothing impressive to look upon. The air inside was crisp and clean. Every surface devoid of dust, dirt, or grime. The room was sparsely adorned with simple furniture of unfinished wood and plain furnishings. The abbot was seated at the table, looking out upon the orchard through the window.

"It pleases me you have returned to us by your own volition," Jacques said, turning to face Sal. "The men who were certain of your guilt will see this, and they will begin to doubt their conviction and wonder as to what a criminal would have to gain by returning to the abbey."

"I'm no criminal," Sal said defiantly. "Nor have I returned by my own volition."

"Not a criminal?" said Jacques, wrinkling his brow. "I see no fetters upon your legs or shackles upon your wrists, but tell me, Brother Tanao, did you not find this man deep in the under-cells of the Magistrate's Compound? Do explain what an innocent man should be doing in such a place." Tanao chuckled under his breath, and a small smile formed at the corner of Jacques's mouth. "As to your reason for returning to Knöldrus Abbey, well, reasons are not so important as the impression you've left on my brothers. By entering the abbey unchained and in good faith, you have given the men of my order reason to doubt their convictions." Jacques gestured for Sal to take a seat.

As Sal stumbled, the abbot merely smiled. "I see you've partaken of the Master Brewer's favored pastime," said Jacques.

Tanao cleared his throat, "I shall take my leave, Jacques, Salvatori."

"Brother Tanao," said Jacques to the monk's back, "if our young apprentice Philip happens to be about the brewhouse, do see he does not once again expose himself in the yard come the evenfall prayers."

Tanao snorted a small laugh. "It shall be seen to."

"And Tanao," said Jacques.

The podgy monk turned around.

"The ring."

"Ah, but of course," said Tanao, slipping the ring of office from his finger and handing it to the abbot.

When Tanao had stepped out and closed the door, Jacques sighed. "It is the decision of the Enlightened Council that you should be given a fair trial for the crime of murder."

Sal's heart sank to the pit of his stomach. It was just as he had feared, coming back to the abbey had been a very bad idea.

"I didn't kill that monk."

"And I believe you," said Abbot Jacques.

"You do?"

"I do. Were it otherwise, you'd still be locked inside the under-cells. But I, for one, know you did not do murder. The state that you were in that night, it was a lucky thing you were even breathing. Yet, there are those on the Enlightened Council who hold a different opinion. They would that you defended yourself before a court of our Holy Order. Let him give his evidence, and let him be judged before the Lord that is Light, they have said to me. Sage council, no doubt, and yet, as many of your judges have already decided upon your innocence or guilt, I fear the trial you would be given would inevitably be unjust."

"Then what is to be done with me?"

"My brothers and I decided a trial would be best. It is the only way to ensure justice is served."

"A trial?" Sal said, unbelieving. "Did you not just say a trial would be un—"

Jacques held up a hand. "For the time being, no dates have been set. I have been able to forestall them, your return to Knöldrus was a stipulation of that bargain, as was your detainment within the abbey walls. You shall be confined to a cell and there will await your coming trial."

"For how long?"

"Only God can know. For now, those who doubt your innocence are satisfied with your confinement, but in time they will thirst for justice, and justice is a thirst that will needs be sated."

"And what, you'll flay me and hang my skin from the abbey gate?"

"There was a time when the brothers of my order would have done no less, but time has gentled us. Were you proven guilty of thievery, we might take a finger, but only life may pay for life, and so death must pay for death. If you cannot prove your innocence before such a time, you must be given to the Lord that is Light."

"Fire?" Sal asked in horror.

The monk nodded, his jaw gritted tight.

Sal swallowed. "And how might I prove my innocence?"

"By obtaining the identity of the true murder."

Sal scoffed. "I ought to have a Sacrull damned time of it too, locked away in my cell."

Jacques cleared his throat. "Yes, well, I have arranged that you should be given freedom of the city. During the daylight hours, and on the condition that you return to your cell before evenfall. This stipulation was fought long and hard by my brothers, but in the end, the opposition relented. Do keep in mind, my reputation is in your hands. Do not fail me."

Sal didn't know what to say. Somehow, he'd managed to live another day, and yet, he wasn't certain he was grateful for the opportunity. After all, everything relied on his ability to find the true killer. As if the wild goose chase weren't enough, he also had no idea as to how long he would have before the monks of Knöldrus Abbey grew tired of seeing his face and decided he would look better as a corpse.

"Well, son, what is your choice?"

Sal considered for a moment, weighing possible responses. He could refuse and walk away, only, would the abbot truly allow him to walk away? He could kill the abbot where he sat, but then, where would that lead?

It didn't take long to realize he was left one, and only one, choice. "That locket I was wearing the night you cared for me, where might it be?"

Jacques smiled and stood from his chair. When he returned from the bedroom, he held a small, gold locket strung upon a thin, silver chain. At the center of the locket's face was etched three parallel lines, one of them blood red.

"An intriguing piece," said Jacques, examining the locket in an open palm.

Sal felt the urge to snatch the thing out of the monk's big hand but let his anxiety out with a slow exhalation through his nostrils.

"There are writings in our holy book, descriptions of a mark. This marking on your locket brings those passages to mind."

Sal clenched his jaw and nodded.

The burly abbot smiled and extended his open hand.

Sal did his best not to reach for the locket too quickly. Though, for an instant, he'd feared Jacques meant to keep the thing. He had a sneaking suspicion the monk knew more about the locket than he was willing to admit.

The gold was cool to the touch, and sent a shock of energy pulsing through him upon contact. Acting as though he'd felt nothing, Sal slipped the thin chain about his neck and tucked the locket beneath his shirt. It felt right, as though a torn remnant of his soul had been returned to him.

"That look, the one you give when you're thinking. It too puts something to mind."

The comment caught Sal off guard. "Might I ask what exactly it puts to mind?"

"A man I knew. Dare I say, a friend. You look very much like him. I noticed it before, but the resemblance is never so exact as when you are thinking."

"Who?"

"Ah, we've not spoken since the Kirkundy Uprising."

"He was a soldier?"

"Of sorts."

"And you, Jacques, you were a soldier?"

"Alas no, I was of the Ducal Forces, but I served as a cutter. My father was a surgeon, and he taught me all that I know of the trade. He'd intended for me to take his place, but as a young man, I had no intention nor desire to stay in that hamlet. I dreamed of adventure, and what I found was more awesome and terrible than a young man could ever have imagined."

"And the man, the one you say I resemble. Where is he now?"

"Ah, but I've much to do this night, and I have wasted away the burning hour with my idle blathering. Do forgive me, Salvatori, but I must be getting along. Come, and I will show you to your cell."

They walked toward a small stone structure, close to the abbot's home. Once within, Sal saw that it was fully furnished. The furnishings were of far higher quality than those within the abbot's own home.

"This is my cell?" Sal asked incredulously.

"These are the guest rooms of Knöldrus Abbey. Seldom occupied, and reserved only for honored guests of the abbey. I have deemed that you be held within these walls for the duration of your captivity," Abbot Jacques said with a wink. "At the request of the Enlightened Council, two guards shall be posted without from evenfall to dawn's break. If you need for anything, simply ask one of the acolytes."

"I don't know what to say, thank you, I suppose."

"You may thank the Lord that is Light, for it is his hand which has guided me. I must go now. Light's blessings upon you."

7

A PAIR OF NE'ER-DO-WELLS

INTERLUDE, SEVEN YEARS EARLIER

"Bagmen," Bartley said, as though he had revealed a brilliant insight. "We hit more bagmen. Scope the routes, just like you did with that fat Svoboda mule. We can pick out the biggest targets and make our move."

"That sounds like a terrible idea," Sal said, leaning on the parapet of South Bridge and looking out on the black water as the Tamber rushed beneath the bridge and pushed out into the bay.

"Hold on, now, you scoped out that bagman just last week. Sacrull's hell, I pulled four off already. Don't tell me it's a terrible idea," Bartley said defensively, "it'll work."

"Look, it worked before, yeah? But think on it, how long can we keep on knocking over Commission sanctioned bagmen before they wise up and turn one on us?"

"Four, maybe five more," said the Yahdrish.

"I'd think closer to once, maybe twice, if we even pulled it off again. The risk just isn't worth the payoff. I say we got lucky once, and we leave it at that."

"Look, mate, I could use the coin, and picking in the markets sure isn't worth the risk either. This is the only plan I've got, and it sure pays better than picking."

"Only plan you've got?" Sal asked.

"Well," Bartley said, "might be you'd want to help me with it some. I know it's not all there, but it's something, right?"

"What if I told you I had another plan?" Sal asked.

"I'd want to know what it is before I make any commitments," said Bartley.

Sal smirked. "Come along now, it isn't far."

"You see that building over there?" Sal said, pointing to the Rusted Anchor.

"How am I supposed to miss it?" said Bartley. "That's a Moretti sanctioned club. I'm not simple, you know."

"Aye, and have you any idea what goes on in there?"

"How should I know? They'd never let me in a place like that."

"Well, in any case," Sal said. "How much coin would you think passes through a place like that on the daily?"

Bartley shrugged. "I wouldn't know how to figure the sums."

"Right, well, I'm sure we can just assume it's a fair bit of coin, yeah?"

"Hold on, you're not—no, surely you're not thinking of knocking over a Commission sanctioned club. Sacrull's balls you're bloody mad, you are."

Sal laughed. "I certainly would have to be. I only asked out of curiosity. The pair of us could never knock over a place like the Rusted Anchor and hope to make it out alive."

"So, why did we come all the way down here?"

"A card game."

"You want to play cards?" Bartley asked.

Sal shook his head. "Every new moon, a card game is held in the back room of the Rusted Anchor. It's one of the biggest games around these parts, high rollers with deep pockets."

"You're even worse than I thought," Bartley said. "You want to knock over a Commission sanctioned card game. How could you ever call me stupid?"

"Well, it's about as dangerous as knocking over bagmen. Both are sure to put us on the Commission's shortlist if we're spotted. However, if we pull this off, we will have enough krom to keep us fed and happy for a few years, at the least. What do you say?"

"I say you're fucking crazy. How is this any better than my plan?"

"Well, it's like I said, we only have to do this once."

8

ONCE A SKEEVER

The locket was cold to the touch as Sal rolled it in his open palm. He ran a finger over the three parallel lines at the locket's center. Abbot Jacques had said the marking made him recall a description from his holy book. Sal wondered how closely the description matched and whether it mentioned the locket. He considered what he knew about the locket and began to wonder if any of it was even true. Nabu had been wrong before, and it could be that what he'd told Sal was nothing more than Shiikali superstition. After all, Jacques had not flinched at the sight of the locket the way Nabu had. Could it be the locket was not so dangerous as he'd come to believe?

He could ask Jacques what exactly the mark made him recall, but he didn't especially want to bring up the locket, in case the abbot changed his mind about letting Sal keep it during his imprisonment. He would needs gain access to the library and find out for himself just what the Vespians' holy book had to say about the thing. Mayhap once he found a reference to the marking, he could find something out about the locket as well.

He rolled the cold metal over in his palm. It had been a long while since he'd dared use the locket to ride the lightning. He had been without skeev for some time, and it seemed the drug was necessary for unlocking the power within the locket. Simply said, no drug, no magic.

Truth be told, Sal wanted nothing so much as to bury his face into two handfuls of powdered skeev. He wanted to smoke the stuff until the cogs in his brain ceased to turn. The physical cravings had not occurred for some time, yet his want for the stuff was stronger than ever, worst when his mind was left to wander.

He disentangled himself lazily from the bed, kicking free of the blankets, made all the more difficult by the soft feather mattress and down pillow. He stretched, yawned, and slipped the thin, silver chain of the locket about his neck.

When his bare feet hit the cold tile floor, he shivered and was tempted to crawl back inside the feather bed. He supposed there would be no harm to him getting another hour of shuteye, he had nothing better to do—did he?

Sal scrambled as realization struck. He shook his head to clear the sleep, shoved a linen shirt over his head, buttoned his doublet with fumbling fingers, and threw on a jerkin. He shoved his legs into a pair of trousers and jammed his boots on his feet before he bolted out the door.

He sprinted headlong for High Bridge, slowing his pace as he neared the steel caps standing sentry. The last thing Sal needed was to be mistaken for a thief on the run. A poleaxe would certainly slow his pace, regardless of where it struck.

From the High Road, he cut over to the Kingsway and doubled back until he reached East Market. It wasn't an unusually busy day, and still, the market-round was filled with shoppers, vendors, and peddlers alike.

There was no sign of her, and Sal hoped she hadn't left. He was over an hour late, judging by the position of the sun. To expect a woman such as her to wait for a man such as him was nothing short of foolishness. Especially after what he'd done to her. His heart sank. His chance to explain crumbling before his eyes like ash. A fortnight of asking, of laying down every shred of pride that remained to him, pleading until she'd agreed to meet with him. All for not.

He turned to leave. The market holding no appeal to him, as Lilliana was nowhere to be seen. He scanned the vendor carts once more, hoping he'd simply overlooked her, but had no luck to that order.

However, he did see someone he recognized across the round. Odie would have been hard to miss twice. As one of the biggest men Sal had ever seen, Odie stood a head and a half taller than the next biggest man in the market.

The big man was in an argument with a Yahdrish vendor. The two men would have been nose-to-nose if the vendor had been taller. As things stood, Odie towered over the vendor, while the little Yahdrish man yelled at his navel.

"Made man or no, I'll not be intimidated by your guild of thieves," said the vendor, jabbing his finger into Odie's chest to accentuate his point.

Had Sal been the vendor, he would have been wise enough to keep his hands to himself. If Odie had ever given him that look, Sal would have shat his trousers and run, but it seemed the little Yahdrish had more balls than brains, as he continued to jab his finger in the big man's chest, like a child prodding a bull.

Odie shook his head, slow and controlled. "Twenty and five is too high. Ten and seven."

The vendor barked a laugh. "I would dump the barrel in the river before I sold you a stone's worth at ten and seven. Twenty and five and you can consider it a bargain."

Odie reached behind his back, wrapping meaty fingers about the long handle of his war hammer, the ball of which had been forged in the shape of a man's fist.

The Yahdrish laughed. He opened his arms wide and lifted his chin to the sky as though presenting himself for the hammer blow. Odie let out an animalistic grunt of frustration and turned away from the vendor, a look of pure frustration twisting his features. Sal considered abandoning his plan but was spotted by the big man before he could change course.

"Oy, Salvatori Lorenzo, back from the dead, are you?"

Sal smiled. "For the time being, how've you managed of late?"

The big man looked over a shoulder and stared daggers at the Yahdrish vendor. "Twenty and five for a stone's weight in snap-powder, what's this world coming to I ask you?"

"Might be he can get the price. The trade tariffs with Shiikal have yet to be lifted, and pure snap-powder is becoming more rare than indigo."

"Used to be I could have bought the whole barrel for twenty and five. Anyone going to do something about them—them what you call em's—tariffs?"

"The duke will needs do something, elsewise half the city will be rioting come autumn."

The big man shook his head. "Might be time someone went and had a talk with them little fishes on the High Council."

"It just might be. Have anyone in mind?"

The big man nodded but didn't deem to tell. "But you, boy, you're supposed to be dead. The way Vincenzo told the tale, you went and got yourself picked up by the City Watch. I been expecting to find you hanging in one of them crow-cages."

"Me, in a crow-cage?" Sal said with feigned astonishment. "I should think not. What sort of stories has Vinny been telling?"

"Says things went south, and you were taken to the Magistrate's Compound." The big man shrugged. "I suppose you wasn't?"

Sal smirked. "You know me. Slippery as a polecat, I am."

Odie seemed to find this explanation satisfactory. "And what is it that brings you to the high-side of town?"

"The women," Sal said with the hint of a smile.

Odie clapped him on the shoulder, "Always knew you was smart, boy. Can't go wrong chasing a rich merchant's daughter or two, so long as you keep them at arm's length of each other once you pinned them down. Course, you go and put a baby in the girl's bellies, they'll be the ones doing the chasing, eh?" Odie laughed and nudged Sal with a massive elbow that nearly knocked Sal to the cobblestones.

"Can't say that's what I had in mind," Sal said as he recovered his balance.

"Aye, well, might be you're not so smart after all. Still, you might want to give it some thought. You could spend a year and a hundred krom courting a rich girl, and she wouldn't be half so interested as she would if you put a baby in her belly."

Sal laughed uncomfortably. He was beginning to think Odie wasn't japing.

"Been working?" Odie asked. "I mean, other than when you're botching jobs."

Sal shook his head. He wanted to steer clear of the subject of work. The last thing he needed was for word to get around the city about his botched job with Vinny. Bad enough he'd have to explain away the arrest after Vinny had opened his big mouth. He needed to talk to the bloody half-Norsic fool before Vinny told the whole Sacrull damned city.

"Been picking up any work yourself?" Sal asked.

Odie nodded. "Always work to do for the Commission. I make collections ten days of every fortnight, and Valla's been running a little crew of her own on the side. Went and got herself made, she did. Can you believe that? A bloody woman's a made man."

"She's as competent as anyone I've ever known, just as smart too, and twice as mean. Besides, I'd have been more surprised if she hadn't made her blood."

"Aye, well you might have expected it, but you're alone in that. Wasn't a single man I know that saw it coming. Been the talk of the whole Commission for months."

Sal shrugged. "With Luca dead, it was only a matter of time before Alonzo Amato filled the opening."

"I reckon you're right," said the big man. "Still, a woman in the Commission ain't happened before, and it might be, it won't happen again."

Sal bobbed his head absentmindedly, and Odie continued to talk, but Sal had stopped listening. A flash of blue had caught his eye in the crowd. A blue dress, not indigo, nor the dark blue produced by common woad, but the deep, full blue of lapis silk, thread-worked with a floral pattern. Her hair was raven black, trailing to the mid-ridge of her back and disappearing into the crowd.

Without a word to Odie, Sal ran after her. He pushed and wedged his way through the crowd, frantically searching for a glimpse of the blue dress or the black hair, to no avail. Anxiety kicked into full gear as he worried he'd lost her yet again.

Just as despair began to sink in, he saw it, another flash of blue. He pushed past a man and nearly trampled a small boy in his haste to reach her.

"Lilliana," he called. "Lilliana!" Damor Nev turned, as did Lilliana—her brow raised in question, eyes burning with cold fury—but Sal didn't care. Just the sight of her made his heart leap. "I'm sorry," Sal said as he closed with her. "I'm so sorry I'm late."

Her frozen stare melted, but that warmth—that warmth he'd known for so short a time—did not rekindle. Instead, she looked as much apathetic as she did sympathetic, a look that swiftly smothered the spark which he'd clung to for so long. She sighed, "Well, you're here, what was it you wanted to talk about?"

"I wanted—look, can we sit down somewhere and talk?"

Lilliana seemed to consider.

"There's a pair of open stools there," Sal said, pointing to an oyster cart at the edge of the market-round.

Lilliana walked to the cart and wordlessly seated herself on a stool. Sal followed, considering how to begin. He could tell her the truth, but what good would the truth do? If anything, it would make things worse.

Damor Nev stood near the cart, lingering just out of earshot, his bastard sword slung across his back.

The vendor asked how many oysters they would like and looked irritated when Lilliana waved him off. Sal ordered a clutch of six to placate the man, and only after doing so, realized he didn't have his coin purse.

Lilliana paid, dropping two iron dingés on the counter in a way that suggested she was thoroughly annoyed.

"Hot radish, pepper sauce?" asked the vendor.

Not wanting to keep Lilliana waiting any longer, Sal waved the man off. "Thank you for coming," Sal told her, "I wanted to apologize, you know, for everything."

"Where were you?" she asked. "Where did you go?"

He'd been expecting the question, and yet, he had no answer. What could he say? Should he tell her he'd been right here all along? Should he tell her he'd climbed down to the bottom of the deepest, darkest pit he could find, tell her about the skeev, his arrest, and the coming trial?

He skewered an oyster and popped it in his mouth. It was chewy and somewhat slimy, the way they get when left in the sun for too long. He swallowed and opened his mouth to explain.

"Forget it," Lilliana said. "What you did for me—I don't know that all things are equal now, but if you go missing for another half a year, don't expect me to forgive you a second time."

"And where you and I are concerned?" Sal asked, holding his breath for the answer.

Lilliana shook her head. "I'll not go away with you, Salvatori."

Sal nodded. This too he'd expected, and still, it worried him more than he wanted to show. If he wasn't able to find the man who'd committed the murder, he would have to flee the city or face the sword of judgment. If he fled, he would be forced to leave Lilliana behind for good.

Though, in truth, leaving her behind would, in all likelihood, be the best thing for her.

"What news of the city?" Sal asked, eager to change the subject. "Surely much has happened while I was away."

"Unrest is brewing throughout Low Town."

"Oh?" Sal said, hoping she would elaborate.

"The High Council has placed a new tax on goods sold within a mile of the city walls. There is talk of a trade dispute. The Naidia Trade Company has threatened not to dock unless the latest tariffs have been lifted. In the meantime, the prices of indigo, saffron, and coriander have risen five-fold."

Sal chuckled sardonically. "All because of a few merchants who want to offload some excess woad."

"Well, I will admit, with the price of indigo so high, no one can afford not to dye with woad. Though it is hardly for the sake of the clothiers and dyers that the High Council has increased the tariffs."

"Oh?" Sal said, smiling confidently. "And who in Dijvois has more sway with the High Council than the Merchant Guilds?" Sal knew the answer. The Commission had more sway than anyone in the city. Only, why would the Commission support the Naidia tariffs? "Well, if not the Merchant Guilds, who?" he prompted.

"Me," Lilliana said, seemingly unable to suppress the smile that formed.

"You?" Sal said, hardly believing what he'd heard. "But—you, what do you mean?"

"I mean to say that I am responsible for all of it," Lilliana said. "It was at my behest that the tariffs were placed, and at my behest that they were increased."

"But what's it all for? Why should you care?"

"I always care. It is my nature to care. But as to what I hope to accomplish, well, my goal has remained the same. I want to stop the importation of drugs into the city. Bliss and skeev, for a start."

"Bliss and skeev, truly?" Sal asked, wondering how much Lilliana knew of where he'd been for half a year and just what it was he'd been doing.

Lilliana nodded somberly. "You've not been here to see how bad things have gotten. Still, I fear the trade tariffs will not be enough. We won't see much, if any, progress until the duke agrees to a full trade embargo with Naidia"

"Embargo? Lilliana, that's madness. Don't you see what a precarious position that would put the merchant houses in? The tariffs have likely hurt them already. An embargo would force them to trade illegally just to stay afloat."

"The merchant houses are not my concern. When children are

in danger, we need to think long and hard about a solution. And thus far, this is the only solution I have been able to surmise."

"And what of the merchant guilds and the Naidia Trade Company?"

"They would be obliged to cooperate, elsewise the High Council would be forced to give right of trade to others willing to obey the law."

"You've thought this through," Sal said, somewhat impressed. "Still, how did you do it? What sway do you hold with the High Council?"

"Why, Daddy, of course. He sits Fourth Seat upon the council. I've put a word in Daddy's ear from the beginning, and Daddy always listens to reason."

"I see," Sal said, their previous conversations regarding trade tariffs cast within a whole new light. Lilliana seemed to know much more of the subject than she had let on before. "Will the High Council impose an embargo, do you think?"

"They will do what is right in the end."

"A vote of confidence I wish I could share."

"You doubt me?"

Sal smiled. "Never. It's those fat lords of the High Council whom I doubt. Behind the closed doors of the High Chamber, I worry the jingle of a heavy coin purse sounds far louder than the cries of the children in the streets. Worse, I fear the merchant guilds have no shortage of krom, and so their strangle hold upon the council may not end anytime soon."

"Daddy holds more sway than you might expect," Lilliana said, rather petulantly. "He is Fourth Seat of the High Council. When he speaks, the others listen. And when I speak, Daddy listens. Believe me, a solution will present itself. God will not abandon the children, and neither shall I."

"I don't mean to be a heel, but it's in my nature to expect the worst of others, those lords of the High Council more than most. But you'll needs excuse my lack of faith. I hold no such apprehensions where you are concerned."

"So good of you to put your faith in me," she said mockingly. "What could I have done to earn such high praise?"

"You can do anything you set your mind too, Lilliana, I've known that from the moment I laid eyes on you."

"Ah, you must be referring to the day you slapped me on the ear? The day of End, was it not? Tell me, was it before or after I hit you back that you decided I was capable of all things?"

Sal chuckled. "I want to help."

Lilliana looked skeptical. "Oh, and what could you do?"

"I hold more sway in this city than you might think."

"So, what exactly are you proposing?"

"Right, well, I'm dammed useful for a start," Sal said, giving her his most disarming smile. "My charm and good looks ought to serve as well, but most importantly, I know Low Town better than anyone else you are like to meet."

Lilliana looked thoughtful, biting her lower lip in a way that made Sal's pulse quicken. "Do you know of anyone who sells the stuff?"

Sal hesitated. Again, feeling that uneasy sense that Lilliana knew more than she was saying. "I know someone who might point me in the right direction. Why do you ask?"

"Could you take me to them?"

"Take you—Lady's sake, Lilliana, what for?"

"Well, I know how the drugs are getting into the city, I think. What I do not know is how they are getting out into the streets. More importantly, who is putting them out there."

"Even if I find someone willing to meet with me and answer a few questions. I'm afraid they'll up and run should they see Damor Nev approaching with that bastard sword of his."

"Just me then," Lilliana said. "Damor would stay behind."

"Damor would never allow it."

"Damor Nev serves me. It is not for him to allow."

"I still don't know, not without time to speak with the man. Besides, even if I talked with him, there is no guarantee he would agree to meet with the both of us. It's not as though I know him that well," Sal lied.

Lilliana didn't seem happy, but she did seem to accept his proclamation. She looked up at the sky and sighed. "I need to be going. It would seem I am late for an appointment. Good day, Salvatori Lorenzo."

Sal took her hand and kissed it. "A good day to you as well, M'lady," Sal said with a smirk. Lilliana smiled back, and Sal felt a rush of giddiness course through him as she stood and walked away.

When she was no longer in sight, Sal returned to his oysters, requesting hot radish from the vendor. He spread the white pulp on each of the five remaining shells before skewering his next bite. As he chewed, thinking over his conversation with Lilliana, an overlarge hand clapped him forcefully on the shoulder.

"Oy, what'd you go running off for?" Odie asked.

Sal turned. He was surprised to see Odie, as he'd forgotten all about the big man the moment he'd eyed Lilliana across the market-round.

"Odie, I—"

"Don't go and wet your small clothes, boy. Only, japing. Had a pretty thing like that to chase, I wouldn't be standing here, now would I? No, the reason I come over is, now Valla's made her blood, she's gone and started a little crew of her own. Looking for a cat's paw, you see?"

Sal flinched. He'd been on plenty of jobs and played a lot of roles, but never the cat's paw. It was a role reserved for the quietest and coldest of snatchers, a hybrid role consisting of second story work, sentry duty, and clean up. Simple enough if things went smoothly, but things seldom went smoothly, and if a passerby stumbled too close, Sal would needs remove them from the situation. He didn't think he had the stomach for that kind of work—no, knew he didn't have the stomach for it. He'd killed before, three men in all, and he'd spent near half a year attempting to forget what he'd done. Justified or not, his hands were stained with blood, his sleep plagued with night terrors, his soul fragmented.

"I'll needs think on it," Sal said.

"Don't go thinking too long. Valla will be expecting an answer within the week."

Odie grabbed one of Sal's oysters, put the shell to his lips and slurped, then wiped his mouth with the back of an overlarge hand. The big man winked and set off, parting the crowd as he walked, head and shoulders above the rest.

Sal pushed the remainder of his meal away, no longer hungry. As darkness clouded his thoughts, he felt an overwhelming desire to climb inside a shell and hide until the end of his pathetic, miserable existence.

The morning market was in full swing when Sal stood from his stool. Gentry and merchant class, for the most part. Still, much of the nobility sent servants to the market in their stead, and yet, Sal felt a beggar among the crowd of well dressed, clean cut, and freshly bathed High Town locals. Keeping his head low, Sal slunk through the sea of people. Although, even down as he was, when a young nobleman brushed shoulders with him, he couldn't help but pick the man's pocket with a soft touch.

Once out of East Market and on the Southwalk, Sal chanced a look at his takings, three coins in all, a gold krom and two iron dingés. Not a bad take for a moment's work. He pocketed the krom and rubbed the dingés together between thumb and forefinger as he walked.

He crossed the Tamber at South Bridge, stopping on the Big Island to take a piss over the parapet and into the bay before he stepped into Low Town.

The Rusted Anchor took its name from the great pitted hunk of steel planted just outside its doors. Sal passed the anchor and turned the corner of the alehouse. The shadowed alley smelled of salt air and rotting fish. He put a hand to the locket about his neck, his mind on the pigsticker tucked in his boot.

"Ticker," Sal said. "Tick, you there?"

A sliver of a shadow split from the alcove some ways down the alley. "Who's asking?"

"Salvatori," Sal stammered. "Salvatori Lorenzo."

"Lorenzo? Haven't seen you in a time. Thought you'd died. What do you want?"

"A cap. I—I need a cap."

Ticker stepped fully from the shadows, his skin pallid, face drawn, creases forming at the corners of his mouth, his eyes rimmed red, and his cheeks sunken. "Just the one?" Ticker asked and smiled, showing yellow stained teeth. "Two silver."

"I'll need a leaf and wick if you have it."

A look of irritation passed over the dealer's pale features. "Coin first," Ticker said, holding out an open palm. "Two and a copper."

"At that rate, I'll take two caps." Sal put the gold krom in Ticker's hand and winked.

Ticker smiled. He turned and walked back to the alcove he'd emerged from. When he returned, he held a bundle of rolled tobacco leaves and a length of wick, along with two golden-brown mushroom caps.

The sight of the skeev caps set Sal's heart pounding and his mouth salivating.

Ticker handed him the rolled leaves and the wick, then the caps.

"Now if that's all, bugger off."

Sal smiled. "With pleasure, M'lord, but first I needs take care of business. You wouldn't happen to have a flame handy?"

Ticker made a sound of disgust as Sal unrolled a leaf and began crumbling the skeev inside. "Not here, you don't. You want to bring the whole City Watch down on me?"

"The steel caps don't care about a little skeev," Sal said. "Besides, when's the last time you saw a steel cap in the Shoe that wasn't on the hunt for a taste?"

"That's just the point. You think them steel caps pay for their fun? One of them bastards catches the scent, I'll be cleaned out." Ticker went back to the alcove and returned with a shard of flint.

Sal tucked the wick and leaves away and gently slipped the caps into his jerkin pocket, then took the flint.

"Now, fuck off," said the dealer.

"Always a pleasure, Tick."

Sal left the alley behind the Rusted Anchor and skulked along the Bayway, peeking into alleys until he found one to his liking. It wasn't deserted, but close enough to count. The alley's sole occupant was curled up in a heap of tattered rags and what looked to be old fishing nets.

Sal took out his half-filled tobacco leaf and skeev cap and resumed crumbling the golden-brown cap into the leaf. His fingertips were soon coated in a thin layer of the powder, making them dry and coarse. Once filled, Sal rolled the leaf, using his saliva to seal the bind.

He frayed the end of the waxed wicking so that it would take to the flame more readily and swiped the flint across the brick of the alley wall, the wicking positioned to take the spark. By the third swipe, he heard a hiss and smelled burning. He cupped his hands about the wick, blowing softly upon the burning red cherry. When the cherry bloomed into full-fledged flame, Sal put the rolled leaf between his lips, his mouth salivating like a rabid dog.

Slowly but surely, he brought the wick to the end of the tobacco leaf, rolling the joint and breathing in quick, short inhalations until the tip burned evenly. The alley soon filled with a smell like tobacco and burning leather.

When the rush hit, the entire world slowed. Color became more vibrant, as though bursting to escape the confines of reality. Sounds sharper and cleaner. Smells more pleasant and easily identifiable. The sense of euphoria quickly spreading throughout his body with a warm, tingling sensation.

Sal laughed, unable to contain his joy and the pure sense of relief that swept over him. He took another hit, held his breath, and exhaled through his nostrils. He leaned against the wall and continued to take long, deep inhalations until half the leaf had burned away. At that point, he snuffed the rolled leaf on a brick and pocketed the remainder of the joint for later.

It wasn't until he'd left the alley that the guilt began to set in. He'd gone neigh on a month without the stuff. He'd survived the cravings, the sweats, and sickness that accompanied the parting, and in an instant, he'd thrown himself right back into the mix.

The great rust-red anchor stood tall as a man, the top loop wide enough for Sal's arm to pass through. By his best estimate, the thing must have weighed forty stone. Might be four men the size of Odie could move the thing, but so far as Sal knew, the anchor had been there since the beginning of time and would remain until the end.

There was no sign nor painted name above the door to the Rusted Anchor alehouse. It was the sort of place that cultured a specific breed of clientele, and rarely, if ever, welcomed outsiders. It was a dockside den for dicers and card slicks, known for its watered ale, oily wine, and poxy whores.

From within, the Rusted Anchor smelled of stale beer and sweat. Smoke hung in the air like a gray cloud. Paint peeled from the shiplap walls to reveal moldy, bug-eaten wood. The rushes so old and dry, they were fit for kindling. A cacophony of voices, cursing and blaspheming in a multitude of tongues, filled the crowded space. All about the taproom, hard-looking men diced or played at cards, winning or losing their fortunes at the flip of a coin.

Sal brushed past a stoop backed man, catching sight of a familiar face across the room as she tossed a pair of dice.

"Care for a roll on the straw, honey?" said a red-haired woman, grabbing Sal's crotch and giving his manhood a playful squeeze.

Sal nearly jumped from his skin in surprise.

The red-haired woman laughed in delight. "Touchy one. What do you think, Brella, should we take him upstairs?"

A blonde woman, older than the red-haired girl, but prettier of face, laid a hand on Sal's arm, gently massaging the muscles beneath the linen. "Might be we could have some fun with this one."

"I—"

"Come now, there's no reason to be so scared," said the redhead. "We won't bite."

The blonde took his hand and began to lead him toward the stairs, while the redhead nibbled at his earlobe and whispered. Sal felt a tremor run down his spine, and he shivered. His manhood swelled rapidly, his self-control began to erode. As terrified as he was excited, his mind whirled. He had the sense to know it would be a bad decision, and yet, he found another part of him felt to go along with the women was the most sensible thing in the world.

"No," Sal said, planting his feet. "No, I think I'll needs pass on the opportunity."

The blonde laughed, and the redhead grabbed him by the crotch once more. "Oh, honey," the redhead said with a vulpine smile. "Seems to me you've got a hitch in your step, and there's only one cure for such an ailment."

"No," Sal repeated. "No, I've other business to attend."

"So, attend your business after you've attended us," said the blonde, unwilling to relinquish her grip on Sal's hand.

Not wanting to look an utter fool struggling with the pair of whores, Sal relented, allowing the blonde to lead him toward the staircase. He sighed. "Listen, ladies, I don't want to be presumptuous, but before we begin, I need to know if the pair of you can afford me."

The women stopped and shared a look of bemused smiles.

"Afford you?" asked the redhead.

"My going rate is twenty krom for the hour, another twenty for each subsequent hour. But seeing as there are the two of you, I could cut you a deal, say thirty krom for the first hour and twenty-five for each hour that follows?"

The blonde laughed, but the redhead narrowed her eyes, a surly look spreading across her visage.

Sal kept his composure and did his best to remain stone-faced.

Just then, a big man with a shaved, tattooed head approached. "Fuck's the problem here?" said the pimp, a blue vein bulging at his temple.

"This one wants to charge us for a hump," said the blonde.

"The fuck," said the pimp, his face reddening. "The fuck you say?"

"Just what you heard," Sal said defiantly. "A man's got to make a living. I can't afford to be giving my services away for free, even to a couple beautiful ladies with such class."

The pimp looked to be as confused as he was angry. "Look here, you scrawny fuck. You take up my girl's time, you pay for it. End of story."

"Your girls? These ladies belong to you? There seems to have been a terrible misunderstanding. You see, I hadn't realized you'd laid claim upon them. By all means, take them."

Sal slipped free of the blonde's grip and made for the taproom, but the pimp grabbed him by the collar and slammed him up against the wall, driving the air from his lungs and sending a dull ringing between his ears.

"You-pay-now," said the pimp through gritted teeth.

A woman cleared her throat.

While keeping Sal pinned to the shiplap, his feet dangling off the ground, the pimp turned to look, revealing the slender form of Valla.

"You don't want to mess with that one, Dirge," said Valla in a cool, collected voice. "That there is Stefano Lorenzo's nephew."

The man named Dirge kept Sal where he was, his feet dangling off the ground. He turned his big ugly face back on Sal, his breath smelled a mixture of rotting onions and sour wine. "You owe me for the fucking time you wasted, for my girls and me. I want the fucking opportunity cost compensated as well."

Ugly and foul-mouthed as he was, it seemed the pimp was not so dim as he looked.

"Opportunity cost?" Sal said, feigning ignorance.

"For every fucking sale my girls missed out on while you was wasting their fucking time."

"You must not have heard me, Dirge," Valla said. "Leave the boy be, and go on with your day."

The pimp twisted Sal's collar tighter. "Mind your own, bitch. Now then, fuck hole, what do I have to break to get me money?"

"Let him down, now."

"Or what, bitch?"

"Or? I think you mean *and*, Dirge. Let the boy down, *and* you leave here with your balls firmly attached."

The pimp scoffed. A spray of spit showered Sal's face. "The fuck you think you're gonna do, bitch—" Dirge screamed, his grip releasing Sal's collar as both hands went for his crotch.

Swift as a silverfish, Valla had closed the distance to Dirge with such feline grace that her movement was nearly untraceable. She had unsheathed the knife at her hip, ducked, and slashed.

The pimp dropped to the rushes, thrashing like a beast in its death throws. His shriek was like that of something primal.

The taproom was silent, all attention focused on the man thrashing on the floor in a pool of his own blood.

Valla stepped over Dirge with a playful hop and took Sal by the hand. As her fingers closed about his, Sal noticed Valla had a new tattoo.

"Sorry, ladies, this one's mine," Valla said.

The pair of whores stared in stunned silence as Valla led Sal to her table.

"You shouldn't have done that," Sal said.

"What? And left you to Dirge?" Valla said, taking a seat and patting the chair next to her. "Are you not appreciative of my interference?"

"No, of course, I appreciate you rescuing me, and all," Sal said, taking the seat next to Valla. "I only meant that you are going to likely be in a spot of trouble for that."

"From who? I own the majority share of this shit hole now, and the City Watch is paid well to stay clear. From who should I fear repercussions?"

"You own most of the Rusted Anchor?" Sal asked.

"A new investment, I plan to buy out the remaining shareholders in short order and move on from there."

"You seem to be doing well for yourself. I noticed you've got something else new," Sal said, nodding to the tattoo of the black cross on her hand. "One of Don Moretti's soldiers now, are you?"

Valla's smile was cocksure. "Made my blood a few months back.

What can I say? All those years sucking Alonzo's little cock finally paid off."

Sal scoffed. "Certainly seems that way, but at what cost, I wonder?"

"Oh no," Valla said. "No, no, not going to get into this with you, Salvatori. I didn't spare your life so that you could criticize my career choice and bring down my evening. If I wanted that sort of company, I'd have sat at table with my father. Besides, after the stunt you pulled in this place, I'm impressed you've got the gall to show your face inside these walls. You never did tell me why Don Moretti didn't kill you."

"Right, forget I asked," Sal said.

"I will," Valla said with half-lidded eyes. "Now, what are you drinking?"

Sal hadn't planned on drinking, as his purse had lightened significantly after buying the caps. "An ale might do the trick."

"Good, tell them I'll have another," Valla said, making a shooing motion. "They'll know what you mean."

Sal stood hesitantly, slightly irritated at himself, and slightly more so with Valla. As he walked toward the bar, he snuck a peek at the entryway and saw only the pool of blood where Dirge had been laying in the rushes. There was no other sign of the pimp or his whores.

"A house ale, and another one for Valla," Sal said to the barman.

The barman looked at him slack-faced.

"Another what?"

"Another for Valla."

"Yeah, sure, another what?"

Sal sighed and rubbed his eyes. He looked to Valla's table, but she had moved to a dicing table and was throwing the bones as Sal looked in her direction.

He turned back to the barman and pointed in Valla's direction. "That woman there. The one who near cut that pimp's balls off not half a turn ago."

"Ah, the boss lady. Why didn't you say?" He turned to the tap, two clay mugs in hand, and filled them until they overflowed with heady foam.

Sal reached for the mugs, but the barman didn't release his grip.

"Is there a problem?" Sal asked.

They stood there, awkwardly staring at one another, each with a hand on the mugs. "The boss drinks free," said the barman.

Sal nodded and tried again to take the mugs, but the barman refused to relinquish them.

"The boss drinks free," the barman said once more, his face devoid of emotion.

Sal sighed. "Give 'em over already, would you."

The barman shook his head, a mischievous twinkle in his eyes. "A copper for the ale."

"Boss said it was free. Need me to call her over?"

"Oh," said the barman, realization sweeping over him. "Boss said that, did she?"

Sal nodded.

The barman pushed the mugs into Sal's hands, slopping ale and foam on the bar and Sal's jerkin. Without another word, the barman moved on to wiping the bar with a dirty rag.

"What took you so long?" Valla said.

Sal only shook his head, thrusting the mug at Valla. By then, it seemed she'd done her dicing and made it back her usual table.

Valla smirked. Then drank long and loud, whipping her mouth when she'd finished.

Sal took a sip. "I'll needs savor this one. Your barboy took me for a copper."

"Willus?"

"If that's the name of the horse behind the bar, I'd say yeah, that's the one."

"Must have taken a liking to you. He usually takes them for a silver." Valla reached into her pocket and flicked him a copper krom.

Sal smiled, tucked the krom in his pocket, and chugged his ale the way Valla had. He set it on the table, opened his mouth to speak, and was cut short by a grunt and a nod from Valla. Sal hesitated, but the arch of an eyebrow from Valla got him to his feet. Taking Valla's mug with him, Sal returned to the bar.

"Two more," Sal called out to Willus. This time, the barman snapped to attention. He took Sal's mugs, refilled them, and placed them on the bar without comment. "This one's for you," Sal said, slapping the copper on the bar and taking the mugs.

When he returned to Valla, she was seated back at her table, a foot tapping as though he'd kept her waiting. "You took long enough at the bar with Willus," Valla said with mock scorn. "Flirting, were you?"

Sal set the mugs of ale on the table and took the seat next to her.

"Now, Salvatori, there is something I have wanted to discuss. Our friend Vincenzo tells me you were arrested. How is it a day and a half later I find you here in my establishment and not in a crow-cage?"

Sal cleared his throat and repeated the question, buying time to think about how he wanted to answer. "Vinny was mistaken. I can see why he may have thought things happened that way, but I assure you, nothing could be farther from the truth. In fact, I'd be happy to lay out the order of events, but I would doubt if you are interested in hearing the story. It is not nearly so droll as Vinny made it seem, I'm certain."

Valla leaned back in her chair and casually reached for her mug. "By all means, do tell."

Sal took a long drink of his ale, a flat yellow substance that was too thin, by far, for his taste. Though, one could expect no less than poor fare from such an alehouse. Men did not come to the Rusted Anchor for the drink and fodder.

"Ay, well, Vinny and I decided to run a small-time job that quickly went awry."

"Bit rusty after your holiday, are you?"

"Wasn't on my account that things went wrong, but that's hardly the point. It went wrong, and we found ourselves in a little rooftop chase with the City Watch. Vinny and I split up, and I wound up falling through a roof."

"You fell through a roof?"

"Yeah, also not the point. Look, I fell through the roof, and when I hit the table, the steel caps burst in, hounds at the lead, and with all the commotion they caused attacking the homeowners, I managed to slip past without a scratch. Now, I assume if Vinny told you he saw me arrested, it was the man that lived in the shoddy hovel I crashed through. If it weren't for him going at those hounds with a long sword, I never would have made it out."

Sal swallowed, and Valla's eyes narrowed.

"The man from the house you fell into was arrested?"

Sal shrugged. "I'd have to assume. Didn't see it for myself, did I? I was too busy getting the hell out of there."

"And you think Vincenzo mistook this man for you?"

"I'd have to think he did, but I haven't had a chance to talk with Vinny since that night."

"And you weren't arrested by the City Watch?"

"If I'd been arrested, I'd be in a crow-cage, wouldn't I? But I'm not, I'm sitting here with you, drinking ale and telling stories."

"That is hard evidence to contradict. It seems one of us will need to speak with Vincenzo about spreading tales when he would do best to keep his mouth shut."

Sal took a drink, averting his eyes from Valla's shrewd stare.

"Well then, seeing as you're here with me, and not stuffed inside a crow-cage, I would like to make a proposition. I'd like you to join my crew. If you're back on the job, that is."

"Why, Valla dear, I'm honored that you should think so highly of me. But I suppose it depends on what sort of work you have in mind?"

"Well, you'll be second-story more often than not. However, I have been in need of a good cat's paw for the bigger jobs." And there it was, the cat's paw. He'd been worried she would bring it up. "You know how hard it can be to find a decent cat's paw, and you fit the bill far better than most."

"Not so well as you," Sal said, winking, and hoping she didn't see the beads of sweat forming on his brow.

Valla smiled, but not the way a blushing maiden smiled, rather, like a cat smiled at a mouse. "Cat's paw is a piece, not a player. You know well pieces don't pull the strings, I need to be where I can coordinate. These days, I play point, but you, Salvatori, you could be my cat's paw."

"So, now Luca's gone you've gone and started yourself a crew?" With Luca out of the picture, it was only natural that Valla had taken charge. She'd always been demanding and had no trouble shouting orders. But Sal wasn't certain he liked the idea of her playing as puppet master. Then again, he'd put up with Luca, how much worse could Valla be?

"Luca was a rat," Valla said. "He has nothing to do with me starting my crew. I was made on my own. My crew is Commission sanctioned because of me, not that rat fuck Luca."

"I didn't mean anything by it, Val. Luca has just been on my mind. I never did learn who his backer was for that kidnapping job."

Valla shrugged. "I never knew who Luca's backers were either. That was for Luca to know, and Luca alone. If you're curious about what he was up to before the end, might be, I have something of Luca's you'd be interested in."

"Oh, and what might that be?" Sal asked, his curiosity peaked.

"You'll see," Valla said. "I'll bring it with me the next time we meet. But first, I'll have an answer from you. What do you say, in or out?"

"I make a decent watcher, that's true, but cat's paw—I'm no killer, Val."

"No killer?" Valla laughed. "I wonder what a killer looks like to your eyes."

"I would say that Kalfi born, Dellan, fit the bill nicely."

"Dellan." Valla nodded. "Dellan was a killer, born and raised for wet work. Though, I seem to recall a rumor about a certain someone who killed Dellan. Burned a hole right through him, if you can believe it."

"Way I heard it, the Lord that is Light struck the demon down."

"A demon, was he? I thought he was only a Vordin, but what do I know? Tell me, Salvatori, how did you put the hole in him? Flash-oil? Black powder?" Valla gave him a searching look. "No, must have been something a Talent cooked up, something rather nasty."

Sal shrugged.

"Not going to say?" Valla asked with a frown. "Suppose it will out in time. But by any means, you killed him, and if you killed Dellan, what then, does that make you?"

Sal didn't know how to answer her. What *did* that make him? Was he a hero having slain that monster or just another kind of monster himself? "I'll want fifteen off the take," Sal said boldly.

"You'll get five."

Sal sighed and took a drink of his ale.

"It's agreed then?" Valla asked. "I have my cat's paw on summons?"

"It's agreed," Sal confirmed.

Valla saluted with her mug and chugged what remained of her ale. Standing, she led Sal to a dicing table.

***

When Sal finally staggered out from the Rusted Anchor, the sun had nearly set. He had wanted to speak with Vinny before the day had ended, but he was supposed to be back within the gates of Knöldrus Abbey before sundown. It was a long walk from the Toe to the abbey gates, and with little time, he would needs run some of the ways. Sal felt it would be both advantageous and wise if he were to smoke the remainder of his rolled tobacco leaf in order to calm his mind and allow him to focus on the task at hand. He returned to the alley he'd used before and finished off the remainder of his rolled leaf.

***

Heart hammering, lungs burning, legs weak, mouth dry, feet sore, stomach sick, Sal ran on. By the time he'd reached the South Market, he had wanted to collapse, but fueled by alcohol and skeev, he was able to push past mere corporeal limitations.

The sun sunk beneath the horizon as he reached Beggar's Lane, and Sal knew, despairingly, that he wasn't going to make it in time. He was going to break the curfew on his first night, and there was nothing he could do about it. He'd as well head for Gold Gate and make a run for it, rather than stick around and await his punishment. His uncle was right, Sal was a God's damned fool. His stomach felt sick, and his throat began to tighten at the thought of what they would do to him if he was caught running. He put a hand to his throat and felt—the locket.

Sal cursed. He really was a God's damned fool. Reaching into his jerkin pocket, Sal crushed a pinch of skeev between his thumb and forefinger, grabbed hold of the locket, and focused his will.

He burst forth like a flash of lightning, bouncing from rooftop to rooftop as he raced the setting sun.

The gates of Knöldrus Abbey came into view. Sal leaped from the rooftop and rode the lightning until his feet hit the ground at a run. The gates were still open. Sal was going to make it.

Sal kicked into top speed, but before he was within earshot of the monks on sentry duty, the gate closed with a resounding thud.

Sal cursed and slowed his pace. He continued on until the gate was within an arms breadth. He called to the monks but received no response. Cursing, he began to pound on the gate with his fist, he yelled out for someone, anyone to open up, and still, he received no response.

"Sacrull's bloody balls!" Sal cursed, kicking the gate. He grabbed hold of the locket.

"A tad upset, are we?"

Sal whirled around. The mousy monk, Phillip, approached at a leisurely pace. He sported a cocksure smile that somewhat clashed with his dun brown robes and tonsured pate, and in his hand, he held a peach, a strange fruit for him to have this time of year.

"You're too late," Sal said. "Gates been closed, and no one is answering. There's no way in."

"No way in?" said Philip in a mocking tone. "But whatever shall we do?"

Sal knew what he had planned to do, but he couldn't very well use the locket in front of Philip.

Philp took a bite of the peach, juice ran down his chin and dripped to the collar of his robe. Then, he moved on down the road, following along the abbey wall in the direction of the Tamber.

Sal followed, deciding whether it was better to take his chances to get inside the abbey or if he should simply put it down for a lost cause and run now while he still could.

Philip dragged his fingers along the stone wall of the abbey as they walked, and to Sal, it seemed an eternity before the monk stopped at the decrepit guard tower that was built into the abbey wall. The tower post was unmanned. Philip withdrew a skeleton key from the pocket of his robes and unlocked the tower door.

Sal felt a pang of sadness, a memory of that tower, a memory of Bartley.

It seemed the tower door had been repaired since his youth, new support beams spanned the walls, and the top half of the stairway had been mended. Though, it seemed the tower remained roofless, as the moonlight shone through the open top. Sal followed the monk inside and up the winding stairwell that led out atop the wall. They followed the parapet in the direction of the Tamber before reaching a wooden ladder propped abbey-side.

Philip finished his peach, tossed the pit off the wall, and descended the ladder.

It occurred to Sal once more how strange it was that Philip had a peach, after all, where did one even get a peach in Dijvois that time of year?

Before Sal had a chance to ask Philip that very question, the monk spoke. "You'll want to tell your guard that you were with the abbot."

Sal nodded. "Thank you."

Philip winked and headed in the direction of the cloisters.

Sal made his way across the abbey yard. When he reached the guesthouse, he found two robed monks standing sentry outside the door. "You're late," said the shorter of the two.

"Yes well, been with the abbot, haven't I."

"The abbot?" said the big one.

"Ay, where else would I have been? Now, it's been a long day, and I would appreciate if I could get in and get some shuteye."

The monks shared a look and parted for Sal.

"My apologies," said the shorter monk as Sal passed.

Once within, Sal breathed deep, feeling the full effects of his run finally sinking in. He slipped out of his boots and outer garments, placed the leaves, tinder, and caps on the bedside table, and climbed into the bed. He laid his head on the feather pillow and closed his eyes.

II

THE CHOICE

The Lord that is Light showed mankind the Way. It was man who fell from favor, man who lost the Way. For the Light will never leave a true believers heart, but harbor deeper within.
—Uthrid Stormbreaker

At times, I wonder if I'm a bad man. Then I remember, there are no good men.
—Luca Vrana

9

THE CARD GAME

INTERLUDE, SEVEN YEARS EARLIER

The new moon rose as the sun dropped beneath the horizon. A clear sky, blanketed with stars, allowed for easy visibility. Sal and Bartley had made their way down to the Shoe early, a full hour before evenfall.

"You're sure it's tonight?" Bartley asked in a whisper.

"Would we be sitting here waiting if I wasn't?" Sal asked.

"Sorry, I was just wondering is all."

"The game doesn't start until a full hour after evenfall."

"An hour after—Why in Sacrull's hell did we get here so early?"

"First rule of the game, always get there early. The last thing you want is someone getting the jump on you."

The little Yahdrish scoffed. "No one has ever gotten the jump on me."

Sal doubted that to be the case. Bartley seemed to be the kind of person that stepped before looking. "Just be grateful we're not sitting in snow," Sal said.

Within half an hour, familiar faces began to show for the card game. Important men, high rollers, one and all. But to Sal, they were no more than marks, pigeons for the poaching. Most arrived in town coaches, others by foot, while one man—some Lord by the look of him—had his skiff moored bayside.

"I don't understand," said Bartley. "Some of these men look gentle-born. What would they be doing this far south?"

"They're here for something they can't get on their side of town," Sal said. "And we're here to give that to them. In truth, we will only be taking our fair due, our compensation for delivering the rush that they're after."

"I'm not sure I understand what you mean," Bartley said. "What exactly will we be giving them?"

"You don't need to worry so much about what you'll be giving so much as what you'll be taking."

Bartley slipped on his mask. It was the sort of mask a child wore on the day of End. The masks had been Bartley's idea. A good idea, as it wouldn't do for either of them to be recognized on this job. For himself, Bartley had gotten a gray wolf, and for Sal, a red fox.

"Not yet," Sal said. "You'll want to wait until we're a bit closer to put that thing on."

"Is that everyone?" Bartley asked.

"Were missing one or two, but this will as good as suit our purpose. You've got the snap-powder?"

Bartley held up a small sack roughly the size of a coin purse. A shit eating grin spread across his Yahdrish face.

"Right then, let's move."

They slipped through the alley behind the Rusted Anchor, their boots scuffing along the cobbles, wool brushing soft linen with a muted swish, swish. They ducked beneath the window sill, Sal's heart thundering in his chest. He looked to the Yahdrish and nodded, and in unison, they donned their masks.

10

THE ORCHARD

Sal woke in the guesthouse feather bed, groggy, sick, and with a crust of sleep in his eyes. He felt far from refreshed, and yet, he could sleep no longer with the sun blaring through the window. It seemed the monks of Knöldrus Abbey didn't believe in curtains, and since the sun rose that morning, it had shone its light directly into Sal's face.

Sal rubbed at his eyes. He felt sick to himself for what had happened the night before, for the way he'd allowed himself to slip right back into the skeev. Apart from the magic, no good had come from the drug before. It was a difficult decision. Give up the drug, and the magic that came with it, or keep what he had, at the cost of all else.

A difficult decision, but one he seemed to have already made. He didn't know what he expected to happen this go 'round. It was only a matter of time before the drug consumed him once more, took over his mind and his body until he was willing to give up everything just for a taste.

Worst of all, he was supposed to be helping Lilliana find and eradicate the source of the stuff.

He looked to the bedside table where he'd left the caps along with the leaves, the length of wicking and the shard of flint. Guilt swept through him like a cold wind. His self-control was pitiful, even more than his betrayal to Lilliana.

He'd kicked the stuff, never wanted to use it again so long as he lived, and now it was all for not. A fortnight of struggling, of pushing the thoughts of skeev from his mind, and in the end, he had given in, wasted all his effort to the contrary.

The worst part of it was how little he seemed to care. Even as the thought of using the skeev sickened him, Sal wanted nothing more than to smoke a cap. He climbed out of bed, stretched his arms above his head, and yawned. He was about to reach for the roll of tobacco leaves when suddenly, there was a knock at the door.

Sal swiped the contents of the tabletop onto the bed and scrambled to cover it all up.

"Ah, I see you have woken," said Jacques. "My brothers and I have finished our morning prayers and now seek to break our fast. Will you join me at table?"

Sal's heart was racing so quickly, he couldn't speak. Instead, he managed a weak nod.

The abbot seemed to find the answer satisfactory. He nodded in response, turned, and headed out of the guesthouse, apparently expecting Sal to follow, which he did after a brief hesitation.

The monks that had stood sentry outside Sal's door were no longer there, likely they were already in the frater breaking their fasts. Sal followed the abbot, not to the frater, but to the abbot's own house.

He took a seat opposite the abbot at his table. A white cloth set the table. Cutlery had been laid out for each of them. There were few furnishings about the abbot's home, an oil painting on canvas, a pair of longswords, and a shield hung upon a wall.

Two boys, likely ten and three at the oldest, bustled about in their brown robes, readying the abbot's meal and dishing out the food, hot from the hearth ovens.

One of the boys brought a sliced loaf of bread to the table, steaming and smelling of fresh dough. The other boy placed a dish of butter and a knife next to the bread.

Jacques motioned with his hands, and Sal took a slice, slapping a healthy portion of butter on the warm bread. He bit into the crisp crust with a satisfying crunch and into soft, white flesh before the butter could melt. Sal felt he hadn't tasted anything so good in ages, yet the bread was far from the best thing he'd eaten that meal.

"I see you are eyeing my swords," Jacques said, laying his slice of buttered bread down upon his plate.

Sal nodded. "Yours?"

"Only, by inheritance." Jacques gestured. "That sword there belonged to my father's father, the shield and the other, my father's."

"Are they sharp?"

"Oh, but are they," the abbot laughed. "Sharp enough to cut a man in two, I reckon. Though, I was never a man of the sword. All my life, I have been a healer, as my father trained me to be. On the latter end, I have been a man of God, but never a man of the sword as my father before me. Come now, let us not waste this fine meal with words, eat your fill, my son."

While the abbot looked to live sparingly, it seemed he lacked for nothing at table. They were served mulled wine with the meal. When the bread had been all but picked to crumbs, the serving boys brought cheese and fruit, followed by poached eggs, bacon, and fried potato slices. When Sal felt he could eat no more, the serving boy placed a lemon custard before him, and Sal found he had room after all.

It seemed Jacques preferred to keep his morning meal spare of conversation, deferring to speak only after they had finished with the custard.

"I was informed you arrived back here after evenfall last night."

Sal froze. He'd hoped word hadn't gotten to Jacques, but it seemed there was no helping it. He would needs tell the truth. "I did."

Jacques cocked an eyebrow. "I can appreciate honesty. I'll not ask where you were, nor why you arrived late. I only ask that you do not do this again. I can only cover for you so often. If you were to have been seen by one on the Enlightened Council, we would not be having this conversation."

"Look I—I'm sorry. I never meant to put you in this situation. If there is anything I can do—"

The abbot waved his hands. "I don't ask that you apologize, only that you correct the error of your ways."

"It won't happen again."

"See that it doesn't. For the sake of us both."

Sal nodded.

"What did you think of the food?" Jacques asked, lightening the mood.

"Excellent, I've not eaten so well in a long while. Much better than what was served in the frater."

"Ah, but the abbey cannot afford for five hundred men to eat so well. The brothers of the Vespian Order are no strangers to sacrifice. We live sparingly as the Lord teaches, but those who do the most work are compensated for their efforts, and as master of the manor, in a matter of speaking, I must be nourished with strength enough to fulfill my many tasks."

Sal smiled. "You no longer share the sleeping quarters with your brothers, I see."

"To lead the flock, the shepherd must be set apart, and in some ways, set above. By this, he will become more visible to those who would follow. To be set apart is my burden to bear."

"You must admit there are certain comforts afforded the position."

"I would not deny it, and yet you seem to be forgetting the responsibilities that come with such comforts and the weight those responsibilities bare. It is no simple task to rule Knöldrus Abbey."

"I meant no offense by it."

"Of course, there was no offense taken," said Jacques. "But tell me, what of your task? Have you found out anything of promise concerning this murder?"

"Nothing thus far," Sal admitted.

"I see," said Jacques. "If anything changes to that regard, I would that you informed me immediately. Anything I can bring to the Enlightened Council could put doubt in their minds concerning your guilt. Find enough evidence, and it could serve to delay a verdict."

"Right, well, I'm innocent on all accounts, ought I to try and tell them this?"

Jacques smiled sadly and held his hands in a placating manner. It would be best if you had some sort of proof of your innocence. Leobald has the rest of the Masters looking for blood, and that is a difficult thirst to quench with words."

"You make my future seem so hopeful," Sal said sardonically.

"I'll not act as though there is nothing to fear. Make no mistake, you must learn the truth of what happened to Brother Dennis and give sufficient proof to support your story, else I fear the Enlightened Council may prove less than merciful when the time comes for judgment."

"And when will that time be?" Sal asked. "I can't just run around looking for something that likely isn't there. All the while hoping that I won't be tried for murder at any given point."

"I understand the predicament. This is an unusual circumstance, but as I have told you before, there is little else I can do on your behalf. Though, I should think you would be more grateful for the measures I have already taken."

"I—I am, grateful," Sal said. "I only fear for the inevitable outcome of this unusual situation."

"Have you considered retracing your steps from that night?"

Sal looked at the abbot skeptically. "And what good should that do?"

Jacques shrugged. "Retracing my steps oft helps me to remember things I've forgotten."

Sal considered the idea. He had not thought much on the night that he'd been found in the cathedral. Could it be that he had seen something that night? When he'd visited the orchard the morning they found the body, Sal certainly felt as though he'd seen something. It was as though he had walked back into a nightmare that day. A feeling he was not eager to reencounter. Yet, the abbot could be right, perhaps retracing his steps was a good idea.

"I suppose I could give it a go."

Jacques nodded, a benevolent smile spreading. "Very well, I have enjoyed your company, Salvatori, but it would seem the hours have not slowed, and I am needed elsewhere. You have my leave to go."

As Sal crossed the yard, he considered what the abbot had told him. His recommendation about retracing steps from that night might be helpful, and Sal decided that was what he would do.

Only, first, there was something he wanted to find out.

Sal made his way back to the abbey guesthouse and was relieved to find his skeev and assorted paraphernalia had not been disturbed. He took one of the tobacco leaves from the roll, crumbled half a cap of skeev, and rolled it in the leaf. He cut a length of wicking and pocketed the flint, then hid what was left of the caps, wicking, and leaves beneath the mattress, before looking for somewhere private to smoke. He decided to simply round the guesthouse, sparking the flint on the stone wall that he kept at his back. With the wicking hot, he lit the rolled tobacco leaf and inhaled the acrid smoke, coughing when he exhaled.

He hoped none of the monks would notice the smell and decided he'd best head out before someone went investigating. With the leaf half smoked, he smothered the joint on the wall and pocketed what was left.

He felt better, much better. His urge to touch and hold the locket increased tenfold. There was certainly a connection between the locket and skeev, though how strong and deep that connection was remained unclear to him. All Sal knew was the magic of the locket was unleashed with skeev.

But what good was the magic, really? It had gotten him out of some sticky situations, had even helped him to murder a man, but for the everyday practical uses, the locket's applications were seriously lacking. The magic was too wild, too unpredictable, and far too powerful to be taken lightly.

Still, the locket held a certain appeal that Sal found irresistible. It was almost like a drug, the more he wanted to be away from the thing, the more he sought after it. In a way, the locket held more power over him than skeev, after all, the locket was the one thing he would not have sold for a taste of skeev. And that included his soul.

The more he thought about it, the more he realized how little he knew about the locket. Nabu had told him of the Sahyasa, wardens of Darkness, the servants of Sacrull. According to Nabu, the locket bore their mark, the symbol of the beasts of six. Still, it was all a touch fantastical. What exactly had Nabu suggested, that the locket contained a demon?

Jacques had mentioned the symbol on the locket as well. He'd said it was mentioned in his holy book. Might be, Sal should have asked him about it during their breakfast.

Then again, what if Sal simply took a look for himself? Only, where would he begin? The holy book of the Vespian Order was not known for its brevity. It would likely take him weeks, if not months, to finish the thing if he went cover to cover. He was no stranger to the holy book, as his uncle had a copy in his solar, but Sal was no expert. However, he was inside Knöldrus Abbey, a stronghold of the Vespian Order. Where better to find a slew of experts on that very book? And where better to find those experts than the library?

Sal knew he should do as Jacques suggested. After all, he only had until the Council decided otherwise to find the monk's true killer, and there was no way of knowing when that would be.

And still, he wanted to know what the rune stood for. At the very least, he felt that knowing that would give him some clue about the locket's origin. An origin that was perhaps less steeped in superstition than the one Nabu Akkad had provided.

He headed for the library, telling himself he would retrace his steps later. For now, the only thing on his mind was the locket. He had only seen the library of Knöldrus Abbey from afar, but according to rumor, the library was a beauty all its own, comparable to Knöldrus Cathedral herself.

The rumors had not lied. Limestone, constructed and carved to match the cathedral, complete with two façade towers. The gargoyles that lined the façade stared down with menacing visages warped by pain, fanged maws opened wide in challenge, and clawed hands threatened to pluck the unwary from their stupors. Some with beaks, others snouts, wicked horns, and bat-like wings. Some crouched to spring, others standing tall and defiant.

Sal found them stunning. Dark, twisted, and depraved—but beautiful all the same. The skill and craftsmanship of the sculptor readily apparent.

Once within, Sal found the library no less entrancing. The ceiling was a latticework of ribbed vaulting. The floors richly veined marble tiles arranged to form subtly elaborate patterns. The stained-glass windows not only shone with light from across the color spectrum, but were arranged to depict scenes of heroism and beauty. Most impressive of all were the walls lined with shelves of oiled mahogany wood, filled floor to ceiling with books of all colors and sizes.

Sal could not imagine where one would even begin to look. He would do best to start by finding a monk to help. He wandered the vast expanse of the library, taking it all in, when he finally crossed paths with two monks wearing the drab brown robes of the Vespian Order. Sal recognized the tall one as a Master on the Enlightened Council, he'd been at the pardimon tree the day the body had been found. Sal did not recognize the other monk, a man with sunken eyes, gaunt cheeks, and a face that showed his displeasure without a hint of pretense.

"What in the Light's name are you—" shouted the monk with the sunken eyes. "You can't be in here."

Sal stopped in his tracks, stunned still by the sudden and surprising outburst.

"Is there a problem?" Sal asked.

"You can't be here," repeated the monk.

"And why not?"

"Access to the archives is exclusive to the brothers of the Vespian Order."

"Truly?" Sal asked, affronted by the man's aggressive nature. "Well, might be you can help me then. I'm looking for a copy of your holy book and if possible someone to help me find a certain passage."

The monk looked as though he might reach out and strangle Sal with his wrinkled little hands. "Access to the archive is exclusive to the brothers of the Vespian Order."

"Right, yeah, you said that already, but I'm not asking for access, just a book, and a little help."

"You need to leave," said the sunken-eyed monk.

Sal looked to the tall monk but couldn't catch his eye. It seemed as though the tall monk had paid no interest to the altercation. At a loss, Sal backed off, turned around, and headed for the exit. He felt the monk's eyes on his back as he walked away. When he rounded the corner, he looked over his shoulder to see if he'd been followed. Neither of the monks had pursued, and Sal decided it was far too early to give up. There was no reason he shouldn't search for a more amiable monk who might agree to help him with his problem. This time, he walked the other direction, admiring the beauty of the carved wood and the stained-glass, when he heard voices.

Sal slowed his pace, moving toward the sound of voices and peeking his head into cloister after cloister, expecting to cross paths with the speakers at any moment.

"Don't play coy with me, you little shit!" said a shrill voice.

Sal stopped cold. He recognized that voice.

"You're not backing out now," said Leobald. "I don't care if you piss your little britches, you're going to do this."

"He knows," said another man. It took Sal a moment to realize the voice belonged to the young apprentice, Philip. "No, I won't do it, not now."

"Keep your voice down," said Leobald. "How could he possibly —look, he knows nothing. Now, we had an arrangement, don't forget what I've promised you."

"What, that you'll make me your prior?" said Philip. "If he finds out what you're planning—"

"What *we* are planning," said Leobald. "Don't forget your involvement so quickly, I for one, shall not."

"Are you threatening me?" asked Philip.

"I am reminding you," said Leobald. "When I am abbot of Knöldrus Abbey, you shall be my prior, and together we can elect an Enlightened Council which is more to our liking."

"Obedient to you, you mean," said Philip.

"Must you be so obstinate?" said Leobald. "You know precisely what I mean. But if you don't act, none of this comes to fruition. You do understand this?"

"I don't think you know what you're asking of me."

"I am asking a simple task," said Leobald. "Now, we should be moving on. I've been gone too long."

Sal heard shuffling from the cloister. Without a moment of hesitation, he turned tail and moved as quickly as he could for the library exit. No one called after him, and Sal neither heard nor saw any sign of a pursuer. Still, he didn't feel safe until he was out of the library and moving across the abbey yard.

His legs and feet moved of their own accord, his mind spinning with a whole new set of questions.

Why was Philip speaking privately in the library with Leobald? What plans had the pair made, and why was Philip so frightened to carry them out? Who was it Philip feared had found out their plans? Could it be that they had something to do with the murder of that monk?

Sal had been looking at the ground, lost in his own thoughts. When he finally looked up, Sal realized where his feet had carried him.

The sight of the great pardimon tree nearly stopped his heart. His pulse quickened, and his head grew light. He was caught somewhere between wanting to flee and wanting to freeze, he settled with walking toward the tree, slowly.

A memory came to him, a man beneath the tree, a hooded man in brown robes—a monk. Only, no, not one man, two men—two monks—and the storm, and a struggle, and the scream.

A blood-curdling scream, just the thought made Sal want to stop walking, to drop to the ground and curl into a ball. It was the scream of a man who knew death was emanant. The scream of a man who had nothing left to him but to cry out.

Sal felt sick to his stomach. The thought of what he had seen finally sinking in. The realization that he had seen the monk murdered, that he had heard the man's final cry for help, and he had not helped. It was no consolation to Sal that he was too sick, too deep in his cups that night. It was no excuse worth using, none-the-less, a thought to find comfort in.

He was nearly close enough to the pardimon tree to touch the wide trunk. Sal stood where the body had laid the morning the monk had been found. A fish-belly-white corpse in drab brown robes.

Sal could see it now. The monks struggling beneath the tree, illuminated by flashes of lightning, the noises of their struggle muted by the storm, and yet, one scream had carried through—a scream that had sent Sal running away when he should have run toward. More than a scream, but a moment of truth, a moment for Sal to learn his true role, a moment where he'd shown his true colors.

Sal touched the trunk of the tree. The next moment, he was leaning his weight against it as he vomited upon the orchard floor.

He pushed off the trunk, staggered away from the pardimon tree, and out of the orchard. He wanted nothing more than to find a deep, dark hole and bury himself within.

He walked toward the Tamber, hoping that he might take refuge from his memory within the brewhouse. The red-faced Tanao called out a warm greeting, but his face quickly changed from quiet geniality to disparate concern as Sal drew closer.

"Whatever is the matter, boy?"

Sal only shook his head, and the monk wrapped an arm around his shoulder and led Sal into the brewhouse. Tanao seated Sal upon a cask while he filled two horns from a tap. When he handed Sal the ale, Sal drained his horn without a word, stood, and refilled the horn—only to drink it all in one swig once more.

"Seems something is wrong here," said Tanao. "Feel free to quell my worry when it suits you, but the sooner, the better, where my heart is concerned. Has something happened, something to the abbot?"

"No, not the abbot. I—it's stupid really, a damned fool of a thing to worry over."

"Ay, well, I imagine there is a good bit for you to worry over of late. Can't say I would blame you if the feeling took you from time to time. Anything you were feeling a need to divulge?"

Sal didn't dare tell Tanao the truth. If he did, the man would— he would—Sal realized he didn't really know what the monk would do. Might be, he would help, and at worst, he wouldn't. Sal was already scheduled to go on trial for murder. Really, there wasn't much Tanao could do to make things worse for him. It could be, telling the truth was his surest course of action.

"I've remembered something. Of the night when they found me unconscious in the cathedral."

"What sort of memory?"

"The unpleasant sort."

"A memory of something you did?" the monk asked, frowning.

Sal shook his head. "It was more to do with what I didn't do."

"How do you mean?"

Sal sighed and refilled his horn with ale. "I ran."

Tanao gave him a blank look. "Why don't you start from the beginning."

"Right, well, I was in the orchard. Went on the abbot's request that I retrace my steps from the night they found me. As far as I could recall, the orchard was the only place I'd been. Had a fleeting memory of that big pardimon tree, the one where they found the monk, and so I walked over not half a turn past. Walked up, and nearly touched the trunk, when it happened." Sal took a swig of his ale, and Tanao did the same. "I remembered what I'd seen that night. Remembered seeing them fighting under that tree, and that scream, I'll never forget that scream. And I—I remembered running."

"Saw who fighting?" said Tanao.

"Monks, only two of them. Saw them fighting under the tree— but the storm—and it was night. Never did get a look at them."

"Yes, I think I understand. I imagine we can presume one of these monks was the late Dennis. A stunning revelation this," Tanao said, taking another long drink of ale. "You are certain you saw two monks, not Brother Dennis and perhaps another man?"

"Two monks," Sal said confidently.

If there was one thing he was certain of, this was it: there were two monks struggling beneath the pardimon tree that night.

"And you were not able to get a good look at the other man?"

"I didn't get much of a good look at either man."

"Two monks, you say. This is quite the charge, quite the charge indeed. To accuse a brother of the Vespian Order."

Sal took a drink.

"I suppose the question is, what we are to do with this information?" said Tanao.

"I'm going to use it to prove my Sacrull damned innocence."

"Ay," Tanao agreed, "but it seems to me you will need more than an accusation to convince the Enlightened Council of your innocence. Thus far, you have Abbot Jacques and myself on your side, and eleven others who doubt your innocence, our dear prior chief among them."

The mention of Leobald jogged Sal's memory. After what had happened in the orchard, he had nearly forgotten all about the incident at the library.

"I think it would be best if we kept this information to ourselves," said Tanao, brushing foam from his mustache. "If what you have told me is true, it is to your benefit if the true killer does not know what you know."

"So, you believe me? About the killer being a monk?"

Tanao shrugged. "Anything is possible in a place as large as Knöldrus Abbey. There are nearly five hundred men living within these walls, a town of its own, if not for the city without. Yes, I suppose it's possible this vile act was committed by a brother of my order."

"And would you believe that monk was Leobald?"

"Leobald?" said Tanao, bursting with laughter. "That scrawny shrew, a murderer? I'd believe him a poisoner of women and children, but a strangler of men? No, not Leobald, the man's craven as a gelded goose." Tanao refilled his horn and drank deep. "I can see why Leobald would be the first name from your lips. The man is a horse's ass, but I have trouble imagining him a killer."

"But I heard him today," Sal said.

"Heard him, heard what?"

"Today, when I was in the library, I overheard him. He was talking about when he was to become abbot."

Tanao laughed. "This would not be the first time Leobald has been talking of becoming abbot. He's made such talk for years, yet he is no closer to the post than when abbot Tarquin still lived."

"Yes, but this was something else," said Sal, the effects of the alcohol taking a noticeable effect. "Listen, he was scolding Philip. Telling him he had to do what they had agreed. Otherwise, Philip wouldn't become prior because Leobald wouldn't become abbot."

"Philip, become prior?" said Tanao, a smile spreading across his broad fleshy face. "I think you've misheard. Philip is a long way from becoming second to the abbot, the boy is an apprentice scribe, for Light's sake."

"Look, I'm only telling you what I heard. Philip said he didn't want to do it because someone knew whatever it was they planned to do."

"And what was it they planned to do?"

"Wish I knew," Sal said, beginning to grow frustrated with the monk. "They didn't say what they'd planned, only that someone was on to them."

"And you don't know who this person was that had uncovered this…plan?"

"No," Sal admitted.

"I think you would do best not to worry over this," said Tanao. "God only knows when my brothers will overrule Jacques and insist on a trial. You should focus your attention on the problem at hand."

"And how would you suggest I do that?" Sal said, his frustration getting the better of him.

"You say that you are looking for a monk. A monk who had a reason for Brother Dennis to be dead. I would start there."

"What do you know of Dennis?"

"He was young. During his time at the abbey, we crossed paths rarely. Though, I had heard his name a time or two involving some rather nasty rumors."

"Nasty rumors?"

"The sort of thing one would hope did not take place in a house of God, but as I have said, when a place grows so large as Knöldrus Abbey, well…" Tanao said, trailing off.

"What did Dennis do?"

"Apprentice, I believe he served as an assistant to the quarter-master. Brother Adolphus is his name."

"I don't know Brother Adolphus."

"Ah, well you can't miss him. Adolphus will be the tallest man wearing the robes of my order."

Sal realized by the description that he had in fact seen Adolphus on more than one occasion. The first time was when the Enlight-ened Council had gathered beneath the pardimon tree. The second had been just that morning in the library.

"Ah, it seems I do know of the man. Tell me, Tanao, where does the quartermaster hold office?"

THE SHIPPING MANIFEST

"Brother Adolphus," Sal said. The sky grew dark as the sun began to set. "A word, if you please."

"I fear it does not please me at the moment," said the tall monk, hardly sparing Sal a second glance.

"Please, I have some questions, about Brother Dennis."

The tall monk froze. "I—no, I don't have the time. The evenfall prayer will begin any moment, and I must return these to the store-rooms before I join my brothers in the cathedral."

"I'll join you," Sal said, lifting a sack of flour.

Adolphus scowled but seemed unable to offer sufficient protest as to why Sal should not help him. Adolphus lifted the other sack and began walking, the pace of his long strides difficult for Sal to match. Sal was grateful he'd slept off the drinking he'd done with Tanao that afternoon, but he still felt groggy, his mind clouded by alcohol.

"Tell me brother, what did Dennis do as your assistant?"

"What all my assistants do."

Sal smiled to hide his irritation. "And just what is it your assistants do for you?"

"Keep track of inventory, move stock between the warehouses

and the Abbey storehouse, co-sign shipping manifests," the monk shrugged. "As I said, all the things a quartermaster's assistant might be expected to do."

"I see, and what was Dennis doing the night he was murdered?"

"How should I know that," said Adolphus. "I do not keep so short a leash on my assistants that I know their whereabouts each waking hour.

"But you could find out for me, could you not?"

"I could check my records."

"The effort would not go unappreciated."

Quartermaster Adolphus sighed. "Yes, well, the necessary documents would be in the storeroom."

The pair crossed the rest of the abbey grounds in silence. The storeroom was connected to the frater, a large stone walled room, packed floor to ceiling with goods and provisions. There was a small work desk covered with a scattering of papers.

Adolphus laid his sack of flower against the wall, and Sal followed suit, looking around the storeroom as Adolphus went to the desk and sorted through the paperwork, eventually pulling out a list written on parchment.

"The South-docks Eighth Harbor, Dennis co-signed the manifest and supervised the delivery of a shipment that day."

"A shipment? A shipment from where? What was on it?" Sal asked, his curiosity peaked.

Adolphus cocked an eyebrow. "See here, I need to be going. As much as I would enjoy wasting away the evening with idle chatter, I don't have time for such luxuries."

"Idle chatter?" Sal asked. "Is that what you think this is? Clearly, you don't realize the severity of the situation here. I'm innocent, and yet you and your Sacrull damned brothers have decided to try me for murder. The only way I will prove my innocence is by learning the truth about what really happened to Dennis. Now, I don't know about you, but I would not consider that idle chatter, I would consider it talk of the utmost importance."

Adolphus cleared his throat and shuffled through the papers once more, head down, unwilling to meet Sal's glare. "Here we are.

This here is the shipping manifest, shows the ship's name, captain and owner of the vessel, harbor inspector, where the shipment is coming from, and an inventory of the goods on board. From what I can tell, there was nothing out of the ordinary. Seems all was accounted for, and the document has all of the proper signatures."

"Would you mind if I had a look?" Sal said, extending a hand.

Adolphus hesitated before handing over the document.

"Shiikal," Sal read. "You're still getting shipments from Shiikal?"

"Oft as not," said Adolphus with a sly smile. "Of late, we have managed to purchase the contracts for eight of every ten. With the tariffs ever rising, bids on the shipments have become far less competitive."

"I'd not be surprised if the tariffs didn't soon choke off all trade from Naidia," Sal said.

"It'll never happen," said Adolphus. "The duke himself could tell his High Council to impose an embargo, but it won't stop the ships from coming. The shipping routes between Nelgand and Shiikal have been open since the fall of the First Empire."

"And what of pirates?" Sal asked. "Once word gets out that the Nelsigh Navy is no longer defending the trade routes, no sane captain will risk the open waters."

"And who do you think will be running the trade goods? Pirates make the best merchant princes on the great waters. They will have no trouble defending their goods, and fewer scruples about trading, whether legal or illegal."

"And you have no qualms with such practices?"

The monk cleared his throat, and Sal thought he would decline to answer such a pointed question, but after a moment, the monk spoke. "There has been only talk of an embargo, but thus far, there has merely been an increase to the tax. I see no way in which an embargo would benefit the duke or the High Council and would find myself in disbelief if an embargo should be imposed any time in the near future."

Sal decided to drop the topic of embargo for the moment and glanced back at the manifest, quickly scrolling through the inventory, when he came across a word he didn't recognize.

"What's that," he said, pointing to the word. "What does it mean?"

"Sorry?" said Adolphus, craning his neck to see.

"Here, this word here."

"Looks to be Shiikali."

"Something you've seen before?" Sal asked.

The monk shook his head slowly.

"Well, but no—I think—no, in all honesty, I don't know what it is."

"You started to say something there. What was it?"

"It was nothing."

"Nothing?"

"I only thought, well, sometimes when a captain is hauling a certain item of less than reputable standing, such goods will be labeled with a coded word of sorts, a name that will be used on the manifest inventory report. This way, when the goods are inspected and the harbormaster, or any other harbor official, sees that the crates are labeled with the same names that are on the manifest, they will assume it to be legitimate by nature."

"You seem to have an awful lot of knowledge concerning this."

"Some men join the Vespian Order when they are young, others join after they are old and have lived full lives. I am of the latter sort. I joined the order in my Forty-second year, but I did not forget what I was before I became a servant of the Light."

"So, this word is—"

"Listen," said Brother Adolphus. "I would like to discuss the particulars of trade for hours to come, but I really must be going. I am expected in the cathedral."

"Could I hold on to this manifest?" Sal asked.

The quartermaster made a sharp motion with his hand as though irritated. Without another word, Brother Adolphus left Sal behind and went for Knöldrus Cathedral.

With the sun setting, Sal thought it would be best if he headed for the guesthouse.

They sat upon the edge of the fountain. Valla lounged, her bare feet dipped in the water, while the younger woman beside her sat upright, arms crossed, brow slightly wrinkled as though she was irritated or perhaps only uncomfortable. Despite her vinegary look, the younger woman was rather cute, in her own way. She had a freckled face, her nose slightly upturned. Though, truth be told, she was a touch skinny for Sal, and her eyes were too far apart, giving her a somewhat fish-like quality.

As Sal drew closer, it seemed the younger woman noticed him. She nudged Valla with an elbow. Valla sat up, stretching like a cat waking from a nap. She turned lazily toward Sal, her eyes flashed, a coy smile played across her visage. Valla raised her hand slowly, like a goddess in a mummer's show. She pointed to him, turned her hand upright, and beckoned him with the seductive curl of a finger, her tongue gently playing across her top lip.

Sal's legs felt stiff, he nearly stopped in his tracks, his heart pounding in his throat. He hated when she toyed with him.

"Who's this?" Sal asked as he neared the fountain of Uthrid Stormbreaker.

"Now, is that any way to address a lady?" Valla chided. "Talk to me that way again, Salvatori, you may find yourself short a prized appendage."

"Dear lady, do excuse my disgracefully tactless entry. It would seem I was momentarily overcome with an inexplicable spell of irritation, brought on by sickening displays of the most unholy nature. I beseech you, tell me your name, for I would be honored beyond all measure if you would bestow upon me the blessing of such knowledge so that I might address you properly whilst I beg your forgiveness."

The younger woman turned away, blushing red as a cherry tomato.

"Fuck sake," said Valla. "You always take things too far, don't you? Can't fucking help yourself, can you?"

"I am what I am, Val."

"Aurie, this is Salvatori Lorenzo," Valla said. "Stefano Lorenzo's little weasel of a nephew. Though insignificant in status and stature as he may be, he still manages to be greatly obnoxious at all the wrong times. Salvatori, this is Aurianwyn. She's been playing snatcher for my crew the past few months. Has the swiftest soft touch I've ever seen."

"The swiftest you've ever seen?" Sal asked. "Better than Anton?"

"Best I have ever seen," Valla said.

"Better than me?"

"Salvatori, she would put those clumsy mitts of yours to shame."

Sal put a hand over his heart dramatically, feigning pain. Though, in truth, the statement did somewhat hurt.

A singer wielding a lute a few paces away had begun to gather a small crowd about him as he strummed the cords of his lute and sang.

> "A diddler will diddle, that's what diddlers do.
> That doesn't mean it should happen to you.
> Piddle on the diddler, tell the vagrant, 'shoo!'
> No, say I, and no, say you.
> Piddle on the diddler, for that's what we do."

"Hold a moment," Valla said, sliding down from the edge of the fountain. She approached the crowd about the singer like a wolf parting a flock of sheep.

> "And if a diddler diddles your—"

The singer cut short as Valla put a hand to the man's throat and whispered something into his ear. When she withdrew her hand, the singer nodded and waddled off quickly, the crowd dispersing in his wake.

"You feeling alright?" Sal asked as Valla returned.

"Fuck yourself," Valla said, sitting back down on the edge of the fountain. "Hate that bloody song."

Aurie smiled nervously, and Sal laughed. For someone with such a sharp tongue, Valla had notoriously thin skin.

"So, I seem to recall you told me you had something for me," Sal said.

"I have a job in the works."

"A job? Well, that's not exactly what I was expecting, but I suppose I'll bite. What sort of job?"

"The sort of job that is in the crucially sensitive planning stages," Valla said. "Word is, a very valuable shipment should be arriving within the week."

"And you want me to do some scouting work?" Sal said with a smirk. If there was one thing Sal was good at, it was scouting a job.

"I've already got Aurie on that. I just wanted to let you know you'll be needed soon."

"And so, you asked me out here today to sit by the fountain and kick my toes in the water while you ladies chat?"

"Not exactly," Valla said, eyeing him suspiciously. "You want what I've got for you or not?"

Sal shrugged. "Already said I'd take the job, didn't I?

"Not the job, you ass."

Sal frowned. "What exactly are we talking about then?"

"Tell me, does the High Keep job ring a bell?" Valla asked.

Aurie sat up straighter, her eyes widened slightly.

"Luca's job?" Sal asked. "What of it?"

"Told you I had something of his that you might want to see, didn't I?"

Sal felt his breath catch in his throat. "Oh, and what might that be?"

Valla pulled a folded, bloodstained piece of parchment from her jerkin pocket with a flourish and waved it before her face as though it were a fan. It took Sal a moment to realize what it was she held, when it suddenly hit him.

"The letter," he gasped. It was the letter they had gone to the High Keep to steal, the letter that Anton had nearly died taking. Sal's hand drifted to his collar where the locket hung. "How? Where did you get it?"

Aurie's brow wrinkled in confusion.

"Went and took a little look around Luca's place after that rat fuck was dead. When I saw this, believe it or not, I thought of you. Thought about how you were asking all those questions about it and the time you asked me what I thought was on the letter and who it was from."

Sal nodded. "Well, what does it say?"

"Ah, ah, ah," Valla said, wagging a finger. "That sort of information will cost you. What I will tell you, free, is that it is not at all what you think."

"Not what I think, what do you mean by that?"

Valla smirked. "I suppose you'll see, now won't you? Once you've paid my price, that is."

Sal sighed. "You're really going to use this as bait for your extortion?"

"Of course I will," Valla said, turning to Aurie. "See, sweetie, when you find any bit of leverage, crank on it until the whole thing comes crumbling down."

Sal shook his head. "Well, Val, name your price."

Valla smiled a big, wide smile and told him the price.

BLOODY NOBLE WOMAN

Valla had been right. The letter was not at all what he'd been expecting. From what he had surmised of the botched job on the High Keep, Sal thought the letter would be something that could be used against Prince Andrej, perhaps for blackmail or ransom. He had expected a shady correspondence which somehow implicated the prince in less than savory practices.

Instead, he'd received an old piece of parchment. So old it looked ancient, it was tattered, torn in places, and stained with dried blood—mostly Anton's blood.

The script on the parchment could quite possibly be a letter. However, Sal had no way of knowing, as he couldn't read the ancient handwriting, whatever it was. Still, something of the script panged of familiarity, yet he couldn't seem to catch hold of the fleeting memory which was associated.

However, he did know one man who might know just what it was he was holding, Lady's sake, he might even be able to read the thing.

Sal didn't bother knocking before he pushed on the door and stepped inside. The shop smelled of stagnant water, mildew, and an undercurrent of spices.

"You ought to light one of those incense you're always burning in here," Sal said, stepping onto the threadbare, Minnian spun rug. "And these cobwebs, Lady's sake, Nabu, have you never heard of a feather duster?"

Nabu Akkad stirred from where he leaned behind the counter. A curious look in his heavily-lidded eyes. His braided black mustache glistened with oil as he stroked it. "Young Salvatori, how good to see you, my boy."

"Nabu, how have you been keeping?"

"Like a stuffed sausage left for the curing, yes," Nabu said. "I had not thought it possible you should keep me curing so long without even a visit to be certain I have not gone to the spoiling."

"I'm sorry, Nabu. I know how fond you are of my perfectly distributed features, but I fear this handsome face of mine is in high demand throughout the city."

"Bah, I have a wife for this thing. She may be older and fatter than she was, but it seems to me, she still has you when it comes to what is between the legs."

Sal scoffed. "There's no denying it, my pretty face is my finest attribute."

"It is not your pretty young face but your business that has been the lacking. You have found another fence, have you not?"

"Nabu, why must we go over this every time I stop by? You haven't lost my business, wasn't I in here just a few months back?"

"I seem to recall a distant memory of a young man brought with him a handsome cloak, but of the man and this cloak, I have seen nothing for nigh on half a year."

"Half a year? Has it truly been so long? Still, as you see, you've not lost my business."

"I can hardly call this, visiting once a year, business."

"Well, in any case, I've not sent my business elsewhere. In fact, you wouldn't happen to still have that cloak about, would you?"

Nabu rested on one elbow and drummed his fingers. Upon each finger, the Shiikali wore rings of gold and silver. The rings clicked upon the wooden countertop with a *tap-tap, tap-tap*, while the gems sparkled in the candlelight. "The sable trim, made of the finest black wool," Nabu said shaking his head. "A fine piece of the cloth. I am afraid, if this is why you have come, you will be most disappointed. It was very easy for the selling."

"Well, no matter," Sal said, trying to hide his disappointment. "I didn't come for the cloak, anyhow. I had only hoped—in any case, I came to ask about something else." Sal reached into the pocket of his jerkin and withdrew the folded, bloody piece of parchment.

"Where did you get this?" Nabu asked after he'd had a moment to inspect what Sal had given him.

"Luca Vrana. Seems this bit of parchment was half the reason for the High Keep job we did all those months back. You have any idea what it is?"

Nabu frowned. "You do not recognize the hand of the First Empire? The greatest kingdom of men ever to scour this world."

"The First Empire. Can it truly be so old as that?"

"That's what I am telling you," said Nabu in irritation. "This writing comes only from that time."

"What does it say?"

"This is only a fragment, a page of a more greater work. This thing you have brought me is the work of Kellenvadra."

"Hold on, I know that name. You've spoken of her before. Kellenvadra, she was some great magicker. The one who made the—"

"She was much and more. The Fifth of the Prophets, the Arbiter to the Gods, the last of the Pure."

"What was she, some kind of ascendant or something?"

"There are those who have made such claims."

"This fragment of parchment, you're saying it could have been her's?"

Nabu nodded. "I am thinking this thing, yes."

Sal laughed, disbelieving. "I still don't understand how you could know that. Did she write her name on it or something?" He had meant it as a jape, but it seemed Nabu was in no mood for joking.

Jaw clenched, the Shiikali's gaze sharpened to a glare. "You name me liar?"

"I would do no such thing. I was just trying to break the tension of the situation. It's only, well, how could you possibly know who the parchment belonged to?"

"I have not spoken of whom they belonged, only from where they came. The books of Kellenvadra, they became called by the priests who assembled the fragments of her writings. Though, long after Kellenvadra's death, this was."

"The books of Kellenvadra, what in Sacrull's hell are they?"

"You ought to know of this thing. It was the books of Kellenvadra which supplied many of the stories told in your so-called holy book."

"My holy book? You mean the holy book of the Vespian Order?"

"They are far from the first cult of the Light which owes its foundation to the works of Kellenvadra. The Forger of the Final path, the finder of the Way, the last of the Pure, there are few cults left which do not owe their origin to Kellenvadra. Yet, it seems there are few in this land who know of Kellenvadra. Why is this thing you might wonder, yes?"

Sal nodded. "You've certainly piqued my interest."

"You know of the men who first walked this land. Those from who your Pairgu descended?"

"I do," Sal said slowly. "What of them?"

"What know you of their Gods?"

Sal shrugged. "I've seen the Godstone in South Market."

"And of this thing, what do you know?"

"Little and less, I suppose."

"And do you know why this is so?"

"I'd have to assume it has something to do with one iconoclasm or another, the Lady knows this city has seen its fair share of those."

Nabu smiled and tapped his temple with a finger. "Very good, yes. You are knowing the truth of this thing. Iconoclasm, very good. When the first empire came to this land, they brought with them iron, beasts of war, new magics, and Gods of their own. It was the First Empire which built this city, long before the Pairgu kings ruled this land, it was but a backwater of the First Empire."

"I know this, but we still worship the same gods of the First Empire."

"Some of them."

"Well, in any case, unlike the Gods of my ancestors, the gods of the First Empire are known. Solus, Tiem, Sacrull, Susej, the Lady White, Malev—"

"I know their names, my boy, but these are scant few, only the names of the Gods not forgotten. Even still, they have changed with time. These names you speak would be unrecognizable to a man of the First Empire. And in the great city of Aduah, this homeland of your Vespian Order, they recognize but one God. The Nelsigh have cast off the rest as pretenders, have they not? But this is the way of it. As one God gains primacy, the rest must fall ever farther."

"And you're saying this is what happened with Kellenvadra, she was forgotten?"

"Removed from the history, I am saying."

"And the parchment?" Sal asked. "What does it say?"

"It speaks of the Arbiter, the Fourth of the Prophets, the mentor of Kellenvadra, and this here—this is something of the summoning. This summoning they intended to stop."

"A summoning?" Sal asked. "What sort of summoning? Why did they try stopping it?"

Nabu laughed. "Many questions and none of them simple. I know not, this is all the page tells."

"That's it?" Sal asked. "All that writing, and it says something about an old dead man and a summoning?"

Nabu bobbed his head side to side.

"So, you're telling me this thing is worthless?"

Nabu's eyes went wide, the apple in his throat bobbing. "Worthless? My boy, this thing—" Nabu frowned and rubbed his hands together, shifting his weight from foot to foot while avoiding Sal's eyes.

"It's not worthless?" Sal asked. "How much?"

Nabu cleared his throat and bit his bottom lip, looking anywhere but at Sal.

"Is it worth a lot?" Sal asked.

Nabu continued to grow uncharacteristically squirrely, an unreadable look in his eyes when he finally looked at Sal.

"Priceless?" Sal said.

Nabu scoffed, but Sal knew it was feigned. Nabu's forehead was beaded with sweat; his hands clasped together in a white-knuckled grip.

"Nothing is beyond price," said Nabu. "Remember this thing, my friend, nothing."

Sal smirked. "I can think of a handful of things I would never sell, but then again, I'm not Shiikali."

"Bah, you Pairgu are even worse. You bleat like pious sheep, and yet you would trade your own Gods for a loaf of stale bread."

"I believe you're thinking of the Nelsigh. If not for their subjugation of our land, my people would likely have stripped naked and scampered back into the forests from where we came. It was those Vespian monks who brought along the façades of piety."

"Of this thing, you may have the right," Nabu conceded.

"Well then, seems I'm not so ignorant of history as you've always claimed."

Nabu scowled. "One can hardly call this thing history. Still, I have said before that you know some of the past of your little city, but what of the greater world, the pools of origin from which men crawled, and the ancient deserts where civilization began? What do you know of the times when men and Gods alike walked the earth?"

"You have me there, Nabu. I know little and less of it. Still, it seems to me you're merely avoiding the question. Now, what is this slip of parchment worth?"

Sal stepped out of the Rusted Anchor, his head spinning slightly with the haze of alcohol, his pockets stuffed with what was left of the fifty krom Nabu had paid him for the slip of parchment. A pittance of what the parchment was worth, but truth be told, he was happy to be rid of the thing.

Fifty krom was a beggar's fortune, and besides, anything worth more than fifty krom was not something Sal wanted to carry about with him on the streets of Dijvois.

He crossed the Tamber at the Bridge of the Lady, making certain to pay his respects when passing the limestone statue of the Lady White. The day was pleasant, the river calm beneath the bridge. He could even make out fisherman on the Little Island.

When Sal reached the High Town bridge towers, the sun had nearly set behind him. Hooded acolytes belonging to the Keepers of the Flame were out with their pole-candles, lighting the street lamps in pairs, doing their part to fight back the dark. Most shops had locked up for the night, while the seedier wine sinks, pillow houses, and gambling dens had only just opened their doors for business. The streets were far less crowded and much quieter than during the daylight hours, but to Sal, the city itself hummed a melody, as though it kept a tune all its own.

He slowed his pace as he considered something that had not occurred to him until then, Lilliana didn't look favorably on drunkenness, and if Sal wasn't drunk, he'd been well on his way before he'd left the Rusted Anchor. He could eat something. Food might mask the odor of his breath and help to sop up the ale in his stomach. Though he was short on time as it was, and it would take some strong-smelling foods to mask the smell of his breath.

His next option was to simply not show up. He would need to tell Lilliana he'd forgotten, and hope she would forgive him for a slip of the mind. He assumed she would be willing to forgive an honest mistake before drunkenness. In the end, he decided to take his chances. He could mask his drunkenness. He'd done it before. If he merely focused, he could pretend well enough to fool his own mother into thinking he was sober. Sal just had to be smart, and Lilliana would never know.

***

"You're drunk," Lilliana said, a look of disgust on her face.

"I—well, yeah," Sal admitted. "I might be a tick flush, but I have good reason, and—"

"You can save your reasons. I'm not interested."

"Ah, but it involves a magic dwarf, a dragon, and a distressed maiden in a high tower. You're certain you don't have a moment to spare?"

Lilliana smiled despite herself. "But I have heard this story more times than I can count on my little fingers and toes," Lilliana said playfully. "Doubtless, you slew the dragon, outwitted the dwarf, and kissed the maiden."

"Kissed? The maiden? Bah!" Sal pretended to spit. "Clearly you are a bit confused about the details, nay, lass, I did not kiss the maiden. No, her, I outwitted. But the magical dwarf, well, he was far too clever for the likes of me. Him, I slew. Oh, don't look at me like that, magical dwarfs are much easier to kill than they are to outwit. And you see, that's my tale, outwitted a maiden and slew a dwarf. Naturally, after such an affair, an ale was required to wash away the memory of my slaying and my missed opportunity to kiss a beautiful woman."

Lilliana looked unperturbed, yet she pursed her lips and narrowed her eyes. "You, Salvatori, are a jackanape."

Sal winked.

"But what of the dragon?" she asked.

"Pardon?"

"The dragon. You outwitted the maiden, slew the dwarf, and you neglected to mention the dragon."

"Ah, well, lass, I had hoped I wouldn't need to tell you, but you see, after a bit of ale I found that dragon wasn't half bad looking, and I had that kiss left me, and well—must I go on?"

Lilliana hit him playfully.

Sal rubbed at his arm, then winked. "So, tell me, what did you have planned this evenfall?"

"Something unexpected," Lilliana said with a sly smile. "You recall what we spoke of that day in East Market? About the tariffs and what I've been doing."

"I do, and I'm sorry I wasn't able to get any more information about the shipments. That contact I told you about didn't know anything. Although, I did learn a good number of the free-trader shipments from all over Naidia are getting purchased by the monks of Knöldrus Abbey."

"The abbey?" Lilliana said in surprise. "And how is it you know this?"

"I did some asking around. I even got to take a peek at the abbey quartermaster's ledger. Seems the monks of Knöldrus are responsible for purchasing eight of every ten free-trader ships out of Shiikal."

"Eight of ten, truly?" Lilliana asked incredulous. "And you're suggesting the abbey is supplying the trade of skeev and bliss?"

Sal laughed. "I don't see how you've made that connection."

"Simple really, we know the skeev and the bliss are coming in from Shiikal. You said the abbey is buying out the contracts on eight of every ten free-traders out of Naidia. Therefore, it would seem you have suggested Knöldrus Abbey is supplying the city's drug trade."

Sal smiled his most patronizing smile. "I see, but I wouldn't implicate the entire abbey, mayhaps, a monk or two. Still, are you not forgetting the Trader Guilds and the Spicers? Free-traders make up one of every four ships running the Naidia route. And even if all of the skeev and bliss was coming in from the free-trade ships, would it not be more reasonable to suggest that two ships of every ten are carrying the drugs? I mean, they wouldn't want everything so spread out. It would increase the chances that a shipment would be found."

Lilliana patted Sal on the head in a most patronizing fashion. "It actually makes sense if you think about it. Spreading the drugs between more ships might increase the chances of one being found out, yet if one small shipment is spotted, they wouldn't lose everything in one go."

Sal shrugged. "I guess you're right. Still, it will be difficult to implicate the entire abbey in a mass conspiracy without any names to start with. Why not look into whoever is buying out the most free-trader contracts, outside the abbey, and start there?"

Lilliana flashed him a cocksure smile. "I've been to the harbor master's offices already. It would factor that the abbey would not have shown up in the records, as they deal strictly within their own regulations, which puts them outside traditional harbor jurisdiction and under separate laws. Therefore, my perusal of the harbor master's records revealed far different findings, and hopefully findings that will take us closer to the answers we're looking for."

"Meaning?" Sal prompted.

"Meaning, I've already found the next largest buyer of free-trader contracts making the routes to Naidia, and I want you to help me break into his home."

13

FOUND OUT

INTERLUDE, SEVEN YEARS EARLIER

Sal wished the bastard would have simply killed him outright, at least then the storm of questions raging inside his head would finally cease. A summons from Stefano Lorenzo, what could be worse?

The little serving man stood before Sal, wringing his wrinkled old hands as he awaited an answer.

"Now?" Sal asked. "Tell him I really don't have the time. Mayhaps, I could reschedule for later in the week."

"It would be best if you did not try his patience, Master Salvatori," Greggings said, a serious look in his eyes. "Come along now. I've brought the town coach."

Sal was sick to his stomach all the way up to High Hill. Questions plagued his thoughts. What did his uncle mean to do with him? How much did his uncle know?

Greggings let Sal out of the coach before the door of Stefano's home.

Alone, he made his way through the heavy oaken doors, along the pale lavender tile of the foyer, and up the stairway to his uncle's solar.

Stefano awaited him in his usual high-backed armchair, a sour look on his face. Behind him, at left and right, stood his lackeys, Hamish Skein and Benitto Ricci. The Kirkundan, Hamish, was half the age of Benitto. He had a full head of curly, red locks and was built like some bronze statue of a God. Benitto, in contrast, was built like a mud toad, with a head of short, patchy hair and a face uglier than Sacrull's hell.

Stefano's eyes burned with a fire that Sal had never before seen. The eyes that usually ignored him with a distinctly apathetic arrogance now bored into him with an intensity that burned his eyes to watering.

"Do you have a death wish, boy?"

Sal stopped dead in his tracks. He dared not approach any closer. His uncle knew. And he knew that his uncle knew.

"Uncle—"

"You dare call me that? After what you did. I ought to strike you down myself, boy. Have you any bloody idea what you've done?"

Sal nearly collapsed. He was sick to his stomach. Uncle Stefano knew. Sal swallowed. What could he say? If Stefano knew it was Sal that had knocked over the Rusted Anchor's card game, Sal was as good as dead already.

"What will you do with me, Uncle?"

"I'll hear it from your own lips, boy."

"Yes, it was me. I did it, and I did it alone." Sal lied. Best to keep Bartley's name well out of it if he could.

Stefano snarled. "Get to your room. Wait upon my answer."

Head hanging, Sal turned, and wordlessly made for his old room.

14

LORD GARRED PEAKS

"You what?" Sal said incredulously. "Hold on—you what?"

"I want you to help me break into his home," said Lilliana, as though she were asking Sal to pass the salt.

"You can't just break into someone's home."

"Don't play the fool with me," Lilliana said, putting her hands on her hips. "I know what you do for a living, Salvatori Lorenzo, or did you think *me* the fool?"

"No, I never—"

"You are going to help me get inside. After that, you may be on your way, but no matter what, I am getting inside. I'm not going to take anything. I am only after information."

"I can't, I mean, you can't," Sal sighed and pinched the bridge of his nose. "Look, you can't just go breaking into people's houses. There is a long list of things that must be done before you even consider a break and enter. Scouting is essential and—"

"I've done the scouting, and I know for a fact he will not be home tonight. He left at evenfall and is not expected to return home until late into the night."

"How could you possibly know this?"

"Because our target is a member of the Open Council, and they are to meet this evening for the Biannual Co-Summit, a gathering between the Open Council, the High Council, and the duke's advisors."

"Who is this person?" Sal asked.

"Lord Garred Peaks."

"Lord Garred Peaks? I—Lilliana, I think you must be mistaken. Lord Garred is a master of the Dijvois Trade Guild and a member of the Open Council. He, of all people, would benefit the least from supporting the free-traders. In fact, it would hurt his own guild sanctioned trade."

"Exactly," said Lilliana. "It all adds up. Why would he be buying free-trader contracts when it directly conflicts with his business as a master of the trade guild? Unless, of course, there was some other benefit which is not immediately apparent."

"You're suggesting that Lord Garred has been supporting the drug trade by buying the free-trader contracts and using them to bring bliss and skeev into the city?"

"That is a theory and better than I've been able to come up with, but what I cannot reconcile is Lord Garred's support of the Naidia tariffs. I have been asking Daddy to convince the Council to increase the tariffs in order to stop the drug trade. According to Daddy, Lord Garred has been one of the most ardent supporters of the tariffs. Which was entirely unexpected, as Daddy had told me Lord Garred would undoubtedly be among the largest obstacles we would need to overcome. Why would Lord Garred support a tax that negatively affects his trade, then buy more of the affected shipments?"

"I think I can help with that. When I spoke with the quartermaster of Knöldrus Abbey, he told me that the tariffs had increased his profit margin on shipments from Shiikal, Minnoa, and Dahuan."

"No," said Lilliana mulishly. "That can't be. If the tax of the goods is increased, the potential profit margins suffer. You can trust me, that is the way it works."

"I thought the same until the quartermaster explained. The higher tariffs have decreased competition because most of the traders assumed, just as we did, that profit margins would decrease as the tax increased. However, the decrease in interest for the shipment contracts and Shiikal goods has driven down the value of both. To top it off, the tax has had the opposite effect in the markets. A scarcity of goods coming from Naidia in the market has developed, which has significantly increased the value of anything from Shiikal, Minnoa, and Dahuan especially. With less competition for the free-trader contracts and the increased value of the goods in the markets, the monks have actually managed to turn a profit off the tariffs."

"So, you're saying that if Lord Garred is supplying the drug trade, not only is he still able to bring in the drugs, but he has likely been profiting off the tariffs as well?"

"Something like that," Sal said. "Though, it might be Lord Garred has nothing to do with the drug trade. Might be, Lord Garred is only capitalizing on a profitable opportunity provided by the new tariffs. Or, he has been behind all of it and was simply using the monks to his own benefit."

"That is precisely what I want to find out," Lilliana said. "So, will you help me?"

"Help you break into the home of one of the most influential men in Dijvois?" Sal asked, folding his arms.

Lilliana smiled slyly, her hands on her hips, her chest leaning noticeably toward him.

"No, I won't do it." Sal said. "You may have scouted the place, but you wouldn't know what to look for to begin with. The risk is too high, and I won't put either of us in such a situation."

Lilliana's features darkened. "If you must know, it was not I, but Damor Nev that did the observing. I asked him to go with me to the estate, and he told me all of the ways he would get inside and when he would choose to do it."

"Damor Nev? What good is the opinion of a bodyguard?"

"Before Damor accepted hire into Daddy's service, he served as a night flower to the House of Norvos in Yardu.

"The House of Norvos, Damor Nev?" Sal said incredulously. Tales of the Dahuaneze royal family and their hired assassins were so well known, they'd reached even as far west as Nelgand. Sal even knew of a made man who had once been one of the so-called night flowers. "Damor Nev, an assassin. I'd always taken the man for a soldier."

"Yes, well, even you can be wrong," Lilliana said flatly.

"So, why not ask Damor Nev to help you? The man is clearly more qualified than me. Unless," Sal looked Lilliana in the eyes, and laughed at what they revealed. "You asked him already, and he's refused you."

Lilliana glared. "I did not bother asking. I know Damor well enough to know there are limits to what he will do. He would say it was too dangerous and that I was not qualified for such a task."

"And he would be right. You're not qualified, and this is a bad idea."

Lilliana began to look more dismayed than disgruntled. Perhaps realizing how badly she had misjudged the situation. "I think the bad idea was to ask for your help," Lilliana said, lashing out. "I might have expected this from Damor, but not you, Salvatori Lorenzo. How else can we learn if Lord Garred is behind the drugs without breaking into his home?"

"What good will it do?" Sal asked, beginning to grow frustrated. "What exactly are you planning to do once you're in there, interrogate the man's servants? I'm no inquisitor, Lilliana."

"I want to get a look at the shipping manifests for all free-trader contracts Lord Garred has purchased in the past fortnight," Lilliana said, ignoring the clear sense of irony in Sal's tone. "When I know which ships to target, I'll have Daddy pull some strings with the Harbor Master and have Lord Garred's ships seized and searched."

"Won't that make him a tick suspicious when his ships have been seized and searched? I mean, what if it turns out you're wrong, and Peaks is not the one bringing in the drugs? What if Lord Garred then traces back the threads and finds us at the end?"

"He would have no way of finding out it was us. Besides, if he did trace back to the source, his trail would lead him right back to Daddy." Lilliana smiled. "What could Garred Peaks possibly do to Daddy?"

"I see your point, but I still think breaking into the estate sounds a dreadful idea."

"Yes, but I know you could get me in. I've seen what you can do."

The bluntness of the statement struck a chord. How much did she know? How honest could he be with her?

"You've never seen me work. How would you know what I can do?"

"I've not forgotten the night you saved my life."

"I did nothing, Lilliana."

"No? You must remember things differently than I. I seem to recall you did things I have only read of in storybooks. You did magic, Salvatori. Real magic."

"I'm no magicker, I only—I can't do magic."

"You are a liar."

Sal felt his blood begin to boil. Suddenly, he felt like shouting, like breaking something, like breaking free of the flesh that imprisoned him.

"You, Salvatori Lorenzo, are a thief, and you know magic. Do not tell me I do not know what I have seen with my own eyes."

Sal clenched his fists and let his fury escape him in a slow exhalation. "Call me a thief. I'll not deny it, but don't name me liar. What you saw that night, I can't explain it. All I can say is that it didn't come from me."

"Oh, sure, and that makes some kind of sense, does it?"

"It makes more sense than this mad plan to break into an estate belonging to one of the most powerful men in the city on a hunch that he might be connected to something that might be happening."

"I see, so you think I am just some damned fool of a noble girl? Some spoiled Lord's daughter that has no idea what she is getting herself into?"

"I think you are the most beautiful woman in the world. I think I would do anything for you, unless it jeopardized your safety, because, while pleasing you is nearly all that matters, keeping you alive is more important than anything."

To his surprise, Lilliana began to laugh. There was nothing

malicious about it, yet her laughter stung all the same. She must have seen something of how he felt because she stopped suddenly, her eyes filled with concern—beautiful blue eyes, like depthless wells of life-giving water.

"How about this?" she said, closing the distance. She placed her hand on his upper leg, gently, yet suggestively. Her breath smelled sweet like mint leaf. Her very presence quickened his pulse. He wanted nothing more than to take her, right then and there.

"How about we do what I want," Lilliana whispered, her lips close enough to his ear to tickle when she spoke. "Then we do what you want."

"What are we waiting for?" Sal said, putting his hands on her hips.

She slipped free of his hold slowly and seductively and made to leave the alley.

***

"Lady's sake," Sal cursed. "I still think this is a bad idea."

"I told you, the moment I am inside, you can leave," said Lilliana. "I know what I am looking for."

"I'm not going to just leave you there. I'll see this through. I just want to be clear that it's not a good idea."

"Yes, I believe you have made your point abundantly clear. Now, shut up and help me climb this."

"Right, left foot there, dig your toes into the mortar there, and swing your right hand up to here. Good, you've got it."

"How are we going to get through that window?" Lilliana asked.

"Worry about getting up this wall first, and hope old Lord Garred doesn't have dogs."

"Oh, Damor said there were no dogs."

"Well, Damor Nev might not be so useless as he looks," Sal said with a smile. "That's it, left hand there, and grab hold of my—that's it, now the other hand—and you're up. Right, now don't panic, but this next bit is going to be a tick more difficult."

Lilliana stood atop the wall, hands on hips, breathing hard.

"You see that tree there, and that branch, the big thick one? We're going to need to jump to that branch. Do you think you can do that?"

Lilliana looked at the branch as though studying it. "You are certain it will hold our weight?"

Sal shrugged. "I think we'd do best to go one at a time."

Lilliana scowled.

"I'll go first," Sal said, readying himself for the jump.

Lilliana put a hand on his chest, her eyes wide.

"It's not too late to turn back," Sal said.

She shook her head. "No, I have to do this."

Sal nodded, focused on his landing point, and leaped. He landed with both feet on the thick branch, hands scrambling for purchase. He managed to snag a willowy branch with his left and another more stable branch with his right. He caught his breath once he maintained his balance, having worried for an instant he was going to fall from the tree.

"Go ahead," he called back. "The branch will hold our weight, and I want to be here to catch you."

Lilliana seemed reassured by the idea of him assisting her, and jumped shortly thereafter. She hit the branch with both feet and began to fall back, but Sal caught her and helped her gain her balance. He then showed her how to climb up the tree. It was slow going, as Lilliana clung motionless to the trunk of the tree. More than once claiming she could climb no farther and refusing to move until Sal encouraged her onward. After the fourth such episode in the short distance they'd climbed, Sal threated to go back if she did it once more. Thankfully, it didn't happen again, and before Sal knew it, he had climbed within reach of the window ledge.

From his perch in the tree, Sal pulled a set of picks from his boot and began to go to work on the window lock. He was rusty with a pick set and eventually resorted to using his pigsticker as a kind of impromptu wedge. Eventually, he managed to ply the lock and open the window.

After helping Lilliana up and onto the ledge, Sal climbed inside. He had no idea what room they were in. Nor did he know where they were headed. It was a scenario in which he had never dreamed he would find himself. No real professional would ever enter a home without knowing the necessary logistics of the job. Sal assumed the best place to look for what Lilliana wanted was in the solar. The problem was, he had no idea where the solar was located, but before he could guess at where to go next, Lilliana poked her head out the door and walked out of the room.

"Lady's sake," Sal cursed chasing after her. "Lilliana, Lilliana."

She seemed not to hear his whisper, or at least, she pretended it was so. She walked into the hall and took a right. Sal followed, frantic with fear. She was going to get them caught, and he was entirely unable to stop her.

"Lilliana," he whispered again, but she held up a hand for silence and continued walking.

Sal nearly shit his small clothes when he saw the silhouette of a man at the end of the hall but soon realized it was only a panoply of armor. Lilliana seemed to know where she was going as she led them through the hall and up a staircase, then down another hall and through the second door on the right.

A single candle burned in the solar, providing a faint orange glow that blended with the soft moonlight penetrating the open window. Bathed in the soft white light of the Lady was a man, seated behind a desk in a most unnatural angle. The man's head was halfway severed from his neck, a black stain about his collar and fringe.

15

THE TRIAL

Lilliana let out a scream, apparently having noticed the corpse of Lord Garred Peaks.

Sal acted without thinking. He clapped a hand over Lilliana's mouth and soothed her with a soft shush as though she were a child. He cursed silently, knowing they had a matter of moments before someone came to respond.

Sal let go of Lilliana, trusting she would keep quiet and ran to the window. A sheer thirty-foot drop to the ground. If the killer had come through the window, Sal had no doubt the man had brought a rope.

"We need to get out of here," Sal said. "Back out the way we came."

"I do not have what I came for," Lilliana said, folding her arms. "We cannot leave yet."

Sal scoffed. "Look, any instant someone could come barging through that door to investigate the source of that scream. I, for one, won't be standing in this room with a dead Lord when that happens."

"Go then, I will summon the City Watch. Someone needs to know what has happened here."

"The hell you will," Sal said grabbing Lilliana by the hand. "We're getting out of here, now."

Lilliana didn't resist, but allowed Sal to lead her back out of the solar, down the stairs, through the hall, and back out of the window. He helped her swiftly down to the cobblestones, and at his brusque encouragement, they ran.

———

The walls of the guesthouse seemed to have shrunken in around him. He'd not left the room for a full day, and he planned to make it two. His guards had initially protested when Sal requested his meals to be delivered to his rooms but quickly relented when he told the monks he was too ill to leave the bed.

He had laid there, curled up in the feather bed, unable to push away the image of Lord Garred seated in his chair with a yawning gash across his throat. No matter how much skeev he smoked, the image returned again and again. Worse was the sinking feeling that there was some sort of connection between Lord Garred and everything else that had been going on around him, but he couldn't put his finger on what the thread was that connected it all.

Sal shuddered, crawled across the bed, and reached for the joint. He relit the end of the rolled leaf with a candle flame and drew on it, long and slow. As he exhaled through his nose, smoke accumulated beneath the ceiling like one great white cloud that blanketed the entire room.

He began to stare at the red cherry of the rolled leaf. He'd given up much and more for this simple pleasure, this fleeting feeling of euphoria. Lilliana, above all else. Though, that could not be laid entirely at the feet of skeev. Sal was so far below Lilliana's station that he was hardly fit to worship the ground on which she trod. He should be honored merely to associate with the woman on such familiar terms, and yet, he found himself left wanting. He wanted more, so much more than her mere friendship, and still, he knew it was never meant to be. He would never be willing to give up what would be required in order to have a relationship with Lilliana. The realization made him sick to his stomach, and he took a long hit of the joint.

It was strange what love could make someone do. The feeling may not have been strong enough to get him to quit skeev, but it was certainly strong enough to lure him into helping Lilliana with her vendetta. Although they'd gotten no further in discovering who was bringing the drugs into the city, the mere fact that Sal had agreed to help was a testament to his commitment to Lilliana. After all, in agreeing to help her, he had effectively agreed to help eradicate the very thing he could not imagine living without.

Yet, no matter how much skeev he smoked, Sal couldn't seem to drive the image of Lord Garred from his mind's eye. He could only imagine how badly the sight had affected Lilliana, but he'd not seen her since escorting her home that night. They never should have been in that home in the first place. It was a damned fool of a thing for them to do, and besides, they walked away with nothing but an unwanted image burned into their minds.

Still, it did seem rather fitting that after Lilliana suggested Lord Garred was involved in illegal activity, they found the man dead. It could be that Lord Garred was involved in any number of questionable activities, and yet, Sal could not help but think there was a possible connection between the dead councilman and the shipment of drugs into the city, especially now. Might be, Sal would ask around about the man. If Valla or Odie didn't know something, surely his uncle would.

Just then, something occurred to him. He went to the drawer where he'd stashed the shipping manifest that Quartermaster Adolphus had given him. There on the document, beneath vessel proprietor, was the signed and printed name of Lord Garred Peaks.

It was as though everything had fallen neatly into place. Lord Garred Peaks, Brother Dennis of Knöldrus, two of the names on that manifest had been found dead. Two of the names on the manifest of a shipment that Sal suspected was used to bring something illegal through the city walls.

As brother Adolphus had explained, the captain of a vessel would often use a codename and a few underhanded coins to slip questionable goods into the city. The monk had even explained to Sal how he had feared that very thing might have happened on that shipment.

Whoever killed Dennis and Lord Garred had done so because of their involvement with that shipment. It was hardly a coincidence that both men had been murdered shortly after.

His head was spinning with implications. He could hardly put his thoughts in order as revelations struck in such quick succession. He needed to speak to Lilliana. Perhaps getting the thoughts out of his mind, he would be able to properly orient them. Stuffing the manifest into his pocket, Sal headed out from the guesthouse and nearly walked headlong into a man in drab brown robes.

There were three of them, monks, big men, one and all.

"You're to come with us," said the monk in the lead.

"With you where?" Sal asked nervously, feeling a sudden urge to run.

"You're wanted in the cathedral," said the monk. "Come now, whole council is there waiting."

***

The great rib-vaulted ceiling of Knöldrus Cathedral loomed high above. A beam of light shone down upon the dais as though Solus, the Lord that was Light himself, were in attendance.

A rope had been tied about Sal's wrists, as though he were some predator, detained, in case he decided to spring to the attack. He stood in the nave, looking up at the high table atop the raised dais, a table filled with men in drab brown robes. Twelve of the thirteen seats at the table were occupied by Masters of the Enlightened Council. Yet, not all the Masters of the Enlightened Council were present. One seat remained empty. One important seat, which belonged to an important man.

The empty seat seemed to Sal the oddest thing of all. It was like a gaping hole in an otherwise complete portrait. An unnatural wound in an otherwise natural scene. Sal had expected the trial would come sooner or later, but more so, he had expected that the abbot, of all people, would attend. And yet, the one open seat upon the dais was that of Abbot Jacques.

"Salvatori Lorenzo," said Leobald in his shrill, disapproving voice. "You stand accused of a most heinous crime. By the power vested in me by the Holy Vespian Order by the Lord that is Light, I charge you with the crime of murder. We of the Enlightened Council have gathered this day to decide upon a just punishment. A punishment befitting the true heinousness of your crime."

Sal looked upon each of the faces in turn, eleven sets of hard eyes met his, including the pale, green eyes of Brother Adolphus and the beady, black eyes of Leobald. All of the monks seated upon the high table looked down on Sal as though they had already decided his guilt, every man of them apart from the master brewer, Brother Tanao. He, at least, seemed displeased with what was taking place.

"What say you in your defense?" Leobald said, his hands steepled before him.

Sal could hardly believe where he was and what was happening. Now was the time for his evidence. But what exactly did he have? The shipping manifest in his pocket held both the names of Dennis and Lord Garred, but what did that show? Other than a bit of conjecture, he had nothing. He knew this day had been in the cards, knew it could come any moment. Yet somehow, he had never actually thought it would. He had been hopelessly optimistic that he would find sufficient evidence with which to prove his innocence, and yet, the time was here, and he had nothing—could prove nothing—and in truth, knew nothing, other than the fact that he was not the murderer.

"Well," Leobald prompted, looking down on Sal over his hooked beak of a nose. "If you would rather confess to your crime, I am certain no one will object. It will make the decision much easier for—"

Just then, the doors of the transept burst open. Abbot Jacques strode to the dais like a man moving with the intent to kill. "What is the meaning of this?" the abbot burst out.

Sal felt a wave of relief wash over him at the sight of Jacques. Surely everything would be alright now the abbot was there.

"I have called for trial," Leobald said, standing. His teeth bared as he glared at Brother Tanao.

It was that look which revealed all. It was then Sal knew just what had happened. Prior Leobald had called for the trial, and he had invited everyone but the abbot. Yet, it seemed the prior suspected Brother Tanao of giving Jacques an invitation anyhow.

Jacques stepped up to the dais and closed the distance to Leobald. "It is my place to make such a decision. You had no right—"

"I have every right," said Leobald. "Or will you now contradict the laws of our Holy Order?"

Sal held his breath.

Jacques looked as if he would put Leobald in his place. To tell him the trial was off. Jacques opened his mouth to speak, closed it, and looked down at the flagstones. It all happened in a span of three heartbeats, but to Sal, it seemed a moment that would not end.

Then, the abbot raised his head, yet no words left his lips. In silence, he began to walk again, and Sal's heart sank as Jacques seemed to accept defeat. The abbot climbed the dais and took his open seat upon the high table.

Leobald wore a victorious smile, oily and malevolent. He eyed Sal like a predator might eye a piece of bloody meat.

"My brothers," boomed Tanao, standing and facing Leobald. His round, red face set in stalwart repose. "As in the time of Abbot Bethelmure, I propose we place the abbey under a state of Hannivour."

The word sounded vaguely familiar, but Sal had no idea why, nor what it meant.

"You what?" said Leobald.

"I am proposing we place Knöldrus Abbey under a state of Hannivour," Tanao repeated.

"On what grounds?" said Leobald, his features twisting with an angry tilt.

"On the grounds of crisis."

"Crisis!" spat Leobald. "Crisis? And to what crisis do you refer?

It seems to me that we find ourselves in a time of stability. The only crisis I can imagine would be for this animal to go unpunished," said the prior, stabbing a finger at Sal.

"There has been open murder done within the walls of our abbey for the first time in a hundred years," boomed Tanao. "That alone would be crisis enough, and yet, it falls shortly after the death of our long-standing abbot. The proximity of Abbot Tarquin's death and the murder of Brother Dennis leads me to suspect we erred in our presumption of natural causes toward the abbot's death and hereby intend to correct that error. I submit before the Enlightened Council that we declare a state of Hannivour, as in the times of old, and we launch a full-scale investigation into the death of Abbot Tarquin."

Sal stood frozen in place, his heart in his throat as he watched the faces of the old men seated above him, a flicker of hope stirring within as each of the Masters looked to have been rendered speechless by Tanao's proposal.

"It is far too late for such a thing," said Leobald, his voice taking on a somewhat higher pitch than before. "We have no use for a state of Hannivour. The death of Abbot Tarquin took place months ago. Therefore, I find your claims baseless and your reasoning unfounded."

"That is not for you to decide." Said Abbot Jacques, standing to tower over Leobald. "I support our Master Brewer's charge. I agree that we find ourselves in a time of crisis, due to further reflection of our situation." Abbot Jacques bore down on Leobald, fixing him with an accusatory stare. "A new investigation will begin regarding the death of Abbot Tarquin. Until the completion of that investigation, Knöldrus Abbey will be placed in a state of Hannivour."

A hush fell over the Enlightened Council, no one willing to take a breath, with fear of breaking the silence. Sal could hear his heart beating like plugs in his ears.

"This is madness!" shouted Leobald. "We are not here to discuss the matter of Hannivour. We are here to pass judgment upon this murderer."

"Know your place, Brother Prior," Said Abbot Jacques, standing. "I have spoken. We shall evoke a state of Hannivour, by the ancient traditions of our holy order."

"I'll not accept this," said Leobald.

"The abbot has already told you, Brother Prior," said Tanao, standing and thrusting his round belly toward Leobald. "Know your place."

Jacques placed a placating hand upon Tanao's shoulder. "This trial shall needs be postponed. Please, undo the bindings upon our guest."

Leobald shouted his irritation, throwing his arms in the air as he swept away from the high table and off the dais.

As one of the monks began to unbind his wrists, Sal met Tanao's eyes and did all he could to wordlessly thank the man.

16

THE UP BEFORE THE DOWN

Sal could scarcely believe his luck. Surely, the Lady White had been watching over him during the trial. Somehow, Sal had made it out alive, something he'd hardly thought possible a day before.

With the scare of the trial, Sal had nearly forgotten the discovery he'd made that morning before the monks had hauled him to the cathedral. The names of two dead men, Lord Garred Peaks and Brother Dennis, both found upon the same shipping manifest. He had the manifest in his pocket, as good a piece of evidence as anything he'd found thus far. He decided he was going to show the manifest to Lilliana. Perhaps they could work out the rest together. Follow up on the rest of the names on the manifest and see what else they could learn. Whatever the case turned out to be. It seemed Dennis and Lord Garred had found themselves caught up on the wrong end of the same raw deal. Sal meant to find out exactly what that deal had been and whoever else had been involved.

Sal crossed the yard as quickly as he could, when he noticed movement in his periphery. He spun left to see Philip standing atop the parapet, pulling a wooden ladder up to the top of the wall.

Sal stopped dead in his tracks, watching the young monk in fascination, laughing to himself about his odd behavior, and wondering where Philip would be going just then. And for that matter, why wasn't he simply using the abbey gate? Could this have something to do with Brother Leobald and the conversation Sal had overheard, or was the monk acting oddly of his own accord? It occurred to Sal that Philip had acted strangely before, on the night he had helped Sal sneak back into the abbey. Where had Philip been that night, and why had he been out past curfew? Philip had been eating a peach. Where does one get a peach this time of year? Sal knew of only a handful of places, and they all came from the land across the sea, Naidia.

Sal broke into a run, sprinting headlong for the gate. Once outside the abbey, he took a sharp left, making for the broken tower, but knew by the time he reached the watchtower, it was too late. Philip had already moved on.

Sal was left with two options, south or east. On a hunch, Sal headed east toward High Bridge. It was not until he'd crossed half the bridge before he caught sight of a dun, brown robe some ways ahead. Once he was within fifteen paces of Philip, Sal slowed, not wanting to give the chase away.

He wondered where Philip was headed. If they were taking High Bridge, the monk must have been headed somewhere in High Town. Though, Philip neither went up High Hill, nor did he cut toward the Kingsway, but instead took a hard turn and followed the riverside path southward along the Tamber. Sal stuck to the road as long as he was able, but after the Ferryman's Ford, was forced to cut down the embankment and onto the riverside path.

He was no stranger to stalking a quarry. It required patience, keen instincts, and a good sense of the proper distance one needed to remain undetected. Sal had mastered the art, but even he was nervous about following Philip down the riverside path. It provided little crowd cover and nowhere to move off the path should his quarry turn and backtrack. If that happened, the chase would be over.

Sal passed fisherman pulling up their nets and stringing their fresh catches on a line. There was a group of children playing circle-round, laughing and carrying on as though nothing mattered outside their little game. An old crone chased off a dog with her boot. The dog—a skinny, ragged thing—ran from the woman, tail between his legs, a mangled fish in his slavering mouth.

The farther south Philip walked, the more confused Sal became. He was running out of guesses as to where the monk could be headed, and as his confusion increased, so did his suspicion.

The monk continued south along the Tamber until he reached South Bridge. To Sal's utter bewilderment, Philip stepped on the bridge and headed toward the Big Island. As he continued to cross the bridge past the Big Island, Sal wondered if Philip did not know he was being followed. Surely the man would not have taken such a roundabout way simply to reach Low Town when he could have walked straight south from the abbey and gotten there in half the time. Unless, as Sal had suspected, Philip did not want to be seen or followed.

As they walked along the Bayway, Sal became convinced of his theory. Philip continued south past the Harbormaster's quarters and down into the very Toe of the Shoe District. When he saw the Rusted Anchor alehouse and the massive rust-red anchor outside its doors, Sal thought he knew just where Philip was headed, and sure enough, the monk slipped into the alley behind the alehouse. Cautiously, Sal followed, stepping softly as a cherub's buttocks. He crept only so far as he dared before he slipped into a shadowed alcove, slowed his breathing, and waited.

For a moment, there was only silence, and Sal's mind began to flood with doubt. Had he misjudged the situation? Had Philip continued on, or had he stopped as Sal had predicted? Had Philip marked him? Did the monk know he'd had a tail before he had slipped into the alley? Might be, he had only gone into the alley to shake Sal.

Sal's heartrate quickened. His palms clammy, mouth dry, his entire body nearly shaking with anticipation, Sal took a step from the alcove.

"You got something for me?" said Ticker.

Sal leaped back into the shadow.

"The next one is coming in tomorrow," said Philip. "Eighth Harbor, evenfall."

"I'll inform the boys," said Ticker.

"It's a big one, bring all the little street gangs you can, White Eyes, Rooks—"

"Bugger off," said Ticker. "I know how to do my job. Besides, I don't need your kind stinking up my place of business."

There was silence for a moment, then Sal heard footsteps and saw Philip enter into his alley. Sal shrugged back against the wall, pinning his body to the mortared stone, as Philip passed right by him.

Once the monk had left the alley, Sal slipped from the alcove and followed. Philip was headed north, moving quickly across the cobblestones. Sal followed him out of the alley and onto the nearly deserted street.

Philip turned and looked back over his shoulder. As though time had slowed, the monk's gaze locked with Sal's. Without a word spoken between them, Sal knew it was all over.

The monk ran.

"Hey, stop!" Sal shouted, but Philip did no such thing.

In fact, he sped up, sprinting headlong up the street.

Sal took chase.

Philip cut into a narrow alley in the direction of the Shoe's heel before he zagged back up another alley and headed for the Bayway.

Sal felt a sense of urgency, more, a sort of terror at the thought of what the City Watch would do should they spot him chasing a man of the cloth through the streets. Still, he couldn't let the monk escape, surely Philip was his way out.

Even if Philip didn't know outright who murdered Brother Dennis, he undoubtedly possessed information that could clear up the matter with Lord Garred and the shipments of drugs.

As they ran north up the Bayway, Sal began to close the distance, slowly but surely gaining on the monk. When they reached South Bridge, Sal was within two arm spans.

They were halfway to the Big Island when Sal grabbed hold of the brown robe, fingers clenching the loose, rough spun cloth.

Philip wrenched free, shouting something inaudible, and losing his footing as he tripped heels first over the parapet of the bridge.

Sal cried out and made a swipe at the monk, but his fingertips only brushed the hem of the robe as the monk toppled backward over the parapet, arms swinging, face contorted in horror as realization struck.

Philip fell, arms flapping in the air as though he meant to fly. The monk seemed to fall forever, until finally, he hit the water with a smack.

Sal watched in sickened awe as Philip's limp body was washed seaward by the current of the mighty Tamber.

III

THE MISTAKE

Life is full of disappointments, and yet, I imagine death will be the greatest disappointment of all.
—Stefano Lorenzo

17

SOMETHING OF AN APOLOGY

INTERLUDE, SEVEN YEARS EARLIER

"Do you know what the Commission is, boy?"

Sal glared back at his uncle defiantly. He'd been kept locked in his room, a day and a night without food or word of what was to be done with him. Now, his uncle stood before him, daring to lecture him as though he were a child.

Uncle Stefano raised his arm and struck Sal across the cheek with the back of his hand.

The blow stung, but Sal was determined not to give his uncle the satisfaction of seeing him wince.

"I asked you a question, boy. Do you know what the Commission is?"

Sal snarled. "The five most powerful street gangs in Dijvois. Novotny, Svoboda, Moretti, Dvorak, and Scarvini."

Stefano closed his eyes and drew a long, deep breath. "It is of little comfort to me that you acted out of ignorance. The Commission is not merely the Five Families. The Commission is a pact, an agreement between those families, and sealed by the Code."

"I know this, Uncle, what of it? I'm no made man, what use do I have for your Code?"

Stefano struck him again, this time upon the opposite cheek with his open palm. "Bloody whoreson! Boy, you'll begin to use that brain of yours, or I'll knock sense into you until you do. You are no son of mine, but so long as you carry my name, I am responsible for your acts of idiocy."

"*My* acts of idiocy? Am I to blame that the coin purse was kept just beneath the window? If we are to speak of acts of idiocy, blame the fool that was hired to secure the purse. Bloody hell, it was a high stakes game. What kind of fool puts the coin purse—"

Stefano struck him a third time, another backhand that sent his ear to ringing.

"Are you deaf or stupid, boy? Do you not realize the severity of the situation? Do you not realize what you've done? I ought to kill you myself, only that wouldn't satisfy Don Moretti. Do you know what I'll have to do? What you've forced me to do with you? War, that is what you've risked here. You have risked open war of the Commission."

"What is this place?" Sal asked as Hamish hauled him bodily from the carriage.

"The Underway," said the hulking Kirkundan, his voice hardly carrying over the howling wind of Lower's Point. "Used to be a crypt."

Sal went stiff. "You don't mean—"

Benitto laughed his big dumb laugh. "Not been a crypt a long time. Not since the empire left, and the city was retaken by the Pairgu. Nowadays, it's a Moretti safehouse."

"What did they do with the bodies?" Sal asked.

The young man standing guard at the entrance jumped into action and opened the door when Benitto barked the order.

No doubt Stefano had sent word ahead. Don Moretti would be expecting them.

They entered into a damp, dank stone tunnelway. The smell of mildew prevalent in the musty air. A well-dressed man approached, his styled hair was such a fair blonde that it was nearly silver. He was young, with big white teeth and too much smile. His clothes were more elegant than most noblemen. There was something about the way the man carried himself that was both comforting and frightening, which made it altogether bemusing to Sal.

"And this stunted, scrawny, little thing is presumably the adolescent who dared to bravely shove his grubby paw within the hive for a taste of the honey?" said the well-dressed man. "Does he not know that bees possess a propensity for stinging?"

"This is the bastard that's robbed you, if that's what you're asking," said Hamish.

"I do suppose it is heartening to know you're not too stupid to know at least that much," said the man, wearing a smile as though he'd just complimented Hamish.

Sal half expected the beefy Kirkundan to launch himself at the well-dressed man, but instead, Hamish scowled and looked away.

"You going to stand there looking pretty, or you going to lead the way?" Benitto asked.

"You sir, are quite the conversationalist, I imagine." The well-dressed man turned his massive smile on Sal. "Can't be certain why, but I expected you to be a smidgeon more mature, more elongated in a vertical sense as well."

"Amato, ain't it?" said Hamish, the scowl still fixed on his big Kirkundan face. "How about you stop flirting with the boy and lead the way."

Sal froze, he knew the name. Alonzo Amato was a known man among all the right people. He was the righthand man of Don Moretti and the official conciliator of the Moretti family.

Alonzo Amato smiled his big, broad smile, showing off his overly large, white teeth. "I see that you gentlemen are quite anxious to make audience with his Lordship. Very well, we can save propriety and formality for a less trying time, and a more welcome trio of guests. That said, shall we gallivant arm in arm through the majestic halls of the Underway until we've reached our destination?"

The stone tunnels were poorly lit, with random offshoots that led off into dark passageways and made the place seem like an endless cavern of tunnels. Alonzo Amato in the lead, Benitto in the rear, Hamish practically carrying Sal by one arm as they went. They followed Alonzo through a series of tunnels that all looked the same to Sal's eyes. Eventually, they reached a cavernous, open room, barrel vaulted ceilings supported by uniform stone pillars. Before Sal, a cushioned throne sat upon a dais. Sal had heard tales of that chair, the Throne of Thieves, it was called.

The man seated upon the throne was squat, rather toad-like with a big flabby face and round shoulders, short arms, and short, stubby fingers. His side-whiskers grew in thick and white, but his jaw was clean shaven, which made his sagging jowls all the more pronounced.

Hamish dropped Sal on the earthen floor before the dais.

Don Moretti glared down at Sal, his wide mouth set in a frown. "Come to beg for mercy, have you?" Moretti asked, then turned to Alonzo Amato and scanned his heavily lidded eyes over Hamish and Benitto. "Lorenzo isn't here, I see. Not brave enough to come here himself? Sends his lackeys. Why, I ask you, does he fear me? Retribution, perhaps?"

"I imagine Stefano is shaking in his little boots after this transgression made by his own blood," said Alonzo Amato. "Stefano surely fears a war within the Commission."

Chest swelling, Hamish cracked his neck. "Stefano ain't afraid of shit. Especially not no fop like you, Amato."

Don Moretti's top lip curled, his nose wrinkling.

Benito put a hand on Hamish's shoulder, and the Kirkundan backed down.

"Best be on with this before tempers rise," said Don Moretti, leaning forward in his throne. The look he gave Sal reeked of disapproval, yet there was a flash of curiosity in his eyes that gave Sal a flicker of hope. "Did you come to apologize? Do you truly think anything you say could suffice for what you've done?"

"I hadn't dreamed it would," Sal said, standing as a rush of defiance swept through him. "I didn't come here to apologize, I came to warn you. What I did at your card game was only a taste of what I'm capable of."

Don Moretti seemed too stunned by the reply to speak. His brow wrinkled, his frown more severe than ever, his hands on the arms of the throne with a white-knuckled grip.

Silence hung over them, when suddenly, Alonzo Amato burst out with laughter.

Don Moretti turned to Alonzo, eyebrow arched in question.

Alonzo spread his hands, palms upturned. "The kid's got balls, though, he said he came here to warn us. What was your warning, boy, that you're…capable?"

"My warning is to be careful because someday, you'll be calling me Don Lorenzo."

Don Moretti sneered. "You think I'll just let you fuck with me this way, boy?"

"Seems to me, you already have. The men you hired to work that card game were clearly incompetent, at the least, undisciplined. I mean, come now, they were asking to be taken. And that banker you hired, the asshole stuck the coin purse right below the window. Could a man be any stupider?"

"The coin purse was beneath the window?" Don Moretti asked.

"All it took was half an ounce of flash powder and a set of picks," Sal said. "Wasn't for that shoddy mask and my uncle's man who'd spotted me, no one would ever have known."

Don Moretti turned to Alonzo, one eyebrow arched.

"I've had Bruno dealt with," said Alonzo Amato.

Don Moretti shook his head, the hint of a smile forming at the corner of his mouth. He looked to Sal. "Don Lorenzo, you say? Best hurry up on that, because the way I see it, you don't have long."

"No?" Sal asked. "And why is that?"

"Haven't you any notion why you were brought here, boy? Your uncle and the rest of the Commission have given me the go ahead. Your life is now in my hands. From this day forward, I decide whether you live or die. And right now, I'm not so certain I much like you."

18

THE SHIPMENT

Her raven black hair sheened in the afternoon sun. She sat alone at the oyster vendor's cart—alone aside from her mustached bodyguard, who seemingly stood aloof a hair's breadth away. Sal knew Damor Nev's disinterest was feigned. Beneath the mask of dim expression, the bodyguard was vigilantly observing everything around his charge.

As Sal drew closer to Lilliana, he could feel Damor's stare boring into him, but couldn't seem to catch the Bauden man looking. Lilliana smiled as Sal took a seat on the stool beside her, a smile that didn't quite reach her eyes—her beautiful, sad, blue eyes. "How are you feeling?" Lilliana asked.

Sal smiled back. His smile genuine, despite everything. "Better, yourself?"

"You have news?" Lilliana asked. "I can see it in your eyes, you are dying to say. What is it? What has happened?"

"Much and more," Sal said, glancing at Damor Nev.

"Well?" she prompted.

Sal told her of the discoveries he had made regarding the shipping manifest. He then told her of following Philip, of what he had overheard between Philip and Ticker, and the chase which had ensued. But when he reached the part about the bridge, his words left him, like smoke in a breeze.

"And what?" Lilliana said, seemingly unaware of his distress. "What happened next?"

"He fell," Sal said, his breath catching in his throat.

Lilliana put a hand over her mouth, her eyes widening like a frightened animal. Even Damor Nev had turned to face Sal, all pretenses of disinterest done away with.

"Where—what did you do?" Lilliana asked.

"Went to the abbey to explain what had happened," Sal said.

Damor grunted, and Lilliana turned on her hired man like a mother addressing a child in need of discipline. "And you would have done differently?" Lilliana asked her bodyguard.

"Pardon, my lady, I didn't mean to interrupt, I only—well—it's like this. Those monks up at the abbey are not what you might call the forgiving sort. A hard bunch, the lot of them. And this one claims he walked right into Knöldrus Abbey, bold as you please, and told them monks he done murder to one of their number? No, no, not on Damor Nev, boy. You want to try and pull the wool over my lady's eyes, you're going to need to do better than that. If you gone to Knöldrus Abbey telling them monks a tale like that, we'd find your corpse strung up on the abbey gate."

Lilliana looked pointedly at Sal, as though silently demanding an explanation.

"Right, well, there are those of the Vespian Order who would have gladly strung me up. More accurately, I was told they wanted to give me to the flames. Though, there were some who wanted to flay me alive and hang only my skin above the gates. Might be, they would have let me walk free after they'd skinned me, it's difficult to say."

Damor frowned. "That sounds a tick more like the monks of Knöldrus. So, what happened? How's it we don't get the pleasure of watching your hide flap in the breeze?"

"That's enough, Damor," Lilliana said, wearing a look of disgust. "I'll not hear that sort of talk."

"Pardon, my lady."

"Well," said Lilliana. "Explain yourself, how is it you are here?"

Sal smiled. "I kept faith."

Damor Nev laughed, but Lilliana's look sharpened to a glare.

"I'm somewhat familiar with the abbot of Knöldrus," Sal said. "After the—the incident, I went to the abbot and told him everything. I left nothing out, holding to the faith that he would do what was right."

Sal laughed, and the other two shared a look.

"Pardon," Sal said. "It's only, he didn't speak after I'd told him the tale. He looked me square in the eyes for a moment, then told me he needed to pray, and then he left. I just sat around, not really sure what I was supposed to do. I thought about getting out of town, but the abbot eventually returned, told me he would speak to the Enlightened Council and that everything would be alright. Sure enough, my name was cleared by morning. It seems the abbot discovered a certain poison among Philip's possessions that was used to murder the previous abbot, along with a bracelet that had apparently belonged to the monk Dennis, who had also appeared on the manifest."

"That's wonderful news," Lilliana said, smiling. "Uh, terrible, but wonderful. And what of this other monk that was on the manifest, this Dennis, could he be questioned?"

"Brother Dennis is dead, he was found strangled on the abbey grounds a month past. Philip, it seems, was responsible for that as well."

"Dead," said Lilliana, "but then, how will we ever know who was bringing in the drugs?"

"I'm sorry, but I thought that was clear. Dennis secured the shipments. Philip, it seems, was the middle man, the coordinator between the street dealers and the shipment. Lord Garred, it seems, was the vessel proprietor."

Lilliana blinked owlishly, and slowly, her eyebrows began to rise.

"What?" Sal said.

"And who was coordinating it all? Who is orchestrating the endeavor? Who is profiting from all of this, and who is killing everyone else involved?"

Sal thought he knew the answer, in fact, he'd accused the man before. Yet, Tanao had not thought it very likely and had declined to investigate any further. "His name is Leobald, the prior of Knöldrus Abbey," Sal said. "If anyone is in charge, it's Leobald."

"Leobald? You have not mentioned that name before," said Lilliana.

It was true, and it was an oversight Sal now regretted. He should have been looking into Leobald from the very beginning. "I'd not thought the name worth mentioning, until now. Yet, now I think on it, he has to be our man. He certainly wouldn't have balked at the murder of Lord Garred."

"What's this now?" said Damor Nev.

Sal went still.

"It's alright, Damor is helping," Lilliana said. "After the incident at the Peaks residence, I thought it prudent to bring in more help."

"And your father?"

"So long as my lady remains out of danger, I see no reason to inform his Lordship. And while I am around, my lady shall never find herself in danger."

"I see, and what think you, Damor Nev?"

"I think we ought to look in on this quartermaster as well as the prior. If you overheard that another shipment was arriving tonight, then clearly, they have not stopped operations. We could be dealing with something systemic, something far larger than we'd anticipated."

"I want to join you when you go to this shipment," Lilliana said.

"No," said Sal and Damor in unison.

"It is not for the likes of you to command me."

"It is for the likes of me to keep you safe, my lady."

"I agree with the brute, you shouldn't go. I'll go alone. I have experience with this sort of thing."

"I want Damor to go with you, at the least," said Lilliana.

"Really, that wouldn't be necessary," Sal protested.

"I would like to join you," said Damor. "We can meet outside South Market, a turn before evenfall. Ought to give us time to reach Eighth Harbor and get settled."

Sal nodded, as though he had any say in the issue.

"Fine then, it's settled," said Lilliana. "But you will report to me when it is finished. I will not be kept in the dark about this."

———

Sal's breath misted in the light of the burning street lamps. The Keepers of the Flame were out in pairs, dressed in their black cloaks and wielding their long pole-candles, which they used to light the street lamps.

The cap in Sal's pocket almost seemed to scream out to him, but he'd left his flint and wicking behind. He needed his faculties at full capacity, and smoking the skeev would have only inhibited him. Besides, he needed the cap for other reasons.

He touched the cold metal of the amulet, and a shiver ran down his spine. Sal pulled up the hood of his cloak, ducked his head, and weaved through the crowd as he moved south. He saw Damor Nev standing near the swaying sign of the boar. The bodyguard wore all black, as did Sal, only slung about Damor's back was his hulking hand-and-a-half sword.

"Shall we?" the Bauden asked as Sal approached.

Sal nodded, and they made for Eighth Harbor.

———

Tucked comfortably against the parapet of the high wall overlooking the harbor, Sal almost felt bad for the crew of porters forced to work through the cold night.

Down below, a crew of stalky porters unloaded crate after crate off the ship. Three separate wagons were being loaded as the men worked. There was another group of men, dock thugs, about half as many as there were porters. They stood around the worksite, laughing and carrying on while the porters unloaded crate after crate.

"That one there," said Sal, pointing, "goes by the name Ticker. I think he's a connected guy, but he's no made man, just a pusher as far as I know."

"Looks to be the one in charge," said Damor. "Most of them dock thugs are Rooks, if I'm making out those tattoos correctly, see a couple White Eyes as well. Doesn't mean this has nothing to do with the Commission. They don't operate like one might expect. Everyone thinks the Five Families are right in the thick of crime in the city, but they tend to sit back and pull the strings. Let them connected guys do the hiring out, that way it's not the made man getting his hands dirty."

Sal knew well the way the Commission operated, but he had seen little of their presence in connection with the shipments. His uncle might know something, but Sal would needs ask him later, as he was rather occupied at the moment.

"That fop with the green hat," Sal said. "Do you recognize him by chance?"

"Some lord's get, I imagine," said Damor.

Sal frowned. A lordling overseeing the unloading. Might be, Lord Garred was not the only noble involved with the drug importation business.

"Well, I'll be—Dominik D'Angelo," said Damor Nev. "But that can't be. The man was bounty hunting the last I knew."

"Who's he?" Sal asked.

Damor gave an irritated snort. "What in God's name would he be doing in a place like this?"

"Looks to be working," Sal said with a smirk.

"You have a loose tongue," Damor said. "See I'm not forced to reign it in for you."

Sal leered at the bodyguard. He had been hit by Damor before, and while it was not a feeling he ever desired to taste again, it wouldn't do to show fear with Damor Nev.

Once the crew of porters had nearly unloaded all of the crates onto the wagons, they began to gather about the loading ramp.

Ticker whistled and made a motion with his hand, whirling it in a circular motion above his head.

Things seemed to slow down. The group of street thugs that

stood around the perimeter of the worksite withdrew crossbows, swords, and daggers and turned upon the porters who had been unloading the ship.

"No!" cried Damor, just before the thugs opened fire upon the porters.

Sal felt his heart drop to the pit of his stomach. The few dockworkers who didn't fall to the quarrels tried to run but were cut down mercilessly and without exception.

The bodies were dragged off the docks and dumped unceremoniously into the bay.

There was some sort of commotion down on the docks near one of the moored cogs. Men began to shout, while others boarded the wagons and drove off.

"With me," said Damor, his voice like chipped ice.

Sal followed in a daze.

They skidded down the steep embankment, running when they hit the cobblestone street. The horse-drawn wagon plodded on just ahead. Two men sat the driver's bench, facing away from Sal and Damor. The wagon bed was covered with a curtain, but Sal had seen something like three to four men climb into the back of each wagon.

It only occurred to him precisely what Damor intended to do when the big man was an arms breadth from the wagon.

Damor Nev unsheathed his bastard sword and leaped upon the wagon bed, blindly swinging his sword through the canvas curtain.

A man screamed.

The men upon the driver's bench turned.

Sal threw his pigsticker, but the blade was meant for stabbing, not throwing. The balance was all wrong, and rather than strike one of the men upon the driver's bench, the pigsticker ricocheted harmlessly off the side of the wagon.

The driver shouted and pulled back hard on the reins, while the man beside him leveled a crossbow at Sal.

Sal cursed, dove, and rolled as the quarrel shattered upon the cobblestones.

Another blood-curdling scream sounded, and a man stumbled out the back of the wagon, clutching at his blood-soaked belly.

The crossbowman was cranking hard, attempting to load another missile, while the driver scrambled from his seat and charged at Sal, a short, curved sword in hand.

Sal reached into his pocket and crushed the cap of skeev in his palm, then grabbed hold of the locket. It was warm to the touch. He was flooded by a surge of energy. Willing all the focus he could muster upon the man, Sal thrust out an open palm and felt the bolt of lightning surge forth.

With an explosion like blast powder, the lightning bolt struck the man square in the chest, propelling him backward.

Sal dropped to his knees as the magic seemed to sap him of his energy.

The man with the crossbow had nearly reloaded his weapon when Sal heard two consecutive screams and saw Damor step from the back of the wagon.

The crossbowman took aim at Sal once more.

Sal dove to his belly and rolled, but just before the crossbowman pulled the trigger, the gleaming blade of Damor arced through the air and struck deep into the man's neck with a wet *thwack*. The crossbowman threw his weapon as his arms spasmed, and his body crumpled to the cobbles. The crossbow clattered to the street and fired of its own accord, quarrel launching with a twang before it ricocheted off a wall.

Sal rolled onto his back, breathing hard.

He could hear Damor Nev approaching, but he had no desire to speak to the man. The fool had nearly gotten them killed with his Sacrull damned heroics.

Damor stood over Sal, hand reaching down to help him to his feet.

"I don't think I can stand," Sal said, not bothering to hide the shame in his tone.

Damor nodded and pulled Sal to his feet, as though he weighed no more than a child, and helped him to lean against the wagon. Damor pulled back the canvas curtain to reveal the blood-soaked corpses of three men, hacked to a bloody mess, their bodies contorted over an assortment of stacked crates.

Damor climbed up into the wagon bed and pried the lid off one of the crates with his sword.

The look on his face told Sal he did not find what he was looking for.

"Look, Nev, whatever it is you're after, let's get it and get the hell out of here before the steel caps come calling."

Damor pried the lid from a second crate and a third but seemed to remain disappointed. Sal tried to peek into the crates but could not see from his low viewpoint. Damor pried the lid from a fourth, cursed, and sheathed his sword.

"Let's be off," said Damor Nev.

"Hold on," said Sal. "What was in the crates? What did you see?"

"Indigo," answered Damor. "Not, but God's damned indigo."

19

SCARVINI PALACE

"The Enlightened Council has put the issue to an official vote," said Jacques. "After the recent discovery of the items previously within possession of the late Brother Philip, Salvatori Lorenzo, your name has been cleared of all charges."

Sal felt a wave of elation sweep over him. He'd known this moment was coming, but something had niggled at him. A worry that it was all too good to be true.

"While you are free to go, know that you are welcome to stay. The guesthouse is not required at this time, and you may continue to keep your residence there, as an honored guest, with the freedom to come and go as it please you."

"Your offer is a generous one, and I must thank you for all that you have done for me," Sal said, "but I can't say I feel worthy of such generosity." Sal took a bite of the bacon and washed it down with mulled wine. As usual, no expense had been spared at the abbot's table. A full spread of dried fruits, cured meats, and aged cheeses was laid out before them.

"I did no more than what God would have expected of me," said the abbot. "You were an innocent man, accused of falsehoods, and you deserved no less than a hand in revealing the truth to those who are blind to such sentiments."

"Still, I owe you a debt, no doubt."

Jacques smiled. "You may seek absolution with the Lord that is Light. For my part, I was only doing my duty."

Sal sighed and took another bite of the bacon. "You monks are all the same," he said through a mouthful, "pious deference and self-abasement on the exterior, but I wonder what you're really thinking."

"Take it from one who has lived among men of the cloth. Many of us possess little more than self-adulation and pious indifference within our shrunken heads. And yet, from time to time, some of us seem to find a shred of dignity within. There are times we find ourselves doing what is right rather than what is in our immediate interest. Philip was a friend of mine. His death angered me as much as it saddened me, though, not so much as the news of his betrayal. Still, I am obligated to do what is right, as much as it pains me to realize just how close at hand the traitor was."

"And yet, I wonder if Philip was working alone," Sal said.

"Are you suggesting there are others within the walls of my abbey that have betrayed us?"

"To me, it would only seem plausible. Clearly, Dennis was responsible for acquiring the free-trader contracts for which the drugs were imported, and yet, there was a shipment received just last evening."

"A shipment?" said the abbot in surprise. "A shipment of what?"

"Indigo, so far as we could tell, but I've a suspicion there was more, much more."

"You're suggesting it hasn't stopped?" the abbot asked.

"I can't be sure. Still, I think you would do best to keep your eyes peeled. I've suspicions about a man, but I'm certain of little and less where he is concerned."

"Pray, do tell," said Jacques, reaching for his cup of wine. "Might be, I can provide some form of clarity on the subject."

"Leobald," Sal said.

It was a moment before Jacques spoke. He set down his cup and wiped at his mouth with a sleeve. "I will not be the first to slander a brother of my own order, but Leobald is a man with high ambitions and low scruples. A dangerous combination at any rate. I will keep an eye out for any suspicious activity on the prior's part, but for my own, I do not think him capable of such a thing."

"Beg pardon, but did you think Philip capable? Yet you found poison among his possessions."

Jacques's features hardened.

"I'm, sorry," Sal said quickly. "I didn't mean—I only—a person's intentions are not always clear."

Jacques reached for a wedge of cheese, and only when he began to chew, did his look soften. "Tell me, Salvatori, how fares that locket of yours? You've not lost it, I trust?"

"No," Sal said, slightly jarred by the change in subject. He resisted reaching for his collar where the locket hung tucked beneath his shirt.

"I only ask as I came across that passage we spoke of when I was at my morning reading. The mark of three, mark of beasts, the mark of Sacrull. Many interpretations as to the meaning and origin of that symbol. Some would say it is evil, others hold that to be mere superstition."

"And what say you?" Sal asked, leaning his elbows on the table.

"Ah, but I am no historian. I am a simple servant of the one true God. It would take mere days for me to divulge all that I know of the holy book. Though, if you must know my thoughts on the subject, I would say the mark is certainly very old. Older even than the holy book. In such a vast span of time, there is truly no telling how much of the truth has been lost or changed."

"And what does your book say of the mark?"

"My book? My son, the holy book is for all the children of the Lord that is Light."

"Even those who hold to other Gods?"

"False Gods, for there was nothing before the Light."

"Nothing but darkness," said Sal, smirking.

"Oh, dear boy. Tell me you do not hold to the darkness, surely you are not a worshiper of Sacrull?"

Sal shook his head. "I'm not so masochistic as that."

"But then, you must hold to the old dark, to the Nameless, those who dwelt before the light, they who birthed the pantheon? I would not have taken you for a man who held to blood sacrifice."

Sal could not help but laugh. The wine had made him giddy. "I hold to no darkness, but to she who keeps the way in the night. I follow the Lady White."

"Ah, but I see," said Abbot Jacques with a grin. "You hold not only to a false God but a God of false light."

"There is nothing false about the Lady's light. Does the moon not shine brighter than any star in the night's sky?"

"In the night's sky perhaps, for night is the domain of darkness, a place for evil to dwell. But at the rise of our Lord, there is no need of the false light, for the light of the moon pales in comparison to the light of the sun. Solus, the Lord that is Light, is the one true God of men. Be not mistaken in this. While the light of our Lord is ever constant, the light of the Lady is ever waning, shifting this way and that. The light of Solus is a blade's edge, but the Lady's light is a mere reflection, and those who would follow her path cannot help but to be mere reflections of men. For without measure, what is matter?"

"A simple monk?" Sal said, grinning broadly. "I dare say I would quake in my boots should a true scholar of your faith accost me."

Jacques bowed his head. "You must forgive me. I am somewhat passionate about the subject. At times, I find it difficult to keep my opinions to myself. Though, I dare say I failed to answer your question. You asked what the holy book had to say of the mark. I fear you will be disappointed to know that there is little in the way of reference. It is mentioned only five times within the entirety of the book, so far as I am aware. Of those references, only one describes the mark." Jacques cleared his throat. "For the possessed man will lash out. Bind him, and he will cry out. He will wail and curse God, with clawing of the eyes and gnashing of the teeth. Men will cut into the man a mark of three, to contain by blood that which pollutes the possessed. For possession is not merely a transgression of the blood, but that of the mind, body, and soul. Just as the

possessed man is taken by mind, by body, and by soul, my brothers
—those who have been indoctrinated have too been taken thus and
must be purged whole. For just as the man marked by the three of
beasts, the indoctrinated man is a danger to himself, his family, and
all those who look upon him."

Sal blinked.

"An obscure reference, I will admit," said Jacques. "It comes
from the book of Mateus, a warrior prophet of old, and a difficult
man to understand out of context. Yet, this one passage contains
two of the five references to the mark of three within the entire holy
book. I must admit, that locket of yours has intrigued me."

Sal was disappointed. None of this was any help, and if the
passage from the holy book had anything to do with his locket, he
for one, could not see how. "Jacques, are you familiar with the name
Kellenvadra?"

"Kellenvadra? No, I cannot say I've heard the name. Should I
have?"

Sal shrugged. "I can't imagine it's of much import, merely a
curiosity."

The abbot nodded. "We must all be allowed our curiosities from
time to time. Speaking of which, do you think that I might borrow
the locket? In order to examine it once more. By no means indefi-
nitely, but I would like to take another look. To satisfy a curiosity, as
it were."

"I, well, the thing is a sort of family heirloom, and you see, and
I'd rather not part—"

"Say no more," said Jacques with the wave of a hand. "As to my
proposition of remaining here as my guest?"

"I would like that," Sal said.

Jacques nodded. "Very well, my son, I have enjoyed this
reprieve, but I must be carrying on with other responsibilities. Do
keep in mind what I said regarding this Lady White, a false path is
no path at all."

Sal laughed and stood to make his leave.

He made his way to the guesthouse. There was a cap of skeev
waiting for him in the guesthouse, and it was calling his name. As

Sal crossed the abbey yard, the cap was the only thing on his mind. He nearly reached the door when a hand clapped on his shoulder.

Sal spun.

"Lorenzo," said Damor Nev. "You need to come with me."

"Lady's tits," Sal cursed. "Nev you scared the piss out of me. How did you know I was here?"

"Never mind that," said Damor, a serious look in his eyes. "With me, now."

"You want me to follow you any farther, you're going to need to tell me where we're headed, at the least," Sal said.

"Best open your eyes, and might be, I won't need to start with the obvious," said Damor Nev.

"The Outers?" Sal asked. "What's in the Outers that you could possibly be after? You have some Bauden kin you want to break the barrel with, chum?"

"Forget the barrel. Make mock of my people again, and I'll break you."

Sal went quiet, it seemed he had crossed a line, something he wanted to avoid with a man like Damor Nev. They walked in silence as they passed through Town Gate and outside the city proper. The Outers was not like the other districts in Dijvois. It had begun as a Bauden caravan camp along the Oliander, when the city was but a budding town. As the city grew, the camp grew as well. Permanent structures were built, and the Bauden inhabitants of the Outers were soon joined by Yahdrish and Shiikali migrants from the east, growing ever larger until, in time, the camp became yet another district of the great city.

"In all seriousness, Damor, I know a bit of your people apart from the typical stereotypes, but I—"

"You can keep them stereotypes to yourself if you're wanting to end the day with all of your teeth."

"I'm sorry for making mock, I only thought a bit of humor might compliment your cheery mood this morning."

The bodyguard grunted.

"Still, it seems the Bauden like color," Sal said as they neared the caravan wagons camped along the Oliander, their awnings a panoply of bright colors, as were the triangular flags that hung upon streamers between the wagons.

Bauden wagons themselves were not as one usually imagined a wagon, they were closer to town coaches, though some of them were as large as houses on wheels. Appropriate, as the Bauden were traditionally a nomadic people. Said to have been roaming Pargeche as long as the Pairgu themselves, the Bauden had never truly found a place they called home. These days, they could be found as far west as Nelgand and as far east as Dahuan.

Sal flinched as one of the horses hitched beside the road reared and whinnied loudly. The horses that used to pull the Bauden wagons seemed a mix between a shaggy mountain breed and the destriers of old. Long, curly manes upon thickly muscled necks and shaggy hair upon their massive shod hooves. They stood a good eighteen hands and looked almost too large to ride, but Sal imagined they could pull a wagon as well as any ox.

"Beautiful horses," Sal said. "Though I wouldn't fancy the task of breaking them."

Damor Nev merely grunted once more.

"Does the tribe of Nev hail from Dijvois?" Sal asked with genuine curiosity. It struck him he knew little about the bodyguard. This Bauden man who followed Lilliana like a deadly shadow.

Damor shrugged. "I wouldn't know. I didn't grow up among my people. I was born in the far south, the city of Krathus. I was the youngest of four. But no Bauden has a use for four sons. I was meant to be a girl, you see. My father sold me to the temple of Tiem when I was but a boy."

"A warrior priest of Tiem?" Sal exclaimed. "You?"

Damor laughed. "No, not I. Though I was a slip of a boy, I was too old by the time my parents gave me up and too willful by half. I was never inducted into the priesthood. I was gifted the sword, not the words. In the temple of Tiem, those of us too old to be inducted into the order are trained in the way of the sword and sold when we are ready to serve."

"Sold?"

Damor gave him a hard look. "I am no man's property."

They passed a pack of children at play. Sal smiled as he saw one little girl tackle a boy twice her size and push his face into the dirt. They turned south and headed into the heart of the Outers, where the buildings were taller, the roads less dusty.

"Lilliana told me you served the House of Nom in Dahuan."

Damor nodded. "I was purchased by the house of Nom the very same day that I was gifted my stripes." The bodyguard rolled his shirtsleeve to show puffy, pink flesh, three jagged scars. Three lines—three parallel lines.

Sal's breath caught in his throat. "That mark—"

"The warrior's stripes," Damor said. "A man earns them when he has proven his worth in the art of the sword."

"The mark of three," Sal said breathlessly.

"I've not heard that term," said Damor.

"The mark of Sacrull," Sal said.

"Sacrull?" Damor Nev exclaimed, his brow wrinkling. "This is no symbol of darkness, boy. This is a mark of Tiem, a mark of the World Mother herself. Each line a gate that the warrior must master." He put a big finger on the first scar. "Order," he said, sliding his finger over to the far line. "Chaos." He moved his finger back to the middle scar. "Balance."

"Damor, have you ever heard the name Kellenvadra?"

"The name means nothing to me. Why do you ask?"

Sal shrugged, trying not to show his disappointment. "So, this mark, the uh—"

"The warrior's stripes," said Damor.

"Yeah, the stripes, they each mean something different?"

"Each stripe is a gate on the path of the warrior. When the gate is broken, the stripe is earned. The stripe of order is given to the initiate when he learns his place of obedience. An initiate must follow orders and take direction. The stripe of chaos is given to the novice when he learns to control the storm within. A novice must think for himself, must be able to see through the fog of the future and build his own order within the chaos. The final gate, the stripe of balance, is given to the master when he becomes one with the sword. Three gates on the path of the warrior, three gates that must be broken."

Three gates, Sal thought. Imagining the mark upon the locket, three stripes, one of them blood red, the other two merely etched into the tarnished gold. He wondered at the significance of this, and if there was any connection between this mark of Damor's and the mark upon the locket.

"So, what is it we're after in the Outers?" Sal asked, pushing his mind back to the task at hand. "What have you discovered?"

"Ever hear of a place known as the Scarvini Palace?" The bodyguard asked.

"I've heard of it. It's a whorehouse. Classiest joint in Low Town, if the rumors are true. You bring me all the way out here so you could catch a piece of snatch?"

"I'm done warning you, boy."

"Nev, if you wanted to get your rocks off you didn't have to drag me—"

Damor Nev grabbed him by the collar, scowling. "Not interested in the place because it's a brothel."

"Well I figured that much," Sal said, placing his hands over Damor's and gently attempting to pry them from his collar. "I'm guessing you think Don Scarvini had something to do with that shipment at Eighth Harbor?"

"I don't know how far up the ladder it climbs," Damor said, releasing his grip on Sal's shirt. "I followed up on the other wagons. They were delivered to a warehouse off Penny Row. A warehouse belonging to none other than Lord Garred Peaks."

"Lord Garred—but he's—and what does Peaks have to do with the Scarvini Family?"

"Well, it wasn't the ghost of Peaks that showed up to check on the shipment."

"Who then?" Sal asked.

"Giuseppe Scarvini."

"The Shark?"

"Ay, that's the one, him and that gangly brother of his."

"And so, you think Scarvini was behind what happened at Eighth Harbor?"

Damor shrugged. "I wouldn't mind knocking a few heads around to find out."

Sal smiled. "So, what's the plan now? Why Scarvini Palace, why not the warehouse?"

"The warehouse is guarded, more than like, it's heavily guarded because of what's inside. As it stands, I wouldn't much fancy the odds of a fight with the Scarvini Family if it came to that. Not with only my sword and that Talent of yours on our side."

"My Talen—saw that, did you?"

Damor shrugged. "I've seen stranger things in my time, and I figure, the way you been cow-eyed with my lady, you ain't much of a threat to her cause, apart from that little prick of yours."

Sal winked. "I promise not to hurt you with my prick, Damor, so long as you finish telling me the plan."

"Not much of a plan," said the bodyguard. "Thought we'd go to this Scarvini Palace and ask around."

"Ask the whores if they've been bringing in the shipments of drugs?" Sal said sardonically.

"Never been with a whore, have you?" Damor asked.

It was Sal's turn to shrug. "I've never considered whoring much of a conquest worth undertaking."

"Ay, well, if you had, you'd know the sort that does. Them that go whoring all have their own reasons for it, God's know I do. But there's a certain type goes because he's lonely. Not so much about the urge in his loin so much as the ache in his heart."

"Loose tongues?" Sal said. "You're thinking someone might have let something slip to one of the whores?"

"Way I figure it, this was a big job. I'm thinking a whole lot of someones done spilled the story to a whole lot of whores. All we needs do is go down to that Scarvini Palace and ask around a bit, maybe take one of them girls to a room and really get to talking."

Sal laughed somewhat nervously. "Sounds like a decent plan. So long as sticking our noses into Commission business doesn't get us killed."

"Don't think this one is Commission sanctioned," said Damor. "As far as I can tell, Scarvini is acting alone."

"Now, you see, that's where you're wrong," Sal said. "The Commission isn't just a collective, it's a pact. If one of the Five Families is involved, all five of the families are honor bound to get involved. Go to war with one of the Five, and you go to war with the Commission."

"Don't you know, boy? There's no such thing as honor among thieves. These bastards are as like to turn on their own, quick as they are us. These Five Families are no families at all, they're not but street gangs, got their chests puffed up and their heads full of false notions."

Sal smiled. "I suppose a man such as yourself has the liberty to make such claims. As for me, I do my best not to bite the hand that feeds me, and I sure as spit don't go around kicking hornets nests. Not anymore, at least."

"A bit of a provoker in your youth, were you?" said Damor.

"You've no idea. Hardly survived my first run-in with the Five Families, and I'm not exactly eager to go repeating the mistakes of my youth."

"Just which hornet's nest was it you went and kicked?"

"Moretti," Sal said.

Damor Nev smiled a big, broad smile. "A tale you will doubtless needs tell me sometime. Though for now, save your stories for the whores. Just keep in mind, you're there for what they know, not for what they do."

Sal chuckled. "I'll keep mine in my trousers if you promise to do the same, priest."

Damor scowled and patted his shoulder where his brand was hidden beneath his sleeve.

Scarvini Palace could hardly be called a palace. A six-story structure in all. The first three floors were built with orange brick, while the top three floors were a mixture of wood and stone in a style Sal did not recognize. A red lantern hung beside the crooked oak door, casting the entryway in a warm, welcoming pink light.

Within, Scarvini Palace was dimly lit, no doubt to set the mood, but more likely to hide the filth and the ashamed looks on the faces of the patrons. Though empty, apart from Sal and Damor, the grand sitting room was filled with old, mismatched furniture: a peach-colored divan, florally patterned armchairs, and a long, squat couch. Strangest of all, a rocking chair carved with reliefs in a style that looked Dahuaneze. The tapestries depicted silhouetted forms entangled in a number of suggestive positions. The marble sculpture at the center of the room depicted the headless form of a woman, back arched suggestively to bring attention to her large breasts, her nipples erect.

There was a soft, *ahem*, from across the room.

Sal snapped his attention away from the statue.

The woman fixed Sal with a sultry stare, though, she was rather a bit old to be playing the coquettish maid. She wore over much rouge, her blouse cut far too low, showing a disturbing amount of the cleavage between her two sagging breasts.

"That there's the hen-mother," whispered Damor Nev, as though Sal hadn't already figured that much out.

"Good afternoon gentlemen," said the hen-mother, licking her lips. "How might I satisfy your needs?"

Sal had no idea what to say. For an instant, he was terribly aware of the odd pair he and the Bauden bodyguard made. How suspicious they must have seemed. He thought it best to just let Damor do the talking.

"We've some friends," said Damor Nev. "A couple of regulars around this part. Well, they was telling us we had to come give this place a go. They said we had to head down to the palace and ask for —" Damor turned to Sal, a puzzled look on his face. "What'd he say their names was, lad?"

Sal only stammered, his mouth opening and closing like a fish on dry land.

"Oh, that's alright, lad, don't go hurting yourself," Damor said with a little chuckle. He leaned in toward the hen-mother conspiratorially. "The boy's a bit touched, he is, can't tell a rhubarb from a rainbow half the time. Don't know why I bother, honestly, suppose I just feel bad for the boy. But I'll tell you what. You find us a couple girls that are worth bragging over so we got something we can tell our friends, I'd much appreciate it."

The hen-mother arched a thinly tweezed eyebrow. "Every princess in the palace is worth bragging about to any and all of your friends. Do you have any preferences—long hair, short hair, thin, thick, pink-skinned, brown-skinned?"

Damor shrugged. "The boy will want someone gentle, willing to share her feelings and allow him to share his."

"We have no virgins here, but I know of some girls that will suffice. For yourself," the hen-mother asked in a husky tone, brushing her nipple with the back of her thumb as though it were accidental. "You look like a man who can handle a more mature woman." She puckered her lips, raised her thin eyebrows, and fluttered her eyelids. She clasped her hands over her legs and leaned forward as her arms squeezed her sagging bosom.

"That I can, my lady, that I can. Though, I find today I'd like someone young, one of the talkative sort. There's something about the voice of a young woman that gets my blood going."

"Pink or brown?" the hen-mother asked curtly, doing a right poor job of hiding her disappointment with Damor's response.

"Either, or both. So long as she's younger than me, with looks enough to boot, makes no matter."

The hen-mother sniffled and whipped her nose into the air. "I shall be but moments, do make yourselves comfortable."

As the hen-mother disappeared behind a curtain, Sal took a seat on the long, squat couch, and Damor sat beside him. Sal turned and raised a brow at the bodyguard, motioning with a hand to all the open seating.

Damor Nev opened his mouth, but before he spoke, the front door opened, and three men entered the grand sitting room. Sal recognized them, one and all.

The man in the lead was taller than his companions. He had the Scarvini look, sunken eyes and jet-black hair. It was his distinctive cleft chin that set him apart from his brothers. He was the oldest son of Don Scarvini, Giuseppe Scarvini, though most everyone Sal knew simply referred to him as: The Shark.

The second man shared Giuseppe's look, the sunken eyes and black hair of the Scarvini blood-royal. Though, more than anything, he resembled a slouching weasel. His eyes flickering place to place as though he felt he was being watched, his movements quick and jittery. His name was Garibaldi Scarvini, second son of Don Giotto Scarvini.

Third to enter was Li Jing, a Dahuaneze man known for doing wet work for the Scarvini family. He was a made man and a well-known one at that. Li Jing was rumored to have served the House of Nom before he came to Dijvois. Around the city, Li Jing was known to be the worst thing to find within a shadow.

Damor leaned close to Sal. "We need to go, now."

Sal scoffed under his breath. An understatement if he'd ever heard one. Three of the most influential men within the Scarvini crime family had entered the room. The last thing Sal needed was to be recognized.

To Sal's relief, none of the newcomers spared him nor Damor Nev a second glance. Instead, they passed through the sitting room and stepped through the curtain. The same curtain which the hen-mother had disappeared behind. The moment Li Jing was no longer visible, Sal nearly jumped to his feet and froze as the curtain swept open once more.

The hen-mother stepped through, two girls in tow like a pair of ducklings. They were both half the age of the hen-mother, though it was the only similarity between them. The girl in the lead was blonde, peach skin, and a cute button nose. Sal took her for a Norsic, but she could as well have been Nelsigh. Her bosom prodigious, her soft curves accentuated by her alluring silk robe, Sal felt himself stiffen at the sight of her.

The girl in the rear had straight, black hair and nutbrown skin. Her big almond shaped eyes, drew Sal in and would not let him free. He assumed she was of Minnoan blood or somewhere in the near-east. She was more slender then the blonde, but had no less appealing a figure. Sal was a touch embarrassed to admit he would be more than happy to be paired with either girl and had to remind himself he was there for information, not to lose his maidenhood.

The hen-mother delicately place her hand over her mouth and made a soft noise in her throat. "Gentlemen, please allow me to introduce Princess Sapphire, and Princess Diamond." The pair of whores sauntered across the sitting room. The blonde locked eyes with Sal and grabbed him by the elbow. The four of them headed for the curtain, leaving the hen-mother alone in the sitting room.

Behind the curtain was a hallway with a pair of doors on either side and a staircase at the end of the hall. They made for the stairs and rounded them up to the second floor.

Damor flashed Sal one last look before they were each led into rooms at either side of the hall. The whore tugged him into the room vigorously, nearly pulling his arm from the socket as she threw him onto the bed.

Without warning, she scrambled for the button of his trousers, ripped them open, and tugged them swiftly down to his ankles.

He made a halfhearted attempt at crossing his legs, but there was no hiding that he was fully erect.

"Hard for me already, are you?" she said, tugging at his cock.

Sal sat up. "I'm sorry, but I don't even know your name."

"Princess Diamond," she said, putting a hand on his chest and shoving him back down on the feather mattress. Her hand slid down his chest over his navel and onto his rock-hard manhood. She pulled his small clothes down to his ankles, along with his pants, with another swift tug.

He sat up quickly. "Diamond, that's not your real name, is it?"

The whore put her hand back on his chest and pushed him back down on the mattress, somewhat more forcefully this time. Without warning, she put his cock in her mouth, and he nearly gave in there and then. It was wet, warm and the best thing he had ever felt. In a sudden flush of guilt, he recalled what he was there to do.

He panicked and did all he could to swiftly remove her. Though, he probably shouldn't have grabbed her by the hair.

Princess Diamond cried out and slapped his hand away. "Fuck's matter with you?" she said, her eyes filled with venom.

"Sorry—I'm sorry—I didn't mean—"

"Bloody hell," she said. "That just figures."

Sal looked at his feet, his manhood shriveling as shame swept through him. "What figures?"

She huffed and rubbed at her scalp where he'd tugged. "Nothing," she said sullenly.

"No, tell me. I really am sorry I did that. But you can tell me what it is you mean. What figures?"

"Madam Dubois told us one of you was touched. Though, she didn't say which one. Just figures it's me what's got to deal with it."

Sal blushed, he felt a bit touched sitting there on the edge of the bed with his pants about his ankles, his manhood now soft as a Fitzen pudding. "I really am sorry. Are you alright?"

Princess Diamond brushed his hand away. "Right then. What is it you want from me?"

"I want to get to know you first," Sal said.

"Look, if I'm to be honest, I'd rather you just let me suck you off so I can get back to sleep before the next one comes through to put it in me. That, or you can stick it wherever you want, let's just get this done."

"Isn't the client supposed to get what he wants?" asked Sal.

The whore shrugged. Even that, Sal found irresistibly erotic. "It's my experience no one gets what they want, not really. Even when they get what they think they want." She was thicker than he thought he would have liked, and yet it made her all the more desirable somehow. "Well then, what is it you think you want?"

"I want to see you get naked for me," Sal said.

Princess Diamond rolled her eyes, but did as he asked. She began to untie the belt of her robe with deft fingers.

Sal put a hand over hers. "Slowly," he said. "Everything, very slowly. I want to enjoy this."

She smiled stupidly at him. The kind of fake smile a whore would give, but it made his blood all the hotter, and his desire for her all the greater.

In an instant, his cock was hard as a sword, and he longed to sheath it within her, but he had a job to do. A job for Lilliana. The thought of her softened him in an instant. He was there for information, not sex.

The whore pulled her other arm from the sleeve and slowly lifted the hem of the robe upward, slowly, it drew past her soft, white round thighs and up to the triangle of coarse, blonde hair above the mound of her womanhood. Sal felt a tremor course through him as she lifted the robe farther to expose the soft curve of her belly, a long slender naval, a cleft in the pale flesh of her soft stomach. The arch of her ribs, each rib defined as she arched her back, her chest thrust forth as the shirt slowly lifted to reveal the pale, round hint of her breasts. Slowly, the full curve and then the darker pink skin of her nipples, cone shaped with soft indents at the very tips.

Sal shivered as the robe was lifted all the way to her collarbone, fully exposing her pale breasts. Then, she pulled it up and over her head and threw the shift aside. Naked from the waist up, the whore reached for her sex and stroked herself with a wanton hand.

"You worked here long?" Sal stammered stupidly and overly loud.

The girl smiled as though she knew a joke that he didn't. Her fingers played in the wiry blonde hair that formed a triangle above the mound of her womanhood.

Sal could not help but stare. His manhood so stiff it hurt. His heart pounded in his chest. His throat too tight to speak. The whore closed in on him, climbing onto his lap and taking his stiff cock in her hand, when the door burst open.

Damor Nev strode through the doorway, "Get the fuck up," the Bauden shouted, "we need to get the fuck out of here!"

Sal shoved the whore to the floorboards.

She hit the ground ass first, with a shout part curse, part squeal.

Sal pulled up his trousers and bolted out in Damor's wake.

A RETURN TO THE HOG

"Watch it," said a man as Sal shouldered past. He slipped a hand into the man's coat and cut the thin purse throng with his finger-knife. Sal stammered an apology as he moved on down the street. A quick feel of the purse revealed it was light, no more than five coins, but it would serve.

Sal was supposed to meet Vinny at the Hog Snout by midday, but he'd overslept. Cursing to himself, he picked up his pace and was nearly run over by a horse-drawn carriage as he slipped from the dense crowd and out into the middle of the cobblestone street. He shoved a man and slipped back in line, just in time, as a pair of carthorses trotted past. Sal nearly lost his balance as he was shoved from the pack back into the middle of the road, but he took it in stride, and without a look at who'd shoved him, he carried on down Penny Row.

When Sal opened the door beneath the swaying sign of the crudely painted boar, he was hit with the smell of meadowsweet scattered amongst the rushes. He was reminded painfully of the night when he'd found Bartley and Bessy, two corpses lying face-down on the floor of Bartley's room. Just the thought made Sal want to flee the spot.

With all the courage he could muster, Sal forced himself to take a step, and then another. His knees shook as he crossed into the taproom, everything inside him wanting out of that place, but he reminded himself that was not his only memory of the Hog Snout. He'd made many more memories in that taproom, every one of them happier than the memory of the night he'd found Bartley and Bessy.

"Oy, Salvatori!" called Vinny. He was seated at a table, a clay mug to hand, and a grin on his face. There were four others seated around the table, all but one of them familiar faces. "I was beginning to think you wouldn't show."

"No, not our Salvatori," said Odie, placing a massive hand on Vinny's shoulder. "Loyal as a pup, that little fish is."

"He'll be loyal," said Valla, turning on him with half-lidded eyes, "I'll make certain of that, but the cat's paw cannot be late on the night of the job."

"Ah, job is it," Sal said, pulling out the remaining empty chair and fixing Vinny with a withering glare. "For a moment there, I thought I might have been lured here under false pretenses."

Vinny had the grace to look ashamed. "Sorry, mate, you might not have come otherwise."

"I don't believe we've been introduced," Sal said, nodding to the unfamiliar man.

"This handsome bastard, is Balliel," said Valla, gesturing. "Best mimic in the city. Works cons like he was born to it."

"Twenty years, I have spent traveling with a group of mummers," said Balliel. "Grew up on the stage, you could say." The man smiled, accentuating his handsome features and showing off his straight, white teeth. Sal took him for a Shiikali, but his green eyes bespoke of possible Nelsigh blood.

"Balliel, like Balliel the bard?" Sal asked.

"My mother loved his songs," said Balliel.

"I've always liked 'Piddle on the Diddler'," Sal said.

"Can't stand that bloody song," said Vinny.

"The Queen's Old Goose?" Sal asked.

"Now there a droll song," said Odie.

"Not meant to be funny, you dolt. That one's a tragedy," said Valla. "Tells about the collapse of this kingdom. It's about the bloody overthrow of the last Pairgu king."

"Don't mean it ain't fun to shout, 'bout getting the noose though, does it?" said the big man, grinning like a child.

Valla nodded to the young woman seated beside her. "You've met Aurie."

Sal nodded.

"Just wait until you've seen her work," Valla said with a smile. "There are spiders who could learn from watching this one climb. Best snatcher we could ask for."

The girl lowered her chin. Her brow creased, her lips pursed tight. Despite all that, she was still pretty, in a common sort of way. Her freckled face and bleached brown hair told of long days in the sun, possibly some farmer's get, but more than likely an urchin that had made her own way.

"Yes, you've told me, she's a better snatcher than me," Sal said. And although he'd intended for it to be playful, it somehow came out sounding bitter.

Valla smiled a wicked smile. "You, Salvatori are no longer a snatcher. You are my cat's paw, and there's no room for insecurity in that little kitty's head of yours."

"I'd say Salvatori's the better snatcher," said Vinny sullenly, his words somewhat slurred. It was never a good thing when he got too deep into his cups. That was when the mean half of the half-Norsic seemed to come out. "Salvatori is kind of man we'd want on the job. Ask me we can do without the girl."

Both Valla and Aurie turned venomous glares upon Vinny, but the half-Norsic seemed not to notice.

"Right, well, it'll be a pleasure to work with you," said Sal, in an attempt to shift the conversation. "Both of you, that is."

Balliel winked, while Aurie's lips curled back in a sort of nervous leer.

"Now that you've observed all the proper pleasantries, perhaps we can continue?" said Valla. "I'll not take up everyone's time going back over every fucking detail from the get-go, but I will need to go over some of the basics for our latecomer."

"Sorry, everyone," Sal said, knowing full well if he had been informed they were meeting about a job, he would never have been late, but the last thing he needed to do was shift any more negative attention back Vinny's way.

"Salvatori, you'll be playing cat's paw," said Valla, looking over the group as though waiting for an objection. "We will want you on the southwest corner of the rooftop. That ought to give you a good look over Penny Row and Town Road."

"Hold on, what building is this?" Sal asked.

"Warehouse thirty-seven off Penny Row. We've had word of a big shipment moving there. We'll be there to remove that shipment before it moves on to the markets. We will meet at evenfall, just off Town Road outside the Square. There is a binder's press on the west side, that's where I'll be waiting. And I won't be waiting for latecomers."

Balliel coughed something inaudible, and Aurie snickered. Valla fixed Sal with a pointed look.

"Right, well, didn't exactly know what I was getting into, did I?" Sal said.

"Continuing from where we were," said Valla. "Vincenzo and Odie will load the crates. Balliel, as you ought to have the horse cart by then, you'll need to help load. When Aurie and I have finished with the remaining guards, we'll join to help load. We take our fill and leave. Simple as that."

"And the guard?" said Vinny. "If he puts up a fight—"

"Certainly, there will be no objections, yes? said Balliel with a disarming smile. "I am not a man so often denied."

Vinny frowned, chin tucked, nose wrinkled as though he smelled something rotten. "And if you are denied?"

"You let me worry about the contingencies," said Valla. "All you need to do is worry about your end, Vincenzo."

"I'm only saying, we might do better to have Odie and I bag the guard from the start. Don't care how tough the bastard is, he's not fighting off the big man. Whereas—" Vinny said, trailing off as he motioned to Balliel.

"Ah, you do not believe I can be fighting this one man, yes?" Balliel asked.

"No, I don't," said Vinny flatly.

"I assure you, there will be no fighting," said Balliel. "As I have told, there is not many a times when I am denied."

"And why send this perfumed mummer to begin with?" Vinny said, as though he'd not heard Balliel. "Wouldn't we do better to find a woman? Better yet, Valla, why don't you—"

"Enough," Valla said with a voice like a whip. "Vincenzo, I'd shut that trap of yours before someone gets upset. I hadn't thought you to be the one to question my judgment, but it seems you take me for some kind of Sacrull damned fool."

"No, I—"

"I'll not tell you again," Valla snapped. "Do you not think I scouted this job? Do you not trust I have mapped out every step of this plan with meticulous care? This will be one more of a countless number of jobs that I have successfully led. What reasons could you possibly have to doubt me? Especially after those rumors you so thoughtlessly began to spread about our friend, Salvatori."

"Rumor tellings, this big blonde one is the jealous type, no?" said Balliel.

"Let's see how that pretty face suits you in a real fight, Shiikali," said Vinny, standing.

Odie put a hand on Vinny's shoulder, and tempers cooled almost instantaneously. Only fools picked fights with the big man. Even deep in his cups and heated as he was, Vinny would never be so foolish. To pick a fight with the big man was like stepping into the dragon's open maw naked as your name-day.

It seemed Vinny sensed he'd gone too far. The half-Norsic quickly took his seat, his mouth no longer moving, the words extinguished by Odie's touch.

"Right, well, how about a round?" suggested Sal. "I, for one, could use a drink."

Valla motioned for the serving wench.

A curvy woman that looked not too unlike Bessy sauntered over.

She had a head of blonde ringlets and wore over much make up for Sal's taste, but she had a bosom like a set of ripe melons that made it difficult for him to look at her face. He couldn't help but think of the whore he'd been with at Scarvini Palace. He did his best to sneak peeks when he thought she wasn't looking and found himself hoping she would find any excuse to bend down in front of him.

The serving wench cleared her throat. "And what for you?" she asked, slightly annoyed, as though she'd had to ask him more than once. There was no sense of flirtation in her flinty eyes. She narrowed them and glared openly to make her point abundantly clear.

Slightly embarrassed that he'd been caught lost in the ponderance of her prodigious endowment, Sal ordered a house ale without thinking, if only to get her to move her attention anywhere else.

"Not so friendly as old Bessy," Sal said conversationally once the serving wench had moved off.

"Yes, well, she's not also a whore on the side," said Valla.

"Easy," said Sal, "Bessy was no whore. A tad loose maybe, but not a whore."

"Tomato, Potato," said Valla. "I call a duck a duck and a fuck a fuck. You want to pretty up the situation with your pedantic bullshit, do it elsewhere. This is a bullshit free table."

"I liked old Bessy," said Odie, "sweet girl. Though, this new one's a shade younger, got a set o' dugs like a wet nurse, she does, and a rump like two juicy hams."

Vinny laughed, and Balliel clicked his tongue, but Valla shook her head, while Aurie turned red as a strawberry.

"A bit of fucking professionalism wouldn't be out of line," said Valla.

"Oy, you want professionalism, you best cross the river," said Odie mulishly.

"And you best watch your tongue before you wind up leaving here with your balls in a coin purse," Valla threatened.

"There's no need for none of that now," said Odie. "I only look at the other girls, but you know you're the only one for me, lass."

"Should have gone to the bloody Anchor. Leastways, I'd be

making a cut off of what you rum-hounds have swilled down," Valla said and stabbed her knife into the tabletop, where it stood erect.

The serving girl stopped short, drinks upon her tray, her eyes fixed on the knife quivering in the table.

"You see what professionalism gets you, woman," said Odie, gesturing to the serving wench as though goading a farm animal.

Vinny and Sal shared a look, and Vinny smiled, clearly pleased to no longer be the center of attention.

The serving wench approached tentatively, her tray shaking slightly as she served out the food and drinks. The instant her tray was empty, she quickly bustled back to the kitchen without bothering to ask if anyone at the table needed anything else.

Things calmed down a tick once the group had fresh drinks and food to eat. As Sal knew well, empty stomachs breed bad company. Sal sipped at his ale, listening more than speaking, keeping one eye on Vinny as everyone talked and drank.

"I'm only saying, six isn't necessary," Vinny said loudly as he conversed with Odie.

Valla looked at Vinny like a hound with a scent, but Vinny carried on as though he hadn't noticed. "I mean, we could do it as easily with four. Means a bigger cut for the lot, don't it?"

"Vincenzo," Valla said, pulling the knife from the table and pointing it at Vinny. "One more word, I will put the point of this sticker right through your eyehole. Understood?"

Vinny turned on Valla with a look dripping of petulance. He must have been deeper in his cups than Sal had thought. "Was only saying the girl isn't needed, and that Shiikali fop—"

Valla moved swift as an alley cat, she had drawn a second dagger, seemingly from thin air.

Before Vinny had stood, Valla had closed the distance.

Moving faster than Sal would have believed possible of such a big man, Odie had moved between Valla and Vinny. With one arm wrapped around Valla's waist, the big man had lifted her off the ground and used his other hand to pin Vinny back down to his chair.

"Let's not lose our tempers," Odie said, smiling. "Keep in mind we're all friends here, and, lad, I suggest you drop the issue before Val opens you up right here in the taproom."

"Sound advice, yes?" said Balliel with a wink.

Valla looked aghast at being lifted and detained, Vinny looked disgruntled, but neither of them argued with Odie, as there was little one could do to change the mind of the big man once it had been made up.

Slowly, Odie lowered Valla to her feet and lifted his hand from Vinny's shoulder. Valla sheathed her blades, and Odie took his seat once more.

Aurie was the only one around the table who did not seem nullified. Her face twisted with anger, she stood, picked up her drink, and poured it over Vinny's blonde head, then walked out of the taproom without a word spoken.

Everyone laughed, except Vinny, who shot a glare at Aurie's back as she walked out of the inn.

"Keep your calm, Vinny. It's not a dagger in the eye," Sal said reassuringly.

From that point on, the afternoon's gathering unfolded without incident. Vinny was the first to depart, saying something about a new shirt and being short on coin. Odie left next, shortly followed by Valla. Sal began to stand, when Balliel put a hand on his arm.

"Please, another drink. You will stay and speak with me, yes."

Sal nearly told the Shiikali he had to be going but found himself waving down the serving wench and ordering another ale.

"That friend of yours, the Norsic boy. I would like a word with you about him."

"Right, well, Vinny might have had a little much to drink, but he won't be a problem."

"Respectfully, I must disagree. You know this Vinny better than I, but it seems I know the ways of men better than you. I have always had a good, you might say, feeling for what is inside a person."

"And what is it you see inside me?" Sal asked.

"Always men are wanting to know of themselves, me, me, me,

when they should be knowing of the things around them, else they are not blind to all that is before them."

"Well, what about me, me, me?" Sal said, winking.

Balliel scoffed and smiled, waving his hands loftily. "There is potential."

Sal laughed. "You're a difficult man to dislike, Balliel."

"This is the way of drinking, yes?" the Shiikali said, still smiling wide.

Sal shook his head. "Alcohol has never kept me from disliking a man. But you, I find I like. Tell me, Balliel who is not the bard, what is it you see inside Vinny that makes him such a problem? I mean, if you think Vinny is a problem, you really ought to have a look inside Valla."

"I have seen inside all of them, all of whom I have met, all who I have known. My Talent allows this at but a glance. In Vallachenka, I see anger, but there is also control. In the one you call the big man, I can see a quiet confidence. In the young woman, Aurianwyn, there is a beautiful flower waiting only to show her face to the sun, but in this Vincenzo friend of yours—"

Sal raised his eyebrows and looked pointedly at the Shiikali, but before Balliel spoke, the curvy wench had returned with their drinks.

Balliel took a swig, but Sal waited, unwilling to look away.

"Right then, you were on Vinny. What is it inside him that you find so disturbing?"

"Betrayal," the Shiikali man said. "I see betrayal in him."

Sal was uncertain what to think of that. He didn't know what the Shiikali was getting at. They were a superstitious people, but this was something else, something strange. "How precisely does one see betrayal inside a person? I'm a tick confused on the process."

Balliel took another drink. "You've heard of Talents, no?"

"So, you're a magicker?"

"Of a sort. There are some who hold many Talents, and some who possess only one. Since I was a child, I have been able to see in men what others cannot. It has made my dealings simple things all my life. It is this Talent which shows me what others desire, and it is with this gift that I have survived. You must believe me when I tell you, your friend is far more of a risk than you surmise."

"And what reason could Vinny possibly have for wanting to betray me?"

"I do not claim to see the reasons nor motivations behind such desires. I have told you what I know, little as that may be. Heed my warning, and remain ever vigilant."

Sal scoffed. "Right, well, I appreciate the warning, but I need to be going. A prior engagement." Sal drained his mug and made to leave the Hog Snout. As he pushed unsteadily through the door, he wondered how well he truly knew Vinny, and for that matter, how well he really knew anyone.

FIRST DATE

INTERLUDE, SIX MONTHS EARLIER

She was wearing the sapphire teardrop earrings. The same earrings she'd worn the first time he'd seen her. She looked stunning in her blue dress. She was always stunning, and yet, today she looked exceptional. The blue brought out her eyes brilliantly, in a way that made Sal want to stare endlessly into them, to get lost within their depths, never to return to the cold world without.

Sal felt a beggar before a Goddess. "You showed?" he said, almost unable to believe his eyes.

"Well, of course I did," Lilliana said with a smile. "Seems I owed you that much for saving my life, did I not?"

"So, it was out of a sense of obligation?"

"I came because I wanted to," Lilliana said with a look of irritation. "But if you would rather I hadn't, I can always just leave."

"I'm sorry," Sal said. "I just never thought you'd show is all."

"Well, you have a funny way of expressing your excitement at seeing me."

"You're right. That was wrong of me, I should never have acted that way. Please, shall we?"

She accepted his arm and allowed him to lead her across the Bridge of the Lady.

"I see you're wearing the cloak," Lilliana said, running a hand over the sable fur lining. "It suits you."

"Thank you," Sal said, feigning a smile.

The cloak was black wool, finely woven and warm. The black sable lining made it worth more than anything else Sal owned, apart from the locket, that is. It had been a gift from Lilliana, her first gesture in return for saving her life.

The first gift given out of obligation? A question he had pondered more than once. He felt a pretender in the thing. Like a boy wearing his father's boots.

"Where is it you're taking me?" Lilliana asked.

"You'll see," Sal told her, doing his best to make his smile look confident. The feel of her arm locked in his sent flutters through his stomach and his heart beating in his throat. It felt good, but he knew the feeling couldn't last.

They weaved their way across the Bridge of the Lady, down Beggar's Lane, and up Town Road until they were within Town Square. A crowd had gathered, some standing upon the edge of the great fountain of Uthrid Stormbreaker, all heads turned toward Town Hall.

Upon the seventh floor, wire cages had been lined up all along the balcony.

"What is this?" Lilliana asked, leaning close to Sal's ear so that he would hear her over the buzz of the crowd. "What's happening?"

Her breath was warm, and it tickled his ear, sent a shiver down his spine, and stirred something in his loin. "You see that man up on the balcony?" Sal asked, pointing. "Watch his arms. He is about to pull those wires."

"What will the wires do?" Lilliana asked.

"Give it a moment. As soon as the sun is directly overhead, the man on the balcony is going to raise his arms and pull those wires tight above his head."

Lilliana narrowed her eyes, her lips pouting, but Sal knew the look for what it was, and he refused to give in.

Within moments, the man atop the balcony raised his arms, pulling the cords which released the doors upon the wire cages. Hundreds of white pigeons flew out from the cages in unison, circling above Town Square like a great whirlwind.

Lilliana gasped. "Doves, it's beautiful." She looked Sal in the eyes. "They're so, so pure."

"Yeah," Sal said quietly, moving in close to her, nary space for air between their warm bodies. "Pure, completely perfect."

The birds circled overhead, Lilliana blushed but looked him square in the eyes. Sal took the opportunity to lean in close, his lips nearly touching hers. She moved in the rest of the way and kissed him back.

They remained, frozen in time, and for that perfect moment, everything was—

Something wet and warm landed on top of Sal's head. As Lilliana slowly pulled away from the kiss—her eyes closed, a smile on her perfect, soft lips—Sal felt the warm, wet something slide down the side of his head, over his ear, and plop onto his shoulder. He looked down at his shoulder, the black wool and black sable fur of the cloak now smeared with a runny, white globule of bird shit.

THE WAREHOUSE JOB

Half a turn before evenfall, Town Road was more crowded than Sal had anticipated. He assumed Valla had made a similar error of judgment when she'd planned for their meeting place. He spotted the big man first, as Odie stood out in a crowd if anyone did. Vinny and the girl, Aurie, were there as well.

Odie was hunched low, in apparent conversation with Aurie, while Vinny stood to the side, arms crossed.

"Oy!" called Odie as Sal neared. "I'd say you was late, but we've yet to see that silver-tongued Shiikali."

"What of Valla?" Sal asked.

"She went to the warehouse early," said Aurie. "Told me to wait here for everyone and give a quick brief before we start."

"Or so this girl claims," said Vinny.

"And what is that supposed to mean?" said Aurie, turning to face the half-Norsic. The scene was comical, as Vinny stood near twice as tall as the girl and must have outweighed her by a good eleven stone.

"Why would Valla change the plan an hour before we're supposed to begin?" said Vinny.

"And what reason would I have to lie?" said Aurie. "You don't like it, bugger off. Valla said to wait here for everyone, and she would meet us on Penny Row."

Sal didn't like what he was hearing. He'd worked with Vinny before, but Aurie was an unknown entity. Her telling him that Valla gave an order meant about as much as if any other stranger had said it.

Sal looked to Odie. Without a word exchanged between them, the big man seemed to know what Sal was asking, and with a nod, he put Sal's nerves to ease. Still, he felt Vinny had a point. Why would Valla change the plan last minute? One thing could be said for Luca, when he was in charge, no one dared question his rule.

"You going to call this off, Odie?" Sal asked. "I don't want Vinny hurt before the job even starts."

Odie sighed. "I forget you been gone so long. This is the way this been with these two. I told Val we ought to lock them in a room and see what comes out first," Odie cleared his throat, "you know, the knives or the—"

Aurie turned on the big man with a look of such ferocity that he cut short and began laughing. Sal started laughing as well, and Aurie seemed to lose steam. Vinny looked sullen.

"Even if this girl is telling the truth, I don't like Valla making changes this late."

"Lady's sake, Vinny, when did you become the Yahdrish mother?" Sal said, punching the half-Norsic on the shoulder.

Vinny turned on him, looking not to have appreciated the jape. Only, just as Vinny opened his mouth, Odie called out in his booming voice.

"Oy, Shiikali, you'd best put a hitch in that trot or Valla is bound to," said Odie. "You've just made us late."

"Balliel, you cocksure little sand snake," said Valla, seeming to have appeared from nowhere. "I ought to wring that skinny, brown neck of yours, just to see how long you could live with all that air in your empty head."

The Shiikali sauntered up to the group, winked, and clicked his tongue.

Vinny looked at Sal, wide-eyed, and cocked his head toward Valla as if to say, *where in Sacrull's hell did she come from?*

Sal shrugged, and Vinny shook his head in disbelief.

Valla, slick with sweat, glistened in the lamplight. She paced for a moment like a prowling cat, closed her eyes, shrugged her shoulders in a most feline manner, and cracked her neck. "Right, well, now that we've all decided to gather," Valla said, shooting a pointed look at Balliel. "I'd like to discuss a few changes."

Vinny and Sal shared a look, and Sal knew they were thinking the same thing.

"It seems they've increased security. This latest shipment was a big one, and something has them spooked. Balliel, this means you're no longer playing the honey pot. You, Aurie, and I are going hunting. Basic cat and mouse, three on three, a simple matter, really. We'll work out logistics once everyone is in position. Salvatori, this changes nothing for you. I want wide eyes and ears. You even sense the City Watch, I want everyone out of there. Vincenzo, I will need you to button up that slit between your legs before your baubles fall out. Apart from that, nothing's changed. Odie, I'll want you street-side, in case of a slip-up. Anything gets out, you're running containment."

Odie grunted and pounded his chest with a fist.

"Right then, if everyone is clear, let's make our way. You two, with me." At that, Valla, Balliel, and Aurie walked on down the street, headed for an alley where Sal knew they would climb until they were moving along the rooftops.

"Right, well, I reckon that means I best head out," Sal said. "The Lady's luck to you both."

Odie nodded, and Vinny winked before Sal departed for the Warehouse District.

***

The night's wind was cold and set him to shivering. It put his clammy hands to stinging and his nose to running so that he had to wipe at the snot with his sleeve. Like a silent gargoyle, Sal had perched himself upon the rooftop of warehouse thirty-eight, the warehouse directly across from their target.

There were three guards, street level, as Valla had said. So far as Sal knew, he was alone on the rooftops. He'd checked around for crossbowmen and had been relieved to find none.

In the street below, the three guardsmen loafed around. One of the men leaned against his spear at one end of the warehouse, while his companions were actually sitting down as they made small talk. Sal wondered what incompetent bastard had hired these men. From what he had seen, they looked more like dock thugs than hired guards.

Without warning, the guard leaning on his spear dropped to his knees as his throat was opened with one of Valla's knives. As he was lowered silently to the cobblestones, the other two guards didn't so much as flinch. Neither seemed to notice anything amiss.

An instant later, Aurie and Balliel had closed in behind the guards. At knifepoint, the guards walked within the warehouse with Aurie and Balliel, swiftly joined by Valla and Odie. The big man dragged the corpse of the third guard with him. Vinny should have already been inside the warehouse to deal with the last guard. If the man was twice as competent as his companions, it might have taken Vinny half a tick to subdue him.

Sal scanned the horizon. Checked up and down Penny Row and Town Road, keeping an eye out for any signs of trouble. He felt a rush of excitement. It was good to be working jobs with a crew again. He had been too long away. Nothing else in life gave Sal the rush of working a big-time job, not even skeev.

Sal slipped a hand into the pocket of his jerkin. The cap was soft and would crumble between his fingers with the slightest pressure. He felt a pang of guilt, a flutter in his chest that was hard to ignore.

The soft clap of hoofs on cobblestones sounded below. As Sal peered over the edge, he saw the Shiikali jump from the driver's seat of a horse-drawn wagon. Moments later, Vinny and Odie emerged, a wood crate—big as a man—carried between them. The pair of them slid the crate onto the wagon bed, while Balliel held the horses still.

Sal sat back on the shingled roof. He reached into his other jerkin pocket and slipped free a rolled tobacco leaf filled with skeev, a length of waxed wick, and a chip of flint. He frayed the tip of the waxed wick, struck the flint, and had the wick lit within two strikes. With short, sharp inhalations, he rolled the tip of the leaf over the flame until it began to smoke.

Sinking deeper back onto the roof, Sal drew deep, long breaths from the joint, exhaling through his nose. Devine relaxation swept over him. He looked out over the horizon and up at the sky filled with stars and the great bright moon, the Lady White.

The baying of dogs set Sal bolting upright so quickly, he nearly fell headlong off the roof. His first thought was of the City Watch, and his heart sank to the pit of his stomach. His head was spinning, and he cursed himself for a damned fool.

A hound howled, and Sal crushed the joint, rubbing the skeev into the skin of his palms. He put one hand to his locket, focused his mind, and felt a jolt of vertigo as he rode the lightning down to the street.

Landing with a roll, Sal jumped to his feet.

"Get the wagon out of here!" He shouted.

Balliel seemed to have heard the hounds, as he was already sitting on the driver's bench. The Shiikali whipped the reins, and the horses kicked into motion. As the wagon clattered off, Sal ran inside the warehouse to warn the others. He passed the bleeding corpse of one of the guards. When he looked up, he nearly ran into Vinny and the big man as they hauled another crate between them.

"Steel caps," Sal gasped.

Vinny and Odie let go of their load at once. The crate dropped to the floor with a heavy crash. The lid popped askew, and an indigo cloud puffed into the air. The crate, it seemed, was full of powdered indigo.

Vinny ran to the door, the big man went the opposite direction —likely to warn Valla and Aurie—whom Sal imagined were watching the hostage guards, assuming Valla had not simply killed them.

Sal decided to join Vinny back at the door but ran into him

halfway there. Vinny brushed a long strand of blonde hair from his sweat-beaded brow. "They ain't steel caps, but that doesn't mean we're not fucked."

Before Sal could ask who it was, the barking sounded just outside the warehouse. A man's voice carried above the baying dogs. "I don't know who the fuck is in there, but you can come out and face your death like men, or we can send the dogs in after you."

Sal recognized the voice. His bowels tightened, and he shook slightly. Vinny had been right, they were no steel caps.

The voice he had heard belonged to the Shark himself—Giuseppe Scarvini, eldest son of Don Scarvini.

The presence of Giuseppe Scarvini could only mean one thing.

"We hit a Scarvini warehouse?" Sal said in disbelief.

"I didn't know," Vinny said, looking dumbfounded. "I swear, I didn't."

"Right, well, a lot of good that will do us now," Sal said, kneeling to draw the pigsticker from his boot-sheath. "Look, we have to get the hell out of here, any ideas?"

"Time's up!" shouted Giuseppe from just outside the door. "Guess we're coming in after you."

The hounds bayed as they padded into the warehouse at a run. There were three in all, sleek black fur and slavering maws.

Sal and Vinny ran.

"We've got to tell the others," Sal said as they rounded the corner, the hounds close at their heels.

One of the beasts barked. As Sal turned, he saw the thing leap. Sal crouched and jabbed up hard with his pigsticker. The hound yelped, but the power of its leap ripped the blade from Sal's hand.

A second hound pounced.

Defenseless, Sal raised his hands to fend the beast off, but before the hound's teeth closed upon his bare arms, Vinny tackled the thing to the ground. He roared as he jabbed his knives into the hound's thick neck again and again.

Before Sal had a chance to recover, the third hound closed with him.

The beast's jaws clenched around Sal's forearm. He screamed as sharp teeth punched through fabric, skin, and muscle. Hot blood welled and dripped down his wrist and hand.

He thought his arm would be ripped clean off as the hound shook its thick head.

A war hammer smashed into the hound's back, and the beast released him, whimpering.

Sal saw the big man lay into the beast's back with another blow from his massive war hammer. The hound whimpered and wheezed as it lay dying before Odie finished it with a third blow, the strike powerful enough to crush the hound's thick skull.

Vinny was still stabbing at his hound, not seeming to realize through his blood lust that the thing had died long ago.

Valla and Aurie had finished off the first and biggest of the three hounds. Valla gave Sal his pigsticker, sheathed in blood all the way to the leather wrapped handle. Aurie helped Sal to his feet. He was shaking, his arm throbbing as though it were on fire. He clenched the puncture wounds with his good hand, doing his best to lose as little blood as possible.

Everyone looked to Valla.

"How many are there?" Valla asked.

"Nine, by my count," said Vinny, blood dripping from his long, blonde hair as he brushed a wet lock from his eyes.

"We can fight our way through," said the big man. "Nine's not so many."

"Half and again, as many as we are," said Valla. "Or near enough as it won't matter. It would mean two for every man. Even if Salvatori here were whole, I wouldn't like these odds."

They could hear talking coming from the entranceway. It would not take long for the Scarvini men to 'round the corner and come face to face with their little party.

"I can't see as we have any other choice," said Valla. "No time to run now."

"There is," said Sal. "You could all go through the window in back. I'll stay here and hold them off."

"Not happening," said Valla. "We're not leaving you to die alone. We all go home, or we all fucking die here."

"I mean it," said Sal, getting to his feet and gritting his teeth as pain surged through his injured arm. "I have a plan, just go—go now!"

Sal put the bloody hand of his injured arm upon his locket and outstretched his other arm, palm out.

Just then, a group of men came clamoring around the corner.

When Sal saw the whites of the first man's eyes, he focused his mind and unleashed everything within him. Blue veins of lightning exploded from his palm and consumed everything before him in electric mayhem.

The men screamed as they spasmed and writhed uncontrollably. The screams grew ever louder as the men took flame, flesh stripped from bone, they combusted, exploding into thousands of pieces of viscera and charred bone. Pools of blood and strewn blackened matter remained where men had been.

Sal collapsed to his knees, drained of all energy. He heaved, tried to take in a breath, and was overtaken by darkness.

TRUE COWARDICE

INTERLUDE, SIX MONTHS EARLIER

Sal watched from afar as she stood beside the limestone statue of the Lady White, yet he dared not approach. He knew he was not worthy, knew he would never be worthy. Lilliana Bastian was meant for a better man than him.

With one last look at Lilliana, he left. Left her waiting beside the statue of the Lady White as he moved back down the road.

Sal slipped the black wool and sable lined cloak off his shoulders and carried it in the crook of his arm. He was done pretending. Done putting on this façade, this hope that things would somehow magically work out between them. It was over, and he knew it.

It was high time she did too.

He stopped before a grime filled window and looked at his reflection. Sickened by what he saw, the face of a coward. He pushed through the door, the smell of mildew and incense in the air.

"Salvatori, my boy," said Nabu Akkad from behind his counter. "How might I help you, yes?"

"You can take this cloak off my hands," Sal said.

"A fine thing, this cloak. You will be wanting a pretty penny. I am presuming?"

"You can have it gratis if you promise to sell it quickly," Sal said. He just wanted to be rid of the thing, wanted it out of his hands and away from him.

Nabu shook his head and reached into a coin purse hanging at his belt. Slowly, the fat Shiikali counted out twenty gold krom and handed the coins to Sal before accepting the cloak.

Nabu held it up high, black wool and black sable fur lining, a beautiful cloak. Truly a fine piece of cloth, something too fine for Sal by far.

The alley behind the Rusted Anchor was a long walk from Penny Row, but Sal could hardly remember making the trek. All he could think of was how Lilliana would feel waiting beside the statue of the Lady White when she finally realized Sal wasn't coming, was never coming.

The alley was cold and dark, despite the hour.

"What do you want?" said a voice from within the shadows.

"Ticker, it's me, Salvatori."

"Yeah, what do you want?" Ticker asked brusquely.

"Two caps," Sal said as Ticker emerged from the shadows. "And a wad of the black."

"Bliss?" said Ticker. "You're blissing now, are you?

"You my dealer or my Yahdrish mother?" Sal snapped.

Ticker scoffed and pulled a ball of bliss from his pocket, along with two caps of skeev. "Coin," he said.

Sal handed over three krom, but Ticker shook his head and rubbed his thumb and forefinger together. Sal gave him another gold, and Ticker handed him the ball of bliss and the caps of skeev.

"A pleasure as always," Sal said.

"Bugger off," said Ticker.

Sal did as he was told and moved off to another alley. It was deserted, and Sal found an alcove to tuck into. He pulled a wad of bliss off the ball and slipped it into his bottom lip. He sat down, and as the drug slowly dissolved in his mouth, tears began to run down his cheeks.

THE MARKED GIRL

The scent of rosemary was strong. As Sal opened his eyes, he realized he was somewhere familiar, but couldn't decipher precisely where that was. His head throbbed, and he felt a dull ache in his arm. The injured arm was bandaged, but how had it been injured to begin with? And where in Sacrull's hell was he?

He sat up in the cot and looked about, taking in his surroundings. He quickly realized why things seemed so familiar.

"Lay back now," said Alzbetta, approaching with a gentle smile. "Here and now, rest is needed. Get more sleep if you can."

Sal yawned and stretched his legs off the edge of the cot. "I don't think sleep is in the cards. I've only just recalled what put me in this state, and I'd like to find out what happened to the rest of my crew. Vinny bring me in?"

"The handsome one that brought you the last time?" Alzbetta asked, sweeping her silver hair behind one shoulder. "Tall, well-made, blonde hair, cute butt?"

"Cute butt, yeah, that's him," Sal said, swinging his legs off the edge of the cot. "How did he look?"

"Oh, my, were he ten years older, I might have done my best to entice him. My work is all-absorbing, but there are itches satisfying work simply cannot scratch."

Sal laughed. "I was referring to his well-being, the condition of his limbs and so forth."

"He was in much better shape than you were, if that's what you're asking. Had a wound on his hand. The bite from a hound, I presume. The same hound that attacked you, I'd wager."

"Different dog, I think. Looking back, it's all a bit unclear what really happened."

"A story you care to tell?" Alzbetta asked, reaching a hand uncomfortably close to his crotch.

Sal flinched but blushed as he realized there had been a rather large sprig of rosemary upon his lap.

Alzbetta's smile was coy as she clutched the sprig and placed it above the flame of a candle. When the rosemary sprig began to smoke, Alzbetta dropped it into a bowl and handed the smoking bowl to Sal.

"Breathe deep," the mender instructed.

Sal did as he was told.

"Now then," Alzbetta said. "Give me the story, and I'll take a krom off the charge for my services."

"How much do I owe?"

Alzbetta hesitated as she seemed to tally the numbers in her head. "Eleven krom, silver. I can make it eight if you're going to pay gold.

"Knock off two more, and you'll get your krom in gold."

Alzbetta smiled and nodded. "I'll have my story first."

"Why, of course. Though, a proper starting point could prove difficult to find."

"Begin where all good stories begin," Alzbetta said sagely "In the middle."

"Right," Sal said and went on to relay the events of the previous evening as the mender removed the bandage from his forearm. He told her of the warehouse and everything that had followed him reaching the rooftop of warehouse thirty-eight, leaving out the dead guardsman and the fact that they'd gone to the warehouse to rob it.

When he reached the end, he decided to leave out the bit about the lightning and the unrecognizable mass of human remains.

When Sal had finished his telling, he was surprised to find Alzbetta intrigued rather than horrified. He supposed her work had calloused her to such imagery long ago, the work of a street-mender was far from the cleanest of work, not to mention illegal under the laws of the Nelsigh Crown.

Sal examined his unbandaged arm, only faint scarring remained where the wounds of the bite had been. He opened and closed his hand, flexing the muscles of his forearm, and felt only slight pain.

"I know of a man who might like to speak with you," said Alzbetta. "Would you agree, assuming I could arrange it?"

"I would prefer to know a tick more about this man before I agreed to any such thing," Sal said playfully. "For instance, is the man a member of the City Watch? Does this man harvest the organs of living humans? Such answers are necessary in order for me to formulate an opinion about whether or not to take such a risk."

"Naturally, and yet, without his permission, I fear there is little I can say." The mender flashed him a placating smile. "For the time being, rest assured, he is neither a member of the City Watch nor does he harvest the organs of the living. Nor, for that matter, does he or has he in the past, to the best of my knowledge, partaken of human flesh. I do hope these are satisfactory answers, and should you have preferred the opposite, I am sure matters could be arranged to fulfill your rather precarious preference."

Sal laughed. There was something he loved about a woman with a sharp wit. "I can hardly object to those terms, though I dare say, I much preferred your answers as they were. When do you presume I ought to meet with this friend of yours?"

"I believe he would want to speak with you as soon as it was possible. I will send for you when I have his answer."

The Shoe smelled of salt air and stagnant water. Sal had pulled his pigsticker from his boot and slipped it in his sleeve. After the time he'd nearly been murdered a mere two streets south by a gang of urchins, he didn't much care to walk around the Shoe unarmed.

Sal put a hand to the locket. He'd felt the reassuring presence of the thing since leaving Alzbetta's but had not thought to take a look and make certain it hadn't been somehow damaged during the events that transpired in the warehouse. The locket felt whole, the yellow gold no more tarnished than it had been the day he'd stolen the thing. Yet, the instant Sal pulled the locket from his shirt collar, he noticed something strange. The mark upon the face of the locket had changed, the two outer stripes of the rune were now both blood red.

Sal knocked, but to his chagrin, it was not Vinny who answered.

Vinny's father was a near mirror image of his son, in a shrunken, warped by time, and drunk kind of way. A sort of pathetic reminder of what a man can become should he let his vices drag him to the deepest depths of Sacrull's hell.

"Hello, sir. Is Vinny home?"

"Knows you?" said Vinny's father, his breath reeking of sour wine.

"You do, sir. You saved my life once. And I'm still grateful for that."

"Hmm, don't seem you was too grateful, seeming is it you don't —wasn't," Vinny's father shook his head, looking somewhat confused, "was you?"

"No, sir, I wasn't," Sal said, hoping he'd made the right choice.

"No, you wasn't, was you?" Vinny's father agreed, taking a long drink from his cup. He looked at Sal rather skeptically. "You're to see—"

"Vincenzo, sir."

Vinny's father harrumphed and turned. He walked into the house, and Sal followed as the Norsic man swayed dangerously with every step.

"Boy, you wake your sorry ass off, damned sleeping. Man here looking." Vinny's father stumbled as he kicked at the bed where Vinny slept.

Vinny sat up and rubbed at his eyes when his father slapped him full on in the face with the palm of his open hand.

Vinny cursed, scrambled to his feet—shoving his father in the process—and swung a fist.

The drunken lout took the punch stoically, hardly flinching as the fist cracked into his jaw with enough force to crumble the man's knees beneath him. Vinny's father dropped to the floorboards like a sack of unwashed onions and curled on his side.

Vinny shook his head to clear it, grabbed a blanket from the bed, and threw it over his father. He picked up the wooden cup that had clattered on the ground. Vinny cursed. Then blinked, as he only then seemed to notice Sal standing there.

"Sacrull's big hairy ones," Sal said. "You think he's alright?"

"He won't be alright until he quits breathing," Vinny said, snarling.

Sal couldn't think of a thoughtful response, and so he left it there. "How are you, mate?"

"My bloody nose stings something awful," Vinny said, rubbing at it. "Did you see the bastard slap me?"

"I was referring to that ugly bite on your hand there. It looks to be a tick swollen."

Vinny looked at his hand and shrugged. "Not near so bad as the bite you took. You'd have thought that mender was going to have to take the arm off. Though, it seems she is a talent among Talents," Vinny said with a grin.

"You may want to see her about that hand," Sal cautioned. "How's the rest of the crew?"

"Balliel is dead."

"Dead?" Sal asked. "When? How?"

"Last night, while we were trapped in the warehouse," said

Vinny. "It turns out only six of the Scarvini men went into the warehouse. The other three must have gone after Balliel. Caught up to him just before Town Road and opened him full of holes."

Sal shook his head. He'd thought if anyone had gotten out of there, it would have been Balliel. Sal had seen him driving away on the wagon. He never would have thought the man would have been dead only moments later.

"It's almost as if they expected us to be there. How else could they have gotten Balliel? They must have set an ambush."

"Light's name," said Vinny. "You really suggesting—"

"No," Sal said flatly.

Vinny pinched the bridge of his nose. "I suppose the question is how they could have known. How did they know we were taking the warehouse in the first place?"

"You know, I probably should have asked this before taking the job, but do you have any idea who Valla's backer was?"

Vinny shrugged. "Don Moretti, I suppose, but I really hadn't thought to ask."

"Well, I'm beginning to wonder if we shouldn't go ahead and do that. Lady's sake, whoever this source was that gave up that warehouse has set us up for death. We broke the Code. Don't you see that? Valla is made under the Moretti Family, and we just hit a Scarvini owned warehouse."

"Look, we're all supposed to meet up at the Rusted Anchor by midday," Vinny said placatingly. "Might be, we'll get some answers out of her then."

***

As Sal pushed through the doors of the Rusted Anchor, he hardly noticed the haze of smoke, the smell of stale rushes, the peeling wall paint, or the noise.

He brushed off the woman that pawed at him, whispering promises of ecstasy to the highest order. Deaf to the shouts of the man he shoved past, his focus dead set on Valla, his rage blind to all in his periphery.

Vinny put a staying hand on his shoulder. "You don't want to go at her like that, mate. She'll eat you alive, she will."

Sal rolled his shoulder and shrugged off Vinny's hand.

"Oy, the magus lives," said Odie, flashing Sal a broad smile as he drew near.

Odie, Aurie, and Valla were all seated at Valla's usual table. There was only one empty chair. It seemed they'd not been expecting him.

No matter, he wanted to remain standing should things escalate.

Aurie looked worried, Odie unconcerned, but Valla had yet to meet his eyes, as though she meant not to notice him.

Sal slammed a hand on the table, causing Aurie to jump. Odie smiled all the broader, and Valla slowly turned to look at him with half-lidded eyes.

Vinny took the empty seat without a word.

"Seems we're all here then," said Valla.

"Not all of us," said Sal, injecting as much scorn as he could muster into the words. "Where is Balliel, Val?" Sal could feel the faces drop around him, but his eyes did not leave Valla's.

"He don't know?" asked Odie.

"He knows," said Vinny.

"These things happen," Valla said with a shrug. "You know the work as well as anyone."

"Yeah, you're right," said Sal. "I do know the work as well as anyone, and these things don't just happen. They only happen when something has gone seriously wrong. Well, something has gone seriously wrong, Val."

"And you're saying I'm the one responsible, are you?" said Valla.

"You were lead," Sal said. "If you don't take responsibility, who should?"

"Come off it," said the big man. "Ain't no need for that."

"You near got all of us killed," Sal said. "And you damned well got Balliel killed. Lady's sake, Val, we broke the Sacrull damned Code."

"Keep your fucking voice down," Valla hissed. "You don't think I know all of this?"

"And that's the worst of it," Sal said. "You knew we were breaking the Code. The Commission Families are off limits; you know that."

"I didn't know," Valla said defensively. "That warehouse doesn't belong to any of the Commission Families. It was listed under the name of a Lord, some member of the Open Council. None of the fucking Commission Families were even supposed to be connected."

"Let me guess, Lord Garred Peaks?" Sal blurted.

Everyone was silent as all eyes turned on Valla.

Slowly, Valla nodded, her eyes fixed on Sal with a beseeching look.

"Who's Lord Garred?" Vinny asked.

"What were Scarvini men doing there?" Sal said. "And Giuseppe Scarvini himself. This must have been something serious if it required the presence of the Scarvini heir apparent. What else was in those crates, Val? It wasn't just indigo, was it?"

"Drugs mostly," said Valla. "Dream-salt, skeev, bliss, poppy oil. The indigo is a fucking façade, just a top layer to get the crates in the city."

"Sacrull's balls," cursed Vinny.

Aurie went wide-eyed, like a rabbit that had seen a wolf.

It all made sense. The harbor inspectors weren't fools and would have seen the abnormalities on the shipping manifests, just as Sal had. They would undoubtedly check what was in the strange crates —bribed or not—and this time, would have found indigo upon a quick inspection. It would be perfectly reasonable to want to smuggle powdered indigo illegally to avoid the high tariff, and any bribed harbor inspector would have no qualms allowing something so harmless as indigo into the city.

"And your source?" Sal asked. "Who is this acumen of stratagem that has marked us all for death? Who was it backing this warehouse job?"

Valla's glare sharpened dangerously.

"Surely something can be done," said Aurie. "They'll have to understand it was a mistake."

Sal laughed. "We killed the eldest son of Don Scarvini. We

killed Giuseppe the Shark and Gods know who else. There will be no understanding. We've broken the Code of the Commission. Our lives are forfeit."

"You killed the Don's son," said Valla, shaking her head, arms crossed over her chest. "You killed all of them. What the fuck was that, Salvatori? What is it you've been hiding? First Dellan, now this."

They were all looking at him now. Vinny, Odie, Aurie, and Valla all stared at Sal with looks spanning a mixture of bewilderment, fear, and awe.

"You killed them all," said Valla.

"I did what was needed," Sal said. "It was you who put us there, you that marked us for death. You were the lead, Val, you."

"Fuck you, Salvatori."

"Look, mate," said Vinny, "I'm sure your uncle can do something. Scarvini pays homage to Svoboda. I'm certain Stefano could talk to Don Scarvini."

Sal laughed. "Don't you get it? There's nothing my uncle can do. We were dead the moment we set foot in that warehouse. Valla is a made man, and she's broken the Code—*we* have broken the Code. Besides, even if the Commission decided to show mercy for the first time in a hundred years, Don Scarvini is never going to forgive us for the murder of his son. Valla has as good as killed us."

Valla stood. "Shut your fucking hole before I cut your cock off and shove it down your throat."

Sal put a hand to the cold metal of his amulet. He raised the other and faced his palm toward Valla. "You want to try me?"

No one moved, but Sal could see the terror beneath the masks of calm. They were scared and with good reason. They had seen what he'd done to those men at the warehouse, and they'd heard the rumors of what he'd done to Dellan. No doubt, they thought he was capable of melting them all where they sat.

Valla exhaled through her nose, cursed, and took her hands off the knives at her belt.

Sal sneered, then turned to leave, little satisfied with the results of the encounter and too angry to stick around and sort things out.

"Where are you going?" Vinny asked.

But Sal didn't bother to answer.

***

The wrought iron gate stood twice as tall as Sal. Forged in the style of the near-east, it was as formidable as it was elegant. Two guards stood at either side of the Bastian Estate gate. One was armed with a spear, the other a poleaxe. Both guardsmen wore the livery of Lord Hugo upon their breasts, the black bull of Bastian.

A third guard walked up the drive toward the estate house. He carried a message for the lady Lilliana, announcing Sal's arrival.

It wasn't long before Lilliana met him at the gates. She looked beautiful, her black hair tied up in a tight bun, a chain of white gold about her neck, and a slip of a green silk dress that accentuated the curves of her figure.

"Let us go for a walk, shall we?" said Lilliana.

Sal extended an elbow, and she took it gladly.

"Did you learn more about that monk, this Leobald character?" Lilliana asked as they headed up the King's Round. "Is he the man we're looking for?"

"Regrettably, I've not had the chance, and worse, things have only grown more convoluted," Sal told her what he had learned of the shipments of drugs. That they'd been backed by the Scarvini Family and how a warehouse belonging to Lord Garred had been used to store them. They were not merely dealing with some small-time scheme cooked up by a couple of monks and a street dealer. They were dealing with something far more extensive.

Lilliana's eyes showed fear when he'd finished his telling.

"Scarvini, that's a gang, is it not?" Lilliana asked. "One of the Five Families, if I'm not mistaken. I should have known that horrid Thieves Guild would be involved in this. So what does this mean? Ought we tell the constable of the City Watch, or better yet, the lord magistrate?"

Sal flinched. "Sacrull's hell, are you mad? Did you not understand? I'm a dead man if I do anything."

"Sounds to me you're a dead man if you do nothing," said Lilliana. "Why not speak with your uncle?"

"I told you, he can't help. Not now."

"But why not speak with him? What is the worst that could happen?"

The worst? His uncle could turn him over to Don Scarvini, and Sal could be executed for killing Scarvini's men, along with his eldest son. After all, it wouldn't be the first time his uncle had turned him over to a Commission Don.

Sal shrugged.

"Exactly, nothing bad could come of it. You need to go to your uncle, now, before it's too late."

"Right, well, if I go, I want you to stay safe. Things around this city could get quite messy in the coming nights. You ought to stick close to the estate for the time being, and by no means should you leave High Hill. The Commission could very well be going to war."

S al clasped the brass ring of the knocker and rapped upon the heavy oaken door. He stepped back and waited.

"Master, Salvatori," said Greggings upon opening the door. "What a pleasant surprise. Do come inside."

"My uncle, is he home?"

"He's only just returned. Shall you be joining us for dinner?"

"I don't believe I shall, Greggings. He's in his solar, I trust?"

The manservant nodded.

Sal crossed the lavender tiled floor and climbed the grand staircase. The third door on the right was his uncle's solar, the most likely place to find Stefano when the man was home. The number of books in his uncle's collection never failed to impress him. Sal could spend the next ten years reading, and he might finish one of the four book-lined walls within that solar.

Stefano Lorenzo fixed Sal with a look of apathy as he entered, trod across the elaborately patterned Minnian rugs, and took a seat in the armchair beside his uncle.

"Gooday, Uncle."

Stefano cleared his throat, grunted, and went back to his book.

Sal picked at a loose thread in the upholstery of the chair's arm. When he looked up, he saw Stefano's eyes glaring over the top of the book. With a sigh of exasperation, Stefano slapped the book shut and dropped it on the side table with a show of indifference.

"Something engrossing?" Sal asked.

"Hardly," his uncle said with a scoff. "An alternate history of the Sundering, proposed by the Dahliish of Shiikal. It has only just been translated to the common-hand, and what an utter waste of time. Never in my life—the man actually proposes the events could be explained without the presence of Gods. Claims the entire Sundering could be explained with figures—figures, I tell you." Stefano shook his head, looking disgusted.

"I'm sorry, Uncle, figures?" Sal said. "But how?"

"Precisely," said Stefano, as though Sal had provided the answer rather than proposed a question. "The Dahliish has scribbled a mess of numbers and symbols about the pages as though this will explain away the consummate nonsense of his assertions."

Sal nodded, pretending to understand.

But Stefano Lorenzo was not a man to be fooled. His eyes narrowed. "All those years I spent schooling you, preparing you for greatness.

"That was my sister—"

"And rightfully so," said Stefano. "She never shamed me, never balked at a challenge, never failed to grasp a concept, but you, boy, you had as well pull an ox cart for all you've retained."

Sal felt a burning urge to tell his uncle where he could shove his concept, but recalled why he had come, and swiftly swallowed his retort. "I am sorry I'm not the man you wanted or expected of me, Uncle."

"We shall see when you have become a man."

"And why should I not be called a man, for my soft cheeks?" Sal laughed, doing his best to keep the mood light. "I see no whiskers on your chops, Uncle."

Stefano did not seem in the mood to be humored. "Japes, yes, japes. You can make a quip, and you can wipe your own ass, I presume, but I wonder, boy, does a real man jape in the face of his own inadequacy?"

"I shall strive to do better."

"Shall you? Tell me then, why should your name have been brought up today while I was at the Commission meeting?"

Sal's heart sunk to the pit of his stomach. He had been too late. His uncle already knew about the warehouse.

"The Commission has made a decision, and it is only thanks to me that your life will be spared," Stefano said, levelly. "The girl cannot be allowed to live; the risk would be too high. She's been marked."

Sal blinked. "Wait, what girl?"

"Gods, do these falsehoods never end with you, boy?" said Stefano. "Ought I to have made of you a mummer? You were seen with her, by more than one man, on more than one account. Did you not think we would have eyes on her with all the poking and prodding she was doing into our business?"

Sal was dumbstruck, what poking and prodding had Valla been doing? And then it struck him, his uncle wasn't speaking of Valla.

"Lilliana?" Sal blurted.

"Ah, and now you admit to it. Well, when you're done playing the fool, take note, she's been marked."

It was as though a hand had grabbed him by the throat. Sal couldn't breathe. His head was spinning, his entire body numb, as though he'd slipped free of his flesh and was slowly drifting away in an ethereal mist.

He snapped back to the present. "Marked? You can't mean—"

"It's already been done," Stefano said. "We'll have news of her passing soon enough."

25

AMBUSH

Sal's heart felt ready to burst, but he didn't dare slow his pace. Evenfall was nearly upon them, and Sal hoped the assassins would wait at least until sundown before they made their move.

When he neared High Bridge, he relented to sense and slowed his pace, lest the steel caps decide he was making trouble and take chase. His lungs burned, and his side ached, and yet, it nearly broke him to simply walk past the bridge towers when he knew any moment, Lilliana could be struggling for her life.

Or dead—but no—he couldn't think that way. He couldn't be too late.

Once past the bridge and rounding the corner to the King's Way, he picked up his pace again. He ran up the entire High Hill, and half the King's Round, before veering off for the Bastian estate.

Three guardsmen stood sentry outside the tall wrought iron gate of the estate.

The man wielding the poleaxe hailed him as he had earlier that day. "Back so soon, are you?"

"The lady Lilliana, where is she?" Sal said, breathing hard. "Tell me, is she safe?"

The guard shrugged. "She's gone off with that crustacean Damor Nev. You know him?"

"Where—where have they gone?"

"That ain't none of your business," said the guard wielding the spear as he stepped forward. "Her Ladyship ain't here, and that ought to be good enough for the likes of you."

"We need to go find her," Sal said, beginning to panic. "She's in danger."

"Don't see how," said the guard with the poleaxe. "Got Damor Nev with her, don't she? You know of Damor Nev?"

"Right, well, Damor's only one man, and Lilliana has been marked by the Commission."

The guard with spear scoffed.

"Marked?" said the third guard, the one in the back wielding a crossbow.

"Yes," said Sal, desperately. "Please, we need to help her. She's in trouble."

All three guards laughed.

"Bugger off," said the guard with the spear.

"You have—" Sal was cut short by a thrust from the spear that whizzed just past his ear.

"Next one goes through your eye," said the guard. "Fuck off."

Sal took his cue and backed off. He kept on moving until he was out of the crossbowman's line of sight. He tried to slow his panic and think. Where could Lilliana have gone?

Then it came to him, clear as a beam of moonlight. Today was Tiems, Lilliana would be returning from Low Town.

Without another thought given to the plan, Sal was again running.

He knew what he was looking for, rather, who he was looking for. Where to look, however, was a question he couldn't answer. He had a hunch they would cross at the Bridge of the Lady, but he also assumed the stalkers would want to spring their ambush somewhere before the bridge, as the sun was nearly beneath the horizon.

Sal saw the black-cloaked women belonging to the Keepers of the Flame begin to light the street lanterns in their pairs. Keepers of the Flame always traveled in pairs, their long candlesticks held high as they walked. He spared the acolytes only a cursory glance, their black hoods drawing his attention as he slipped past them.

He crossed the crowded bridge as quickly as possible, weaving and bobbing his way through the mass of bodies. The entire time pushing away the notion that it might be too late, that Lilliana might already be in trouble.

The moment he passed beneath the Low Town bridge façade and onto Beggar's Lane, his true predicament became fully apparent. What if they'd crossed to High Town already? What if they had passed him on the bridge, only he hadn't noticed in his rush?

He could only hope he wasn't too late. He cut off of Beggar's Lane and went straight south. The farther south he traveled, the less populated the streets became. As he ran, he wondered if he shouldn't have waited beside the entrance to the Bridge of the Lady. Doubtless, they would have crossed that way, unless they didn't. What if they'd decided to take South Bridge?

His uncle was right, he was a Sacrull damned fool, and he would never be anything more than a stain on society. He'd never done anything worthwhile, and even when he tried to do right, he did it wrong.

As Sal passed another pair of cloaked and hooded Keepers of the Flame, he slowed and gave himself a moment to catch his breath.

The street was empty aside from the two hooded acolytes. Then suddenly, Sal saw them.

Lilliana and Damor Nev emerged from an alley and began walking up the street in Sal's direction.

He nearly shouted for joy, the elation of their arrival kicked him back into action, and he waved and called Lilliana's name.

Another pair of hooded acolytes stepped onto the street. It seemed the Keepers of the Flame were out in droves that evening.

Lilliana waved, a look of bemusement passing over her features.

It was then Sal realized there was something strange about the pair of acolytes behind Lilliana and Damor Nev—neither of the acolytes carried a pole-candle. Sal craned his head around and looked at the pair of acolytes he had passed moments before, and sure enough, neither of them carried a pole-candle either.

"Damor, Lilliana is marked!" Sal shouted and ran for Lilliana as he reached into his pocket and crushed what was left of the skeev in his palm.

Damor Nev reacted without hesitation. With one swift motion, the bodyguard reached over his shoulder and drew his bastard sword. He turned about, taking in the entire situation.

The acolytes behind Lilliana threw their cloaks free to reveal crossbows.

Damor rushed them, his bastard sword raised for the strike.

Sal grabbed hold of the locket, and a shock of energy rushed through his palm. He wrapped his other arm about Lilliana, focused his mind, and felt a rush of vertigo as he lurched forth, his feet lifting from the ground as though propelled by an invisible force.

In a flash, Sal and Lilliana were flattened against the roof, the alley far below.

Without looking at her, Sal released his hold.

"Wait here," he said before leaping from the roof and riding the lightning back into the alley.

He rolled across the cobblestones and stumbled to his feet. The engagement was behind him. Sal spun on one foot, only to see a man charging him, black cloak whipping in his wake, a curved sword held high.

The locket in a death grip, Sal thrust forth his palm as he fell back. His ass hit the unyielding street. A bolt of ethereal blue lightning burst from his hand and struck the swordsman square in the chest.

The man's feet lifted into the air, his black cloak rendered weightless before he dropped, his back striking the cobblestones.

A second man had charged, but Sal felt too drained to focus. His hand closed, involuntarily spasming of its own accord.

The cloaked man was nearly upon Sal. When he stopped suddenly and emitted a squelch as a sword struck into him from behind, cutting deep between his neck and shoulder and severing his head half off.

The curved sword clattered as it fell to the street. The cloaked man sunk to his knees and fell forward, dead before his face struck the cobblestones.

Sal closed his eyes and laid back slowly. The muscles in his forearm so tight, he couldn't open his hand. His head felt foggy, his thoughts flowing like sticky sap.

"Up you go," said Damor Nev.

When Sal opened his eyes, the mustached bodyguard stood over him, a hand extended.

Sal took the proffered hand and let Damor assist him to his feet.

He doubled over, hands on his knees. Weak, drained of all energy, his head light, his stomach queasy, he looked upon the four bodies lying in the street and felt a sudden urge to be sick.

"What in the Mother's Name was that?" said Damor Nev.

Sal turned his palms to the air and shrugged.

Lilliana called down from the rooftop.

"You really are a magicker," said Damor Nev. "A damned magicker, and not just some Talent, but the real bloody article. By the Mother, boy, I suppose there's something more to you than I'd thought."

"You killed them?" Sal said in astonishment. "All of them, just you."

"Oh, now, wasn't as though you could have called them formidable. Only killed the three and two of them hired-knifes had crossbows. Didn't do them much good when I was close enough for a kiss. Other one, well, he was running away," said Damor with a shrug.

Lilliana cleared her throat, and Sal met her stare.

"Besides," Damor said, grinning and looking back at the man Sal had killed. "Can't go giving me credit where it ain't due. I reckon you could've cooked that last one up on the spit if you'd had a mind too. That magic of yours really makes a mess of a man, don't it?"

"Damor," Lilliana said, arousing Sal from his stupor. "That will be quite enough. Now, if you are finished, I would like my feet touching solid ground."

"Yes, my lady," said Damor Nev, all joviality driven from his tone. "And, uh, how, do you suggest I fulfill that desire?"

"Not to worry," Sal ejaculated, summoning the last reserves of his energy as he stood. "I'll be up in a tick." He took hold of the locket and in the blink of an eye, rode the lightning to Lilliana, landing almost elegantly upon the rooftop. Sal held out a hand and helped Lilliana to her feet. He wrapped an arm about her waist and told her to hang on tight.

The guardsman wielding the spear was the first of the three gate guards to see them coming. His eyes went wide. He straightened up and acted as though not was amiss. The guard with the poleaxe was the next to notice them. He nearly jumped out of his boots and did an even worse job hiding his surprise than the first guard had. It seemed the crossbowman hadn't noticed them until they were nearly within an arm's reach.

"Bloody hell," exclaimed the crossbowman. "M'lady, what's happened?"

The other two guards looked at Sal. They seemed terrified, and rightfully so.

"Open the gate, fool," said Damor Nev.

The Bauden bodyguard had sheathed his bastard sword, but the evidence of the encounter was spelled out in the blood that streaked his front.

The crossbowman hurried to obey, unlocking the great black iron gate and swinging it open as fast as the hinges would allow.

"Will you join us inside?" Lilliana asked.

"It would be droll, no doubt," Sal said. "Though, I fear my true problems have only just begun. I've still more to do this night."

"We can help, Daddy and I," Lilliana said. "Or Damor, and any man in Daddy's service, should you require."

"I may take you up on that offer," Sal said. "For now, you need to get to the safest place you can, call the house guard to action and fortify the estate. You've been marked, and until I can do something about that, you need to stay safe. They may come after you yet."

Lilliana took his hand, pulled him closer, and kissed him upon the cheek.

"Thank you, Salvatori."

Sal flushed and did his best to recover with a wink before he turned and walked away.

As he left the Bastian estate behind, he found that although his eyes were open, he walked blindly through the street, moving one foot in front of the other, aimlessly progressing along the King's Way. He knew he ought to look into his hunch about Leobald and his possible involvement with the drug importation, and yet, he was lost in his thoughts about what approach to take regarding his predicament.

No doubt, he would be marked at the next Commission gathering, if he wasn't marked already. He and the other three who'd joined Valla on her fool's errand, they were all dead men, and women, for that matter.

Unless they took action.

Sal stopped, he'd heard the sound of shoes scuffing on the cobblestones. He tensed for a fight, quickly reaching for his pigsticker. He snapped upright and held the knife level with his attacker.

A girl, no older than nine, stood frozen, eyes fixed on the point of the blade as she stepped back and thrust forth a roll of parchment with both hands.

Sal tucked the pigsticker into his belt and reached for the parchment.

Once he'd taken the parcel, the girl ran without a word of explanation.

Sal called after her but to no success. Instead, he opened the parchment. It seemed it was a note from Alzbetta, wishing him to join her at her place of residence as soon as he could. He'd forgotten all about her request and was surprised to hear back from her so soon. She had told him about a man who would wish to meet with him, but he knew little else. He had no reason to mistrust

Alzbetta. She had saved him from death no less than thrice. If she had wished him harm, Sal imagined he'd not be alive. Giving little more thought to the subject, Sal made his way for Alzbetta's.

———

Alzbetta's home smelled of incense and sweet herbs. The dim candlelight flickering as the door was closed.

"Tell it true," said Alzbetta, "do you enjoy terrifying little girls? You seem to have put the fear of the Gods into my granddaughter."

Sal swallowed. "I am dreadfully sorry. Do you think it would help if I apologized? I never meant—"

Alzbetta chuckled. "No, no, an unworthy jape," she said. "I should never have sent her to you. She has made a terrible habit of sneaking." She took Sal by the arm and led him into the next room. There was a round table, large enough for the circle of four chairs about it. Seated on the opposite end of the table was rather large man. Nothing so large as Odie, but there was a formidable cast to his lack of neck, thickly muscled arms, and barrel chest.

Sal didn't know the man, and yet, there was something familiar about him. The man didn't seem to recognize Sal. He scratched his stubbled chin, but his eyes seemed to take Sal in, as though assessing him and determining whether he was a threat.

"Salvatori Lorenzo, this is Dominik D'Angelo," Alzbetta said, gesturing.

Dominik stood and gave a curt nod. "Thank you for agreeing to meet with me," he said, pulling out a chair for Alzbetta.

Sal took a seat across from Dominik, feeling a bit like a cat that had agreed to a meeting with a dog. By the look in his eyes, Sal would have thought the man was harboring something deeply seeded, a contempt that might burst from him at any instant.

Sal wondered again how it was he knew this man. Perhaps, Dominik only reminded him of someone he knew, but then, he couldn't square who that was either. And so, the feeling merely niggled at the back of his mind, refusing to manifest and reveal itself fully.

"Now then," said Dominik, exhaling through his nose. "A wise man once said, the enemy of my enemy is my friend. And this is what I would propose of you, Salvatori Lorenzo."

Sal swallowed. "So, who is this common enemy of ours?"

Dominik cleared his throat. "I mean to make war with the Commission."

Sal went cold. "Sorry," Sal said, his voice cracking. "You would make war with the Commission?"

"Ay," said Dominik. "I would all meself, if that's what it took, and a good beginning it would make."

"And an end they would make of you," said Sal.

"Might be, they would," said Dominik with a shrug. "As I said, war would only be a beginning. First, however, a simpler task. Giuseppe Scarvini was only one of five deaths which I plan to ensure. I would bring an end to the line of Scarvini, and in that, I would ask for your assistance."

"You're not japing," Sal said, still trying to digest what the man was saying. "You want to bring an end to the Scarvini line?"

"I do, and I would assume you as much want the same," said Dominik D'Angelo

Sal looked to Alzbetta. "But—but how? I never mentioned Scarvini—"

"It was rather obvious," said Alzbetta. "I can put one and two together. That warehouse is all the talk with the right crowd."

"Listen," said Dominik. "I don't need an answer tonight. Take some time to mull it over. Just keep in mind, Don Scarvini won't wait forever. If he doesn't already know who hit his warehouse and who murdered his son, he'll find out soon enough. And when he does, you can rest assured every Scarvini thug, crony, and killer will be out hunting for you."

Sal sat back in his chair. His mind numb, his stomach twisting with uncertainty. It was madness, complete and utter stupidity of the highest order. Make war with the Commission? This man was completely mad, and yet, he seemed confident, cool, collected, his eyes entirely devoid of insanity. Something about his demeanor calmed Sal, comforted him enough to want to trust the man. "And what is it you have against Don Scarvini?" Sal asked. "Why should anyone wish an end to a man and his family?"

Dominik's features hardened like stone, and for an instant, Sal thought his eyes had begun to well up.

"There are things a man can do that don't warrant mercy," said Dominik.

It was then that Sal realized where he had seen Dominik, why the man had looked so familiar to him. "Eighth Harbor?" Sal said.

Dominik flinched at the question.

"You were there," Sal said. "You were one of the porters, but how did you—they killed everyone."

"Not everyone," said Dominik, a vein bulging in his forehead. "What happened on Eighth Harbor was hardly the beginning. Trying to kill me was one thing, but no man harms me, family."

A certain tension hung in the air. Sal considered what Dominik had said. A moment of silence that shattered like glass when Sal next spoke.

"I'll do it," Sal said. "I'll join you."

"Sounds right and good," said Alzbetta, beginning to stand. "It is—"

Sal held up a hand for silence. "I'll join you on the condition that you are able to help me," Sal said.

Dominik turned his hands, palm up.

"I want to know who else is involved in the smuggling," Sal said. "The Scarvini Family had partners, and I want to know who they were."

Dominik chuckled darkly. "Dead men, far as I can tell," said Dominik. "Though, that's the problem with hydras, isn't it? Cut off one head, and two more grow right back. Scarvini will find more help, have no doubts. This will only end with the death of Don Scarvini. So long as the man lives, we will have changed nothing."

"They're all dead? All of his associates? Everyone who was involved with the smuggling outside the Scarvini Family? There were no, say, monks of Knöldrus Abbey involved?"

Dominik gave him a penetrating look. "Far as I know, there is someone from the Abbey making sure things are handled with customs. Might be, they're involved on the distribution end as well."

Sal nodded. His heart was hammering in his chest.

"Got to warn you though, I looked into it meself. Seems they already rooted the snake out. The boy's dead, some fella they called Brother Philip. It's only, the monk's supposed to have died some days past, but if that's so, I can't figure why the shipments never slowed."

Sal smiled. "I think I have an idea why. Alzbetta, any chance you'd be willing to make me a tracer?"

26

THE MONK

The rain was more a mist than a proper rain. It seemed to hang in the air, waiting for him to come to it rather than simply falling.

The abbey gates were closed for the night, and Sal was entirely out of skeev, but he knew of other ways to penetrate the walls of Knöldrus. He walked riverward beside the great stone wall until he reached the lonely guard tower, abandoned and neglected into disrepair, yet the spiral stair of the tower remained structurally sound and mostly intact.

Sal encountered the first snag when he stood atop the parapet and looked down upon the abbey grounds below. He'd neglected to bring either rope or ladder and cursed himself once more for not buying more skeev. In the end, he found himself scaling the slick stone face, jamming his fingertips and toes into the mortared crevices and crannies as he descended at a slow, steady pace.

When his feet hit soggy ground, boots sinking into soft mud, Sal pulled the hood of his cloak up over his head and stuck tight to the shadows.

He would go to the abbot the moment he had proof of Leobald's involvement. All he would need is a shipping manifest with the monk's name on it or some of the Scarvini Family's trade goods, supposing Leobald had been paid off in goods for his services. Might be, the greedy charlatan had stolen something for himself. Either way, once Sal wrung a confession from the dear prior, there would be no denying his involvement. Sal meant to conduct himself in the manner of the old inquisition, willing to get Leobald's signature at the threat of blade and flame if that's what it took.

The locket was cold to the touch, and the energy it emitted sent a shiver through him. The thing would be no use to him, not here and now, not after he'd used the last of his skeev cap earlier that night. He would simply need to do without it.

First, he would needs make his way to the prior's quarters. He'd never been, but from his time spent within Knöldrus, he'd learned the thirteen Masters of the Enlightened Council slept apart from the rest of their order. Each was given a room of his own between the two cloister-like structures.

The most difficult part would be finding a way inside without waking any of the monks. He didn't know where it was that Leobald slept. With twelve rooms divided between the two structures, it would have been nigh on impossible to decipher which room belonged to the prior, had Sal not come prepared.

He pulled a sodden swatch of cloth from his pocket and felt a warm tingle emanating from the tracer. A feeling similar to that of the locket, but nowhere nearly so powerful. The tracer seemed to take control of his feet as he began to walk with no inkling of where he was going but confident that if he moved one foot after the other, the tracer would do the rest.

There was no sign of a single soul out of bed as Sal crossed the abbey yard through the misting rain until he came upon two structures, each about twice as large as the abbey guesthouse. The tracer seemed to provide the inkling that he should enter the south building. He circled the buildings at a distance, looking for a point of entry. There was only one door in or out, and Sal had to assume it would be locked until he could check. All the windows were closed. Though, that didn't mean they were latched. There were seven windows in all, one for each room, and another that led into the central hallway.

With a prayer for the Lady's luck, Sal closed the distance to the south building, keeping low and sticking to the shadows when possible, he moved to the door. The iron handle budged only slightly. It was locked from within. After a moment of examining the lock tumblers, he decided he would have no luck with his picks and rounded his way to the backside of the building. Sal slipped his pigsticker from his boot, wedged the blade into the window, and pried. To his great astonishment, the window was unlatched and swung open with little resistance.

Sal slunk through the window, like a polecat sliding over a log on its belly, and hunkered low once within the dim, moonlit corridor. It was good to be somewhere dry, yet, his heart beat all the faster, his palms grew clammy, and his bowels tightened. His task was far from accomplished.

Slowly, he crept along the corridor, allowing the tracer to be his guide. When he reached the third room on the right, Sal knew he had the right door. He felt a faint urge to kick the door down, but as better sense took hold, he thought it would be best to check if the door was locked.

For the second time that night, it seemed the Lady had answered his prayers as the doorknob turned and the door opened. The hinges creaked, and Sal flinched, holding his breath as he listened for any signs that the monks were stirring.

When he heard nothing more than a bit of snoring from a room across the hall, he continued to open the door and slowly creep into the room, his pigsticker in hand.

He could make out the sleeping form of the monk clearly, laying rather stiffly upon his bed.

Sal would need to be swift as running water. Getting Leobald out of the building and into the guesthouse would be impossible without the monk's cooperation. And yet, Sal was confident Leobald would cooperate with a knife to the throat.

He closed the door as quietly as possible, then practically ran to the bed, clapped his free hand over the monk's mouth and put the point of the pigsticker upon the apple of his throat.

Leobald did not stir.

The monk felt stiff and cold, and for an instant, Sal was at a loss. When the realization hit him, Sal scrambled back in revulsion, dropping his pigsticker and tripping onto his backside.

He took a deep breath to center himself and stood to reexamine the corpse.

The moon was his only source of light, and still, Sal could make out Leobald rather clearly. His face slightly contorted, as though he remained in agony. The usually pale flesh of his neck was dark and blotchy, as though horrifically bruised. His hands were stained with dried blood, and yet, Sal could see no visible wounds on the prior's person.

Sick to his stomach, confused by the incident, Sal backed away from the dead man and wondered what forces of the cosmos had aligned to subject him to such malevolence. It was the fourth time in the past year he had stumbled upon someone who'd been murdered. He was beginning to see a pattern. A pattern that had begun with the heist on the High Keep. The night he had stolen the locket for Anton. Sal touched the cold metal of the locket. He pulled it from his neck, ran his finger over the three simple lines engraved into locket's face, the two outer marks now blood red. The mark of three, the mark of beasts, an unlucky thing, Nabu had told him. How true that was proving to be.

Even still, there was more to it, much more. Somehow, Sal had a feeling it was all connected, though he couldn't for the life of him tell how. He decided it would be in his best interest to get out of the prior's quarters as quickly as possible, before he was discovered and subsequently blamed.

Going out the way he'd come in, Sal wondered who could have possibly killed Leobald and why. He didn't doubt the man had enemies within the Vespian Order. Leobald's pompous manner had likely rubbed plenty a monk in the wrong way, and it had been a monk who'd killed the initiate Dennis beneath the pardimon tree.

Although, Sal had thought the monk who'd killed Dennis had been Philip, yet now it seemed that may not have been the case.

Then again, it could have been a Commission assassin, someone sent by Don Scarvini to tie up loose ends. Scarvini might have gotten cold feet after the death of Philip and his son Giuseppe, and Leobald's death was merely a side effect of the symptom.

Regardless of who it was and why they'd done it, Sal needed to get to the one man who could help him.

He slipped out the window once more, closing it quietly behind. The mud sucked at his boots as he crossed the abbey grounds through the misting rains.

Smoke rose from the chimney of the abbot's house, as the windows glowed with warm light. The hour was late, but it seemed luck had joined his side once more. The abbot looked to be awake.

Sal knocked on the door, but there was no answer. Feeling some-what panicked, he knocked again, louder and all the more insistent, and still, he heard no response from within. Deeming the matter more urgent than the abbot's privacy, Sal checked to see if the door was unlocked, found it so, and burst through the threshold.

What he saw within the abbot's home chilled his blood and froze him to the very spot.

Abbot Jacques was seated in a chair wearing not but his small clothes. He was in the act of wrapping a bandage about his abdomen. Near his ribs, a blossom of blood had begun to soak through the linen bandage.

"Ah," said Jacques, pain apparent in his voice. "But it seems you will not be delayed. Come in, my son. Take a seat."

Sal stared, too stunned to move his mud-caked boots. "What happened?"

"I confronted Leobald," said Jacques as he resumed wrapping his bandage. "The things you told me. Your suspicions of the man, they were true. That man was the reason for the death of Philip. He was the true killer of Brother Dennis. It was Leobald all along."

"Leobald?" Sal said. "You believe he was the man responsible?"

"I know he was. He said as much before stabbing me with this."

Jacques picked up a blood sheathed dagger, brandishing it in the air before using it to cut the bandage.

"He stabbed you?" Sal said, eyes flitting to the blossom of red on the abbot's side.

The abbot flashed a gentle smile. "The evidence of that is apparent, is it not?" said Jacques. "Come now, take a seat."

Sal thought on his encounter with the dead Leobald and all that had happened since he'd scaled the abbey walls. Suddenly, something came to him. The door to the Master's Quarters had been locked, yet the door to Leobald's room and the window had been unlocked, but why?

"You went to his room to speak with him?" Sal asked.

Jacques nodded.

"You went alone, in the middle of the night, to confront a man you knew to be a criminal and suspected to be a murderer?"

"What are you suggesting?" said Jacques, his brow wrinkling.

"I only wonder as to why you should make such a visit in the night, climbing in and out of windows like some kind of common sneak thief."

"I see," said Jacques. "Strange, really, I knew he sent you the first time. Only reason I bothered to keep you alive as long as I did. But I never thought he would send you for this."

"Sent me?" Sal asked, suddenly feeling out of his depth. Until that moment, things were finally seeming to make sense. "Don Scarvini, you mean?"

"Don Scarvini?" said Jacques. "Is that who sent you?"

"Who did you think had done?" Sal asked.

"I was told the Scarvini warehouse had been hit," Jacques said, his eyes searching Sal for some kind of cue. "But he wouldn't dare. And you, why would Scarvini send you? You're not one of his."

"No, I'm not."

"No, no one? No one has sent you, you've truly come all your own?"

Sal was feeling sick to his stomach, his head spinning. By the Lady's sake, what was Jacques suggesting? Who was it the abbot thought had sent Sal? If not Don Scarvinni, who else was involved that the abbot could fear?

"Misfortune, it seems, has befallen you, my son," said Jacques as he stood and shook his head slowly, the dagger still in his hand.

Jacques was a big man with a sturdy build and a strong jaw. His teeth gritted as he stood, the wound in his side blooming red through the bandages. Yet it seemed he, the abbot, possessed reserves of energy and an abnormally high tolerance for pain.

Sal reminded himself that Jacques had served among men of the sword before he'd become a man of the cloth.

Sword. The word sounded in his head, and his gaze fell on the shield and swords hanging upon the wall.

As the abbot moved toward him, Sal ran toward the table and threw a chair in Jacques's path.

He reached, wrapped his hands about the sword's hilt, tore it from the wall, and swung as he turned.

There was a hard thud. A jarring reverberation rattled through his arms as the blade sunk into the skull of the abbot.

Jacques made a gurgling sound in his throat and brandished the dagger as though he meant to stab Sal. He took a step forward, determination plastered across his face as blood streamed down his brow.

The monk stopped moving, dropped to his knees, convulsed, and slumped the rest of the way to the floor, dead as the dawn was certain.

THE LADY WHITE

INTERLUDE, SEVEN YEARS EARLIER

"How did you live?" Bartley asked, shaking his head, his expression one of incredulity.

It was a fair question; one Sal was not quite certain he knew the answer too. He and Bartley had broken the Code of the Commission. They'd robbed one of the Five Families and Sal had been caught in the act. Yet, somehow, he had come away alive.

Surely, this was a miracle.

Sal shrugged. "I suppose Don Moretti liked what I had to say."

Bartley laughed. "I hope you weren't coerced into a payment of flesh."

Sal shoved the Yahdrish kid and laughed. "No, nothing of the sort. Though, if I'd have stuck around the Underway much longer, I fear that Alonzo Amato might have tried to have his way with me."

"I still can't believe your uncle turned you over to Moretti. What happened to blood being thicker than water and all?"

Sal shrugged. "Suppose where Stefano is concerned, my blood's been watered down a bit."

"How do you mean?"

"You know," Sal said, shrugging, "bastard-born and all."

Bartley nudged him with an elbow. "Chin up, mate. I never knew my da' neither, and look how I turned out. There's hope for you yet."

Sal smiled. "Suppose there is at that."

"Still, you should have told me your uncle was an underboss of the Svoboda Family."

"I didn't think it much mattered."

"Yeah well, I've never had any family worth bragging about," Bartley said. "Never had much of any family, that is."

Sal grinned. "So how are you really certain that you're Yahdrish?"

"What do you mean?

"I mean that you piss and moan like a Yahdrish mother, but if you never knew your da', how do you know you're Yahdrish?"

"The Yahdrish are of the chosen. They are the Pure, just as I am. The blood of the First Empire. It was we Yahdrish who were given the Way."

Sal laughed. "I've heard of the Pure, in the same myths that tell of magickers who can move mountains and raise the dead."

"The Pure are still around," Bartley said defiantly. "The royal line of Pargeche is said to be a remnant of the First Empire."

"I've always been told I look a bit of a royal myself," Sal said with a wink. "Might be I'm one of these Pure."

Bartley shook his head. "How is it you know you're even Pairgu?"

"I knew my mother," Sal said. "She was Pairgu, full blood, just like my bastard of an uncle."

"And your father?" Bartley asked. "Your mother ever tell you what he was?"

"She always told me she would tell me about my father when I was ready, though it seems she never did get around to it."

They walked up Beggar's Lane, quiet for a time before Bartley brought them back around to the beginning of the conversation, a somewhat annoying habit of his. "So, what was it you told Don Moretti? How in Sacrull's hell *did* you get out of there alive?

"I told him I would be the boss one day."

Bartley laughed. "Now you know that's a lie. You'll be my underboss. It's me that'll be running things."

Sal smiled. "Whatever you say, boss."

A pair of grubby urchins put out their hands and begged for food. Bartley sneered and swatted the hands aside, but Sal pulled out an iron Dingé from his pocket and flicked it their way.

"What'd you go wasting coin on the likes of them for?" the Yahdrish asked.

Sal shrugged.

"So, what about your uncle?"

"What about him?"

"How did he take to you breaking the Code? Aside from turning you over to Don Moretti and all."

"You know what, bugger my uncle," Sal said as they neared the Low Town bridge façade. They passed beneath the façade when Sal saw her. The limestone statue of the Lady White, the very goddess the bridge was named for. Something occurred to Sal, a feeling that this was a sign of some kind.

Sal put a hand on the hem of the Lady's dress, and Bartley's eyes went wide.

"You'd take the Lady White as your patron goddess?" Bartley asked.

"She's the patron goddess of the unwanted, isn't she?"

"You have a point," said Bartley. "You certainly are that. Unwanted, that is."

"You ought to join me," Sal said.

"I'd as soon keep the god of my father," Bartley said.

"Suit yourself," Sal said. "But if you change your mind, I imagine the Lady will be right here waiting."

THE PLAN

The fiddler sang, accompanying his words with the jaunty tune of his fiddle.

> "A diddler will diddle, that's what diddlers do,
> that doesn't mean it should happen to you.
> Piddle on the diddler, tell the vagrant, 'shoo!'
> No, say I, and no, say you.
> Piddle on the diddler, for that's what we do."

The taproom livened with the song. Some clapped or stomped in time while others sang along to the bawdy words.

> "And if a diddler diddles your mum,
> you've a right to feel it wrong.
> Piddle on the diddler, it's what he deserves.
> Piddle on the diddler, we'll all take turns.
> A diddler diddles on and on,
> he'll diddle till the piddling's all but done.
> Piddle on the diddler, do what's right,
> the diddler won't put up a fight."

Sal crossed the taproom of the Hog Snout and took a seat across from his friend.

Vinny brushed a blonde lock of hair behind his ear and nodded before he went back to clapping.

> "A diddler often diddles his own,
> it chafes the Gods deep to the bone.
> Piddle on the diddler, the man is sick.
> Piddle on the diddler, it is no trick.
> A diddler's riddle is oft done alone,
> he'll touch himself 'till he's full grown.
> Piddle on the diddler, in the name of the Gods,
> he'll diddle himself by all the odds."

"The others coming?" Sal asked.

"Far as I know," said Vinny. "They all agreed. Valla, though—"

"I know," Sal said.

> "For when a diddler diddles a dame,
> to his house there falls great shame.
> Piddle on the diddler if you know what's good.
> Piddle on the diddler as right you should.
> A diddler tries to shrug the blame,
> but all who know will curse his name.
> Piddle on the diddler, for all do see,
> the diddler's ways bring infamy."

Sal began to tap a foot along with the rest, letting the song settle his nerves.

> "And if the diddler diddles your sis,
> well go on now, give the diddler a kiss.
> Don't piddle on the diddler, give him a pass.
> Don't piddle on the diddler lest you keep the lass.
> Now everyone knows there is no crime,
> half so bad as a woman diddled in blind.

Though before you go piddle, consider you this,
if not for that diddler who'd diddle your sis?"

Odie entered the taproom, his broad-shoulders casting a shadow upon the entire entryway. The big man was followed by Aurie and Valla, the latter of which looked none too happy to be there.

"'Hypocrisy,' the diddler would scream,
for diddling is not all diddling seems.
He'd point the finger, they'd fall to their knees.
The diddler would smile, for the diddler'd be
     pleased.
At long last the diddler would be, vindicated and
     piddle free.
He'd hold up his hands, and he'd make a big scene.
Then out from his mouth would come the obscene:
'Everyone's a diddler, you fools, don't you see?
We all ought to piddle on you, not me.'"

Odie took the seat next to Sal, while Aurie and Valla took the seats on either side of Vinny.

"Oy then," said the big man, clapping Sal on the shoulder. "What's this meet up all about?"

"All in due time, my big friend," Sal said.

"I'd like to know now," said Valla. "Want to know if I shouldn't just be on my way."

Sal shrugged. "How much do you like living?"

Valla stood. "Is that a threat, Lorenzo?"

Vinny put a hand on her arm.

"Easy now," said Odie.

"No threat," Sal said. "A solution."

"Go on," said Aurie.

"I—we're still waiting on one more," said Sal.

Just then, the door of the Hog Snout swung open. A short, muscular man, with arms like a smith and a neck thick as a bull's, stepped through the threshold. He stalled, looked about the taproom, and caught Sal's eyes.

Dominik D'Angelo crossed the room and took a seat at the table.

———

"I'll need to go underground for a tick," Sal said.

Lilliana eyed him with one-part worry, two-parts suspicion.

"Go underground where?"

"Right here in the city. Like I told you, I'm not going anywhere, not ever again. I'll be here, but I'll need to disappear until I'm able to clear our names."

"Clear our names?" asked Lilliana. "What might that entail?"

Sal sighed. "Much and more."

"Will it take you long?"

"Every moment it keeps me from you is too long."

Lilliana narrowed her eyes, but there was a flicker of a smile at the corner of her mouth.

Sal leaned close. His heart beat so fast, it sent throbbing plugs in his ears. His head went light, his knees started to shake, and he felt the blood start to go to his groin.

Her soft lips puckered so close to his, he could practically taste them.

He put a hand on her back and pulled her close.

"My lady," said Damor Nev, appearing around the corner. "We needs be going."

Lilliana flushed and swept a lock of hair from her eyes. "Take care of yourself, Salvatori Lorenzo."

Sal winked at her, nodded to Damor, and turned to leave.

Thus ends
A Fool of Sorts
Fall of the Coward, Book Two

If you loved
A Fool of Sorts,
Never miss another novel from Taylor O'Connell by joining
The Taylor O'Connell VIP List
at
Tayloroconnellbooks.com
and get your free novel,
A Turn After Dawn,
a VIP List Exclusive

The Man in Shadow
Fall of the Coward, Book Three
available soon
Continue on for a sneak peek

THE MAN IN SHADOW

VENDETA

"What in Sacrull's hell is taking them so long?" Vinny asked as the sun sank below the horizon, and dusk slowly settled in. The torch in his hand aflame, black smoke willowing into the night.

"It shouldn't have taken—you don't think someone stopped them?" Aurie asked. She wore all black, tight fitting cloth that hugged the subtle curves of her slender figure.

"We should go around the other way," Vinny suggested.

"She'll be here," Sal said, putting his ear up against the cellar door and listening for footsteps. "I mean, it's Valla."

Odie leaned against the alley wall and shifted from foot to foot. His great war hammer was unslung, the well-defined muscles in his massive forearms rippling as he tightened his grip on the leather wrapped ebony stalk. The polished iron head of the hammer, forged in the shape of a fist, glinted with the torchlight. The big man snorted and spat to the cobblestones.

"Lad's right," said the big man. "We all need to take a breath. They'll be here."

Neither Vinny or Aurie looked convinced, but Sal thought it best to move forward regardless.

"Right then. You two," he said, motioning to Vinny and Aurie.

"It's time you took care of our little dog problem, and I'll go ahead and get myself set up. Big Man, you just wait here for Valla and Dominik, and the three of you can make your way in together."

It seemed no one had any objections, until Vinny raised his hand high for attention, a broad grin spread across his visage.

"That was the white one that needed poisoning, right?"

Sal smirked, and the big man let out a little chirp of a laugh.

Aurie narrowed her eyes. "You had best be japing."

Vinny winked and clicked his tongue, but Aurie only shook her head, unimpressed.

"Right then," Sal said with a nod.

He waited a moment at the alley mouth, took a deep breath, and slipped out, rounded the corner, and went through the door of the unmarked building.

The foyer was empty, but he could hear the faint hum of a crowed somewhere close by.

As Sal moved down a hall the noise grew louder. He went down a stairway through a door and into a big open room. The man on his immediate right put a hand out to halt him. His look was skeptical, he seemed to be readying himself to speak when Sal cut him off.

"I was just in here," Sal said, as a large hand clapped him on the chest, just before he could slip through the doorway. "Had to find a place to piss."

The door guard grunted, and gave Sal a skeptical look. After a moment's hesitation, he nodded, and slowly pulled his hand away.

The arena hall was massive, yet so packed the crowd stood shoulder to shoulder. Even still, due to the slanted floor, Sal could see the arena all the way from the back.

At center of the hall was a shallow pit, a sand floor and a short fence that lined the edge of the circular pit. Men leaned up against the iron grates, spitting and shouting, jeering and laughing.

Two dogs, massive beasts that rippled with slabs of muscle, fought at the center of the pit. Powerful jaws snapped as slaver flew. Growls rumbled like rolling thunder, barks pitching above the cacophony of crowd noise as they fought on.

Sal made his way through the crowd, a hardened lot of alley

pushers and dock thugs, cheering on the dog fight. Sal approached a solitary man, smoking a wooden pipe. The man seemed as focused on the crowd as he was on the pit. On his neck was the tattoo of a black raven, the sign of the notorious street gang, the Rooks.

"Who'd you put in on?" Sal asked the Rook, nodding to the dogs in the pit.

The Rook looked to the fighting pit. "I didn't bother. Pot was too low. Everyone knows Barbari fights them too early. That black is a big one, but he's a pup yet. The mottled bitch is just biding her time. You'll see, soon as she gets an opening, this one is over."

Sure enough, just as the man stopped speaking, the black hound yelped and reared. The mottled bitch dropped low and lunged, sinking her massive jaw about the black dog's neck. The mottled bitch's entire body snapped taught, locking still like an iron padlock.

The black hound arched, and for an instant attempted to wriggle free before he hunched to the dirt as the mottled bitch dragged him down like a stone anchor.

Sal turned away. Not wanting to watch the rest.

"What did I tell you," said the Rook, as Sal scanned the crowd for any sign of his mark. "Hope you didn't have your krom on that black pup. Age will out over beauty everywhere 'cept the whore-house, and don't you forget it."

"I'll keep it in mind," Sal said absently, his eyes still flicking through the faces of the crowd.

"Next fight should be something more of a crowd pleaser," said the Rook. "Two of the dons going to go at it. Well, Dvorak, he's a don, the other's just a don's whelp. Still, aiming up to be a fight with some real promise. For a tick I was worried it wouldn't happen."

"Oh, and why is that?" Sal asked, feigning ignorance.

"Well, the whelp, Garibaldi, aint no secret that fop is craven. Way I hear it he hasn't left the Scarvini stronghold in a week, and well, on account of what happened to his brother and all—guess I'm just saying I didn't think he would show."

Sal flashed the man the emptiest smile he could manage, hoping it would convey the proper amount of pitiable stupidity to keep the Rook talking.

"You do know what happened to Giuseppe, don't you?"

Sal shook his head. "Who?" he asked, as the memory of burning hair and charred flesh, blood and viscera flashed through his mind.

"The Shark," said the Rook looking somewhat incredulous, loud enough to turn a few of the heads around them in their direction. "You telling me you don't know Giuseppe Scarvini?"

Sal frowned and shrugged.

The Rook's eyes went wide, lips pursed. He shook his head and took a draw from his pipe. "How can a man live in this city and not know of Giuseppe the Shark?" he asked, smoke rolling from his mouth. "God's be damned if you aint new to Dijvois."

"What gave it away?" Sal asked.

The Rook scoffed, and nudged Sal with a friendly elbow. "Just you wait. This next one is going to be something. Don Dvorak himself is pitting one of his own. Dvorak, their one of the Five Families of the Commission, you know?"

Sal nodded. "Sure, sure, the Commission, right."

The Rook smirked and shook his head. "Top level gangs around the city. This Don Dvorak is a pretty big deal. Shit, even that Scarvini whelp has a name with some clout, not on account of anything he's done, mind you. But around here, not even Don Novotny, the Golden Dragon himself, is more important than Don Scarvini. This is the Pit, and the Scarvini Family owns the Pit." The Rook took a hit from his pipe and shrugged. "Still, Kael Dvorak has raised more champions than any other breeder in the city. Some think the pup he's brought today could be too young, but he's come from a champion's line. The stud that sired him and the bitch that whelped him were both undefeated in the Pit in their time."

The way the Rook went on about it, one might almost think he was speaking of something other than a Sacrull damned blood sport. Sal hated dog fighting, it was truly sadistic. Yet, there was something in the way the man spoke that peaked Sal's interest, even while it made him sick to his stomach.

Sal almost felt bad, yet what was the price of one hound's life?

Surely, it was a small price to pay in exchange for the lives of six people.

"And the other one, this Garibaldi Scarvini?" Sal asked as he watched a pair of young men turn the soil in the pit, where a pool of blood stained the sand from the previous match.

The Rook wrinkling his nose. He looked over both of his shoulders conspiratorially, before he leaned close and spoke in low tones. "Everyone knows Garibaldi's not half of what his brother was. He's craven, but this beast of his is nothing of the sort. A red-eyed mongrel that looks to have been fatted on whole sheep and unwary children. A right monster, he is. This will be his third fight in the Pit, and let me tell you, the last two didn't last long enough for him to show half of what he's capable of doing."

An uproar sounded, and Sal looked toward the pit, as a sharply dressed man stepped onto the sand. He wore Minnian leather boots, a silk cravat, and a sharp tailored coat. His name was Don Kael Dvorak

The don looked down at the dark patch of sand where the black dog had laid dead moments before. Don Dvorak then looked out at the crowd, raised both arms above his head, balled his hands into fists, and roared like a savage beast. Don Kael Dvorak then straightened his jacket, slicked back his hair, and exited the arena, poised as though he had just delivered a manifest diatribe, rather than acted like some war leader of a barbarian horde.

"It's been good chatting," Sal said to the Rook.

"What, just as it's getting going?" The Rook asked. "This is the big one, you've got to stay and watch."

Sal wordlessly slipped through the crowd and down the slanted floor to the lower-level. He cut back, and went through a door that led him out of the main arena room and into a hallway. Sal could still hear the noise of the crowd, though it was dulled to a hum by the closed door. He knew what he was missing, and he wasn't the least bit sorry.

Very soon, Garibaldi Scarvini and Don Kael Dvorak would release their dogs into the fighting pit. The beasts would come out snarling, hackles raised, teeth bared.

Sal moved along the hall and down another stairway before he found himself in another hallway, three doors on either side, and a pair of neckless guards at the other end.

One of them turned around slowly, as though the very effort taxed him. "Oy," said the guard, reaching for the cudgel that hung at his flabby hip. "What are you doing down here? The fights going to start, you know."

A burst of excited cheers, shouts and boos, expelled from the room just beyond the door. Sal imagined the rat-faced Garibaldi releasing his red-eyed beast, a smug smile twisting his peevish features. Don Dvorak roaring as his hound padded onto the sand, the blood of champions flowing through its veins. A tension over the entire crowd, bated breaths awaiting the outcome, an outcome that Sal already knew. One he'd known since before he'd even set foot in the Narrows that evening.

So long as Vinny and Aurie managed their part, that is.

"Which room is Garibaldi Scarvini using?" Sal asked.

"And why should I tell you that?" said the neckless guard, his shelfed brow wrinkling.

The other guard turned around. He was equally as fat as his companion, only every bit of his exposed flabby flesh was tattooed in the Dahuaneze fashion.

"I have a gift for Garibaldi," Sal said. "He'll be expecting it after his bout."

The guards shared a look, then the first man turned back to Sal. "Aint going to tell you to bugger off, but I can't go letting you into people's rooms and all. See, that's what were here for. To, uh, stop that from—well, you know."

"I was told to deliver the gift to Garibaldi in his room, directly after his bout. Win or lose he'll be expecting me. How I can deliver his gift to him if you're unwilling to tell me which room is his?"

Sal heard another boom of crowd noise from beyond the door at the end of the hall. He imagined things were just about over. Garibaldi Scarvini would soon be in a mood to celebrate.

"Well," said the guard rubbing his chin, an aloof look in his eyes. "Suppose you could just give me the gift and I can give it to old Garibaldi soon as the match is over."

Sal smiled placatingly. "Let's just say it's not that kind of gift. You, uh, wouldn't want me giving it to you, and you sure as Sacrull's hell wouldn't want to be giving it to him yourself."

The guard's eyes widened with realization. It seemed he wasn't half so dumb as he looked. "That one there is his room. Should be unlocked. Bjorn here is got the keys if you needs them."

The tattooed one grunted as though he'd not been so quick on the take, but Sal didn't give him time to object before he moved for the second door on his left and tried the handle.

The door was unlocked.

*

Seated upon the divan, Sal could hear them as they laughed and jeered in the hallway just outside the room. He breathed deep, and rubbed his hands together feeling the thick coating of the skeev dust on his fingertips. Nerves on end, he crushed more of the cap between his thumb and forefinger.

The door swung open.

Garibaldi Scarvini had his father's look. Sal had seen Don Scarvini a handful of times at his uncle's home, and there was no doubt Garibaldi was his son. Still, there was something about this Scarvini that seemed to fall short of the name. Some quality of his father's which he lacked.

But as Garibaldi's eyes met Sal's he knew what it was that seemed wrong. The handful of times Sal had looked into the eyes of Don Giotto Scarvini, it had sent a shock of fear right through him. Yet when Sal looked into the eyes of Garibaldi Scarvini, all he saw was fear. Not the predatory look of his father, but the wild look of fleeting prey.

"The fuck is this then?" said a second man, entering just behind Garibaldi. An unfamiliar face, lean and hard. He gestured to Sal. "Baldi, you know this one?"

Sal sunk more deeply into the divan, as though he were relaxing all the more. When in truth, his nerves felt taught enough to snap.

Garibaldi Scarvini shook his head. His weasel-like face showing only bemusement.

Two more men filed in, and stopped short, just as the others had, upon seeing Sal lounging on the divan.

"Who are you?" asked Garibaldi, a slight tremble in his voice, his left hand shaking ever so slightly.

"Name's Salvatori. You must be Garibaldi." Sal said in his most sultry tone. "Giovani sent me over."

Garibaldi didn't show so much as the hint of a smile. His restless eyes narrowed and flicked quickly between his companions as though gauging their reactions.

It was then Sal realized his mistake. He'd had Vinny drug the wrong dog. If they'd have drugged the white bitch, and Garibaldi had lost, he might have come back to the room alone. Dispirited, he may have been somewhat moody, but might still have been interested in the bait, for a source of comfort.

Yet in his high spirits, hot on the heels of his victory, it seemed Garibaldi was in the mood for companions to share in his revelry. And the God's only knew just how open Garibaldi was with them about his preferences.

Sal ran his tongue slowly across his top lip. "There's no reason to be nervous," he said, sitting up and patting the divan cushion.

"Close the door," said Garibaldi, slinking toward Sal.

As Garibaldi neared him the look in his eyes changed. He no longer resembled a deer, so much a mischievous weasel.

Sal wondered just how stable Garibaldi Scarvini was, and whether he ought to abandon the rouse there and then.

Garibaldi's nose wrinkled, his top lip curling slightly. "You said Giovani sent you?"

Sal nodded.

The door closed with a thud and the others moved in behind Garibaldi. There were three of them: a slender bloke with a knife at his hip, a fat one with a cudgel already in hand, and a thickly-muscled dock thug that slipped a pair of iron knuckles from his pocket as he neared the divan.

"Giovani? He sure did. Wanted me to make sure you weren't too heartbroken if you had lost—and if you won, I was told to show you a good time."

Garibaldi nodded, but his eyes were filled with suspicion and his pursed lips frowned at the edges. "Giovani sent you did he?"

Sal maintained his composure on the outside, but inside his confidence had shattered like a pane of stained-glass.

"My little brother didn't send you," said Garibaldi, the tremble in his voice readily apparent. "Giovani's never done nothing for nobody in his bloody life. Now who in Sacrull's hell sent you?"

Sal realized his initial approach was bound to fail and so he swiftly switched tact. "I'm here to deliver a message. A message concerning Giuseppe Scarvini."

Quick as that, the weasel was gone, and Garibaldi looked like a deer readying to run. "What's this about Giuseppe, what's your fucking message?" he asked, his voice just short of panicked.

Sal stood up from the divan and calmly stepped past the muscular thug, addressing Garibaldi directly.

"His killer wants to make peace."

"His kill—and just who the fuck are you?"

"Like I said, my name's Salvatori," Sal said with a wink. "Salvatori Lorenzo."

"Lorenzo?" said Garibaldi. "As in Stefano Lorenzo?"

Sal shrugged. "I suppose we're related."

"So, what's this? You telling me the Svoboda Family is responsible for my brother's murder?"

"No," Sal said. "I'm not with Svoboda, nor am I here on my uncle's behalf. I've come seeking peace on behalf of your brother's killer. My message is from him. We aren't associated with any of the Five Families. We're a family of our own, you could say."

"The fuck? You saying you're responsible for Giuseppe's death?"

Sal shrugged, "Some might look at it that way."

All four of the men tensed, Sal could feel it, the energy of the room shifting with that admission. It was as though they didn't know whether to be upset or frightened. Though it seemed they quickly settled unanimously on the prior option.

"And what other way is there to look at it?" asked Garibaldi, a vein in his neck bulging.

Sal shrugged. "Might be, you would need to hear my message to understand."

Jaw clenched, the vein in his neck pulsating dangerously, Garibaldi turned his hand palm up, as though asking Sal to hand the words over.

Sal grasped the locket with his skeev coated hand. A rush of energy cascaded through his veins. Without warning, he focused his will, and released it through his open palm.

A blue bolt of lightning struck the closest man square between the eyes.

His head exploded like a melon, and the muscular, headless corpse collapsed to the ground.

Garibaldi let out a scream.

Sal spun on the skinny one, who'd drawn his knife by then. He focused once more, and unleashed another bolt.

Lightning consumed the skinny man like a web. He writhed on the ground as blood streamed from his eyes and the corners of his mouth.

As Sal turned, the fat one swung a cudgel. Yet he swung as though his club were a sword and he meant to split Sal in half from his head to his middle.

Sal dodged, but the cudgel clipped his ear.

The fat man swung again.

As the cudgel whistled past Sal's head on the backswing, Sal focused his energy, and felt the electricity course through his veins, down his arm and out his palm.

The bolt he unleashed was so powerful that when it struck the man, what was left of his body was thrown across the room and slammed against the far wall.

Sal was panting, his heart hammering in his chest, his limbs weak and rubbery, but he kept standing and turned to face Garibaldi.

Only, Garibaldi Scarvini had disappeared.

Where the man had stood, there was now merely a puddle of piss.

But as Sal looked about, he noticed a pair of fine black leather boots poking out from behind the divan he'd been seated in when the others entered the room.

Sal sighed, relieved that Garibaldi had chosen not to fight back. Exhausted as he was after pulling thrice upon the locket's power, Sal doubted he could have so much as raised his arms high enough to fend off a punch—even a punch thrown by Garibaldi Scarvini.

"Come on out, my lord," Sal said. "The fighting is all done."

The boots quickly disappeared behind the divan, and Sal couldn't help but hate the man for his cowardice.

"Look, Scarvini, you saw what I did to your men, yeah? What makes you think that bit of furniture is going to make a lick of difference if I choose to unleash my wrath?"

"I'll have your balls for this!" Garibaldi cried out, his voice pitched high with fear. "You're a fucking dead man. There are twenty men outside this room, twenty Scarvini soldiers, killers to the man."

"By my count only seventeen men remain you, and all of them are outside this door."

"Think it through," said Garibaldi from behind the divan. "There is only one door in or out of this room, one door and no windows. Just how do you expect to get out when you've finished with me?"

"A valid point," Sal said. "Though, if my predictions prove correct, the two men outside your door ought already be dead."

Garibaldi laughed, yet it was a laugh that rang of false bravado. "What sorcery is this? The guards outside my door will gut you the instant you try to leave."

Sal moved slowly to the door, scuffing his boots loudly as he walked so that Garibaldi would hear.

When he turned the door handle, he looked back over his shoulder to see Garibaldi peeking over the back of the divan. Sal opened the door. The fat body of the tattooed guard slumped through the doorway and thudded on the flagstones.

Garibaldi let out a shrill cry.

The fat body of the tattooed guard was dragged out of the way by his thick ankles, before two people entered.

Valla sauntered in., followed by Dominik.

"Help!" Garibaldi cried out, but too late.

Dominik closed the door behind him. The cry might have been heard just outside the door, but there was no chance anyone in the clamoring arena hall would have noticed a thing.

"Fucking mess you made of this one." said Valla, wrinkling her nose.

"Who—who are you people?"

Dominik crossed the room and rounded the divan. He grabbed Garibaldi by the leg and dragged him out, kicking and screaming. Dominik had to stop dragging Garibaldi once or twice to stomp on him until he stopped his flailing.

When they reached the center of the room, Dominik put a boot to Garibaldi's chest and pinned the man to floor.

"You want to know me name?" Dominik said looking down on the terrified Scarvini.

"A dead man!" Garibaldi said, his voice cracking, a fresh stream of piss puddling on the flagstones beneath him.

Dominik snorted, and drew his knife. "Me name is Dominik D'Angelo. But you can just call me the reaper."

AFTERWORD

I hope you enjoyed the second installment to the Fall of the Coward series half as much as I enjoyed writing it. If you were one of those who disliked the ending, or were simply left wondering where the rest of the book is, allow me a short explanation.

The Fall of the Coward was drafted and initially intended to be written as a single epic novel. After years of work, I came to the realization that the story of Salvatori Lorenzo would be better served if I broke the project into multiple novels. So, for those of you wondering where the rest of the book is, do not worry, the answers are coming.

Just as The Hand That Takes was a long time in the making, many of the chapters used in A Fool Of Sorts were written seven years before the novels release. Although, I'll bet you can't guess which ones.

I especially want to thank everyone who helped with the making of this novel. To my Beta readers, Allan, Kyle, Eric, and Phil, your feedback was invaluable. I also want to thank my cover designer Stuart Bache for his art work. And finally, my editor, Ashely Wyrick with Dream Edit Repeat, for her vigilance and discerning eye.

Without your contributions I have no doubt this novel would not be half of what it is.

Lastly, I want to thank you, my readers for your support. Without you, none of this would be possible.

Taylor O'Connell
Bennington, Ne
August 9, 2019

ABOUT THE AUTHOR

Taylor O'Connell is the author of *The Hand that Takes*, *A Fool of Sorts*, *and The Man in Shadow*. And very much looks forward to presenting the final pieces to the series: *Fall of the Coward*; *A Throne for Thieves*, and *For All that Ascends*.

Taylor primarily writes fantasy, but loves books of all genres. When not lost within the city of Dijvois, he spends most of his time with his beautiful wife and children.

For more information or more novels by Taylor O'Connell, visit Tayloroconnellbooks.com